"Am I drunk, Dick? I feel drunk. I feel . . .
let me see, I feel like taking my clothes off."

"I sure wish you wouldn't do that, Niqui. I'm a little mixed up, too, but I seem to remember reading something somewhere about it being naughty to make it with a nun. Jesus, what on Earth did they put in those beans?"

Niqui said, "I wish you wouldn't keep talking about my husband. I'm feeling a little cross with Jesus, tonight. You see, our marriage has never been consummated and they told me it was a sin to relieve myself with my hand, but, damn it, a girl has feelings!"

Captain Gringo was having feelings, too, but he was still fighting them when Niqui slipped her habit off over her head, placed it on the ground, and reclined stark naked atop the folded cloth to ask him, with an inviting smile, "Would you like to consummate me, Dick?"

Novels by Ramsay Thorne

Published by
WARNER BOOKS

Renegade #10

THE GREAT GAME

by
Ramsay Thorne

WARNER BOOKS

A Warner Communications Company

WARNER BOOKS EDITION

Copyright © 1981 by Lou Cameron
All rights reserved.

Cover art by Chuck Sover

Warner Books, Inc., 75 Rockefeller Plaza, New York, N.Y. 10019

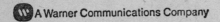 A Warner Communications Company

Printed in the United States of America

First Printing: September, 1981

10 9 8 7 6 5 4 3 2 1

Renegade #10

THE
GREAT GAME

The trade winds hit the north-east shoulder of Venezuela cool and scented with the clean iodine tang of tropic seawater. But as they blew inland across sixty miles of the fetid swamplands of the Orinoco Delta the trades grew sluggish and began to smell like a crocodile's fart. The noonday sun glared down through a malarial haze as the river port of Tucupita dozed by the sluggish coffee brown waters. It was Siesta Time. The shops and cantinas were shuttered and the streets and boardwalks were deserted. Even the stray dogs and chickens had taken shelter from the merciless sun. Tucupita had a police force. A pretty good one, since it was the provincial capital as well as a major Venezuelan port. But like everyone else with a lick of sense, the cops of Tucupita were home taking La Siesta. For who, by the beard of Christ, would be out in the noonday sun?

Men with serious business, of course. Professional killers tend to ignore discomforts, and La Siesta was the one time they could move a tripod mounted Browning machinegun in broad daylight without having to answer a lot of embarrassing questions. They had to set up their ambush in broad daylight because that was when Captain Gringo's steamboat

7

would arrive. It was hot sweaty work getting themselves and the machinegun up to the flat roof of a warehouse overlooking the steamboat landing, but when one's been sent to assassinate the most dangerous man in Latin America, one does not worry about a little sweat. As they hauled the machinegun up on the gravel-topped roof, one of the killers grimaced and said, "Jesus, it's like a frying pan up here!" But another shrugged and soothed, "Hey, better the frying pan than the fire, eh? He'll never expect us to be up here on this hot roof."

The leader told them to shut up as he directed them to a spot overlooking the steamboat landing. There was a gap in the brick parapet of the roof. The machinegunner and his loader-sidekick carefully positioned the pads of the tripod before lowering the heavy weapon on to it. The gunner sighted down the waterjacketed barrel, traversed to cover the probable target area better, and grunted, "Okay, let's load and lock." The leader said, "Load but don't put that gun on safe. The people who are paying us say Captain Gringo and that little Frenchman he hangs about with can both move like spit on a hot stove. I don't want to give him any possible break. They say he has an annoying habit of taking advantage of any breaks you give him."

Another member of the team asked, "Is it true he once turned the tables on a Mexican firing squad, after they had him against the fucking wall?"

The leader shrugged, trying to ignore the furnace heat against his shoulders as he said, "They say a lot of things about Captain Gringo. After today, they're going to say he's dead, if you boys don't blow a good thing."

But despite his words, and the heat, the leader felt goose bumps as he swept his eyes over his ambush, wondering if he'd covered every bet, and remembering what they'd told him about the man he'd been hired to kill.

There were seven of them up there waiting to ambush Captain Gringo and his sidekick, Gaston Verrier. None were Venezuelan and the leader wasn't sure the people who'd hired him were, either. The leader was a one-eyed ex-officer of the Hungarian Cavalry who'd learned private parties paid more for his killing skills than the Emperor Franz Josef. The one-eyed Hungarian was backed by his personal pistol-pack-

ing bodyguards. The machine gunner and his assistant, along with the rifle-carrying back-up team were expendable. This gave some comfort to the Hungarian, although he was damned if he could see how two men walking into a seven man ambush had a chance in hell.

One of his bodyguards wiped a sweaty face and said, "That steamboat is late, Chief. Maybe they tied up, somewhere up the river, to wait out La Siesta, huh?"

The Hungarian fixed his one good eye on the sluggish upstream waters and said, "That's ridiculous!"

"This is a ridiculous country, Chief."

The leader shook his head and said, "You don't stop a steamboat to cool off, damn it. The only decent breeze for miles would be the air flowing over the decks as the boat moved through it. I know these greasers all take to the shade from eleven to three, but they have shade on that boat and the paddle wheel does all the work. They do seem to be running a bit late. That's to be expected in such an uncivilized country. But sooner or later the boat will get here. Thanks to the wonderful new invention of Professor Bell, we know they passed San Felix early this morning, moving downstream with the river high. They're coming this way, and fast, even if the paddle wheel falls off."

As they spoke, a mass of tangled timber from the flooded lands up the river came around the bend they were covering and as it drifted toward the landing the Hungarian smiled thinly and added, "See what I mean? The greasers crewing the boat don't have to lift a finger to get here. Just sit tight and it'll soon be over."

The machine gunner wiped his own face and pulled the brim of his straw hat lower to shade his eyes as he chimed in, "It's a good thing this gun is water cooled. I haven't fired a round and I'll bet you could brew tea in the jacket right now. I've got the muzzle trained between those two mooring poles they'll drop the gangplank between, Chief. But it's likely to be a little messy, from this angle. The guys we're after will be coming down the gangplank with a lot of other people, no?"

The one-eyed Hungarian shrugged and said, "That's their problem. The people we work for don't care one way or the other about innocent bystanders." He chuckled and

9

added, "It's too bad we're not being paid by the head. But our clients want Captain Gringo bad and we'll just throw the other killings in for good measure."

One of the riflemen, picked for having keen eyes, said, "Smoke plume up around the bend, Chief." And the leader said, "I see it. Get ready, boys."

The machine gunner said, "I've been ready long enough to die of sunstroke. One question, though. Didn't you say this Captain Gringo's with a dame?"

"Yes, they call her Bubbles and she's supposed to be great in bed. How did you think the people we work for knew Captain Gringo was aboard that steamboat? Bubbles phoned from Soledad right after she picked him up in the main salon."

The machine gunner squinted down his sights with a frown and observed, "Okay, so the dame fingered him for us, and now she's with him, and he's coming down the plank into my sights. Has anybody warned her to stay the hell clear of him? This Captain Gringo guy's supposed to be good and you only get to miss him once if you want to go on breathing."

The one-eyed Hungarian shrugged again and said, "Don't miss. I told you nobody cared about the others who might be in the line of fire."

"Including the dame?"

"Of course. Who needs her, now that she's done her job?"

The machine gunner didn't answer. Like his assistant, he'd been recruited for the job from among the drifters and adventurers haunting the Banana Lands in the wake of the Great Depression of the '90s. He knew the one-eyed Hungarian by rep. He had no idea who he, and they, were working for. He'd been promised a fast five hundred for this job, to be split with his partner after they were paid off. He had no idea who this dame, Bubbles, might be, but he could see how she was getting paid off, and it was making him nervous.

The steamboat came around the bend as the raft of timber proceeding it passed the landing to lose itself downstream in the sweltering jungles of the delta. Below the killers on the rooftop, a couple of cotton-clad dockhands came wearily out on the landing to wait for the steamboat's shore

lines. The one-eyed Hungarian said, "This is it. Remember what I said about doing the job right. The people we're working for don't tolerate mistakes and if Captain Gringo gets by us, we're all dead."

Thirty odd miles up the braided Orinoco, Gaston Verrier swore softly and asked, "Well, my old and rare, do you know any other short cuts?"

Captain Gringo stared morosely at the quarter-mile-wide channel of muddy water they faced to their north and reached for a cigar in his damp shirt as he muttered, "This wasn't supposed to happen. I looked at the map when we slipped ashore at Barrancas. We're supposed to be on the fucking north shore of the fucking Orinoco. That's the main channel back there behind us, right?"

"If you say so, my mundane explorer. But regardez, we would seem to be lost in a maze of floodwater channels and as I speak my boots are filling with ooze!"

Captain Gringo lit his smoke, tipped the brim of his panama hat back to ease his sweaty brow, and wiggled his own toes inside their water-filled mosquito boots as he muttered, "Yeah, we'd better backtrack to higher ground and find some shade while we dope this out."

His smaller and older comrade gave a startled, goatlike laugh and replied, "Higher ground, in the Orinoco Delta? Surely you jest! Damn it, Dick, I told you we had no business getting off that steamboat this far down the river. It's a maze of islands even in the dry season. Why do you suppose the early Spanish explorers named the country after Venice?"

Captain Gringo shrugged and led the way through the reedy saw-grass to a tree-covered hammock they'd passed getting this far north. Gaston followed, grousing, "No doubt we'll meet at least a crocodile and a barrel of snakes amid that thrice accursed brush, but anything is better than this sun. It's so bright it blinds me just to look around at all this *grass!*"

Captain Gringo said, "They don't have crocodiles down here. They call them caymans, and they eat snakes, so what the hell."

"*Merde alors*, is there any important difference between a crocodile, or a cayman, once it grabs your leg?"

"No. But we're both packing guns." Captain Gringo grinned, as, suiting actions to words, he drew his double action .38 and kept going. Privately, he was more worried about snakes, but he knew his small French sidekick was still moody about that bushmaster who'd bitten him a while back, so he didn't mention snakes as they approached the shady glen of moss-hung trees ahead. They had to have shade. He was an old enough tropic hand to know it would be getting hotter before it started getting cooler, and it was obvious they weren't going any farther north until they'd had time to build a raft. Building a raft without machetes was possible, but trying to do it under an afternoon sun down here was suicidal. As he moved up on the low hammock to higher ground and scouted the sandy surface under the trees he saw no obvious reptiles and said so, adding, "We can hole up here until it cools off."

Gaston made an unpleasant remark about the tall American's mother and said, "*Sacre* Goddam, it *never* cools off in these lowland swamps. Why do you suppose all the white people dwell in the highlands, Dick?"

"Look, we don't have to stay here in Venezuela long enough to raise a family, damn it! I told you we just have to get to Cunama or some other seaport on the north coast and haul ass out of here!"

Gaston spotted a fallen log, looked over the far side to make sure nothing important was hiding there, and sat down wearily before he snapped, "Species of idiot, we were on our way to a seaport when you took it into your thick blond head to leave the steamboat and flounder through these swamps! You're crazy, Dick. I have said this many times in the past, but never with such sincerity! They told us on board the river steamer that ocean going ships put in at Tucupita. Tucupita was just downstream and you had a stateroom with hot and cold running Bubbles. But were you content to glide swanlike into Tucupita holding hands with, or shall we say, blowing Bubbles? *Mais non,* like a madman you grabbed me away from the lady I was working on in the salon and the next

12

thing I knew, here we are, wherever are is! I thought we were going into that river port to buy a drink, or even more ammo. But this is all too *fatigué!*"

Captain Gringo found his own log and said, "Shut up, I'm trying to think."

"You mean you really *think*, Dick? At times I have suspected you of being the natural son of Jack In The Box! Don't you see that by this time the steamboat, and M'selle Bubbles, have arrived in Tucupita, while we, in turn, face an evening with the mosquitoes out here in the middle of nowhere?"

Captain Gringo blew a smoke ring, stared morosely after it as it drifted in the still hot air, and said, flatly, "Bubbles was a plant. She was waiting for us aboard that steamboat."

"Eh bien, that was to be expected. We made a certain amount of noise adventuring through Brazil with its various factions shooting at us. But when we first met the mystery woman you told me she'd said something about wanting to meet you. She was recruiting soldiers of fortune for some action here in Venezuela, non?"

"Yeah, that's what she told me while I was kissing her. She said the people she works for wanted to meet me, in Tucupita."

"And so we abandoned ship at Barrancas to squish our way to points unknown? I seem to be missing something, Dick. We are soldiers of fortune. We get paid to meet people in places like Tucupita."

Captain Gringo took a drag on his cigar, decided it was shitty tasting, and snubbed the cigar out as he explained, "I didn't like her story. She kept trying to suck me off every time I wanted to get down to the brass tacks."

"If you don't want that Havana Claro, I'll take it, Dick. I wish you'd told me how tiresome you found the poor child's oral efforts. I'd have been willing to sacrifice myself for you. She wasn't a bad looking diversion. A trifle cheap and stupid, perhaps, but . . ."

"She wasn't all that dumb. Nobody could have been. She was setting us up for something, Gaston. The last time I met a gal who screwed with eyes *that* calculating, she was an Apache squaw Geronimo had sent to lull what he hoped to be a green cavalry officer."

Gaston shrugged and said, "I know your habit of reading

13

minds at the most peculiar times, Dick. But what if she was working on you for her boss? If she wanted you to join some outfit down here, she might have simply been trying to offer you some fringe enducements, hein?"

Captain Gringo shook his head and said, "Take more than she had between her legs to sell me on a revolution down *here!* I can't explain how I knew there was more to it than that, but even if she was on the level, we're still better off out here than mixed up with her and her whatever. I was talking to that guy we met on board who works for the Venezuelan government, remember?"

"Ah, oui, the man in the white suit."

"Bubbles was trying to keep me away from him. That's when I began to wonder. Anyway, I did get to chat with some of the other passengers, when she wasn't screwing me silly, and the mess they're about to have down here is not one any soldier of fortune with half a brain cell would touch with a ten foot pole. It's not the usual fight between the guys who won the last election and the guys who didn't. It's big stuff with the Major Powers involved."

"*Merde,* what major power wishes to overthrow the Venezuelan government? What would anyone important *do* with this bog if they grabbed it?"

"Nobody wants Venezuela. But Queen Victoria wants a strategic chunk of it. You know the British own Trinidad, and Trinidad lies just off the mouth of the Orinoco, right?"

"*Oui,* but what of it? We can't go to Trinidad. The British have this distressing extradition treaty with our old countries, and a couple of others who may still be looking for us."

"Screw Trinidad—I don't want it. Venezuela doesn't want it. But Her Majesty likes neat maps. The Venezuelan delta country lies between her offshore Trinidad and British Guiana, here on the mainland to the south."

"You call this mainland? But I see the madness in Queen Vickie's method. The British do have this odd desire to paint the map of the world pink. I take it they are moving north-west from British Guiana to include the delta in their empire?"

"That's what the Venezuelans are afraid of. The Royal Navy seems to think controlling the mouth of the Orinoco

makes strategic sense or something. They say the local Hispanics aren't strong enough to hold the delta lands if some other Great Power decided to grab it. So, to save everybody a lot of worry, Britain's going to grab it *first*, see?"

"*Tres fatigué*. But let us be *practique*. Who *is* about to stop the Royal Navy if they decide they'd like control of the Orinoco, Dick?"

"Uncle Sam. El Presidente Cleveland has just told the Royal Navy to keep its royal mitts off the little kids on his block. The Venezuelans I talked to sure hope he means it."

Gaston laughed incredulously and replied, "*Très fantastique*, Dick! We all know how tiresome your country can be about its Monroe Doctrine, but surely, this time, you Yanks are bluffing, hein?"

Captain Gringo sighed and said, "The Brits seem to think so. They've moved some muscle into Guiana and sent a couple of diplomatic battle cruisers into Trinidad. So we'll all know, any minute, who's bluffing whom."

Gaston whistled softly under his breath and said, "Ah, running away from this fight no longer strikes me as such a bad move, my old and rare!"

Captain Gringo nodded grimly, and said, "Yeah. I'm a machine gunner, when I have a machine gun. I can't think of a fucking thing anyone down here would want with our usual services. If the Brits invade Venezuela nobody's about to stop 'em with anything *I've* ever fired! If The States back down, the Brits will win in a walk."

"And if your truculent Grover Cleveland is not bluffing, Dick?"

"The U.S. goes to war with the British Empire and it gets noisy as hell down here. Uncle Sam's navy is smaller but his army is better. I ought to know, since I used to be in it. The Yanks won't be dumb enough to run a smaller fleet between two British colonies, but they'll land a full sized army somewhere near Caracas and march south across the *llanos*. I mean, with infantry and cavalry and the best damned field artillery on earth. The Delta, here, will be the battleground. Do you really figure on being here when those two major forces smash head on into one another?"

Gaston grimaced and said, "You're right. Bubbles was either fibbing or insane. Neither side would hire soldiers of

fortune. Both will swat any armed irregulars they meet like flies. You'll hang if the American Army captures you. Maybe the British would hire us as scouts?"

"Hey, Gaston, I'm an *American*, damn it!"

"Ah, oui, one forgets idealism as one gets older. I confess I would not enjoy shooting Frenchmen, even though they put a very rude reward on my head when I deserted the Legion years ago. Fortunately, we are too far from French Guiana to worry about that, but for your own peace of mind, I agree we should, how you say, get the hell out of here?"

Captain Gringo nodded and said, "We'll wait 'til it cools off a bit and then we'll raft ourselves across that channel. The grassy llano on the far side should offer easy walking after dark. There'll be a full moon and the land's dead flat."

"Dead flat where it is not water, you mean! What if we run into yet another triple-titted stream that has a mind of its own, Dick?"

Captain Gringo shrugged and said, "Shit, we'll cross it when and if. I told you I looked at the map, Gaston. Once we get away from the flood lands it's open llano almost to the north coast."

"Perhaps. I look at maps, too. Forgive me if I seem less active, but I make it over a hundred of your miles to the Caribbean, Dick."

"So?"

"So, *merde alors,* that is one *très formidable* walk, even with nothing in the way, and you just told me this triple-titted country was about to explode in a most alarming major war!"

At the steamboat landing in Tucupita the one-eyed Hungarian was tight-lipped as the last of the passengers left the area, and the deck hands prepared to cast off again. The machine gunner wiped his face with the back of his hand and muttered, "That dame in the big picturehat was Bubbles,

16

right? I didn't see anybody get in that hotel hack with her, Boss."

The leader of the hired killers swore softly in Magyar and said, "Be still, I'm thinking. She looked nervous, even if she didn't spot us up here. Something's gone wrong."

He turned as he heard movement behind him. The team member he'd sent down to check things out came across the flat roof to say, with a shrug, "He's not aboard, Chief. I checked with a deckhand at the cantina over there. Soon as they finish unloading, they're going back up to Barrancas. That's their home port. Deckhand said everybody got off here."

The one-eyed Hungarian shook his head and said, "Impossible. There's no way we could have missed Walker and Verrier in that small crowd. They disembarked on one narrow gangplank. Everyone who left that vessel walked right through our gunsights!"

The man who'd scouted shrugged and insisted, "He got off somewhere else, then. Neither Captain Gringo nor the Frenchman are on board now. We'll just have to tell the big boss this set-up didn't work."

The one-eyed Hungarian repressed a shudder as he considered that. At least, he tried to repress a shudder, but the man he'd hired to man the Browning was an old pro, and he'd been thinking. He glanced at his sidekick, the only man in the team he knew enough to trust. The sidekick was an old pro, too. He nodded and said, softly, "Yeah, that's the way I see it, too."

As the hired gunner glanced around below to see the waterfront starting to clear, another pick-up member of the team asked the one-eyed Hungarian, "Hey, we're still going to be paid off, aren't we? I mean, it ain't our fault the guys we were after slickered us, right?"

The Hungarian snorted, "Are you crazy? The people I work for don't allow for failure!"

The semipro who'd asked didn't notice the signal the Hungarian gave one of his bodyguards. But the machine gunner had been expecting such a kissoff ever since he'd heard how casual they were about ladies who fingered people for them. His belt-feeding partner had, too, so they moved as one when he crabbed around to the far side of the tripod

17

mount, swinging the muzzle just as the body guards were going for their own guns. The results were spectacular.

The one-eyed Hungarian went down, torn to bloody shreds in the cross fire as the quicker-thinking hired gunslicks drew down on the machine-gun crew without waiting for an order. The machine gunner opened up with his clumsier but far deadlier weapon at the same time and proceeded to make hash out of everyone on the rooftop even as he died in a hail of pistol rounds! The Browning fell silent as the gunner died with his hands on the grips and his wounded partner started crawling away, sobbing and trailing blood. A bullet-riddled rifleman, totally confused but still upright on his knees, fired instinctively at the only moving target left and blew the beltman's head to bloody froth before he, in turn, fell forward on his smoking rifle to die with a defeated little sigh.

There are certain limits to La Siesta, even in the tropics, so after a time a couple of Tucupita police officers got around to investigating the most astounding noise coming from the waterfront. A deckhand from the still standing steamboat pointed up at the smoke haze hanging above the flat-topped warehouse, and so the cops went up a side ladder, gasped, and hurried back to headquarters to report the massacre.

As is the case in most police departments, most of the men on the Tucupita force were just doing their job and were as confused about the bloody mess on the roof as anyone else might have been. But the people who'd hired the one-eyed Hungarian hired lots of people, and so, as soon as he had a chance, a certain police sergeant made a phone call.

In a luxurious plantation house outside of town the man who took the call listened bleakly, interjecting a question now and then as the other rather sleek men in the fan-cooled room tried to follow the one way conversation with worried glances at one another. The conversation didn't take long. The plantation owner cradled the telephone, sighed, and said, "Well, Señores, I told you this Captain Gringo was good. You'll remember it was my suggestion we try a gentler approach. But I was outvoted, eh?"

A fatter, oiler man brushed a fly from his face and asked, "Get to what happened, damn it!" and the man by the phone said, "They got our executioners. Don't ask me how. No witnesses report even seeing a tall blond gringo and a small dapper Frenchman. Nobody remembers them even

18

coming ashore from the damned boat. But they most obviously *did!* Don't ask me how."

Another man in the room frowned and asked, *"Madre de Dios,* you say they got past the Hungarian?"

The man who'd taken the call smiled thinly and said, "You weren't listening. They didn't get *by* the Hungarian. They *got* the Hungarian! He and his whole damned team. *Seven* of them, Señores! Seven picked killers, waiting in ambush and well hidden. The policeman I have on the payroll says it looked like a slaughterhouse up there, and the people who reported the shootout say it was over in one short furious burst. Our own machine gunner seems to have gotten off a few rounds, but if he hit that big blond or the Frenchman he didn't slow them down very much, since they are nowhere to be seen and there wasn't so much as a drop of blood anywhere but atop the roof of my warehouse. I *warned* you something like this might happen, remember?"

The fat greasy man stuck out his lower lip and said, "It must have been a double cross. They had friends here in the delta, or maybe the killers you hired had a falling out and . . ."

"Damn it," the planter exploded, "nobody but us had any way of knowing he was in the damned country! Our female agent met him aboard that steamboat and contacted us at the next landing. You voted liquidating him as the safest way to deal with a wild card and I reluctantly agreed. I agree he must be heading this way to get in on the war we seem to be about to have. I sent my best man to kill him before he could contact anyone else in Venezuela, and we know he didn't use the phone, once, upstream. So forget about confederates here in the delta. The big bastard most obviously didn't *need* them! As for our men having a disagreement, I can count. I sent seven to assassinate Captain Gringo and all seven are dead. Santa Maria, do I have to draw you a picture? The big Yanqui is on to us and he plays just as rough as everyone told us he did!"

A cooler man in a corner regarded the tip of his cigar, thoughtfully, and asked, *"Es verdad,* we underestimated this Captain Gringo, or perhaps we overestimated the Hungarian. But what's done is done. What's our next move?"

The man who'd taken the call grimaced and said, "I was hoping nobody would ask that. I don't know about the rest of

you, but I'm about to pay a visit to my hacienda on the llanos, far upstream."

"Your cattle spread is rather far from here where the action promises, no?"

"That's what I just said."

There was more than one telephone in the delta area and more than one Venezuelan public servant taking money on the side, so on the far side of Tucupita another man was hanging up with a puzzled frown. His name was Greystoke and he worked for British Intelligence, although he didn't announce this very often. The cool blond buffing her nails in Greystoke's study looked up and asked, "Trouble, Darling? You look like you just met a ghost in the loo."

Greystoke smiled fondly down at her, running wistful eyes over her nude curves, as he said, "I think I know who the ghost is. Pity, I was rather looking forward to the rest of this siesta, but duty calls and all that rot."

Greystoke was one of those Oxford types who managed to look dignified stark naked, but as he reached for his pants the blond looked startled and asked, "You're not going out in this heat?"

"Have to, Old Girl. No phone line to Her Majesty's flagship off the coast and even if there were, the perishing Yanks would have it tapped. I'll try to get back by midnight. But I might be tied up with this bloody little war business, so, if I don't make it, start without me."

The blond ran a hand over her own flesh, teasingly, and laughed. Then she said, "Honestly, I wish you weren't so eternally secretive, Darling. You know *I* work for Whitehall, too."

Greystoke smiled and added, "Quite. Never do for me to talk in my sleep with anyone *else,* eh what? I'm not being sneaky, Pamela. It's that damned Yank, Captain Gringo, again."

The cool-looking blond, who wasn't as cool as she looked, raised an eyebrow and said, "Oh, is *he* going to play

20

the Great Game with us again? I didn't know he was anywhere near this soggy place."

Greystoke started dressing as he replied, "I didn't, either. But I just got a report that's changed my mind. Dick Walker apparantly ran into a rather good hired killer called *the Hungarian* and I must say he did a lovely job on the bugger."

"Really? How do you know it was your old chum, Walker?"

"My informants tell me the Hungarian had been sent to kill Captain Gringo, and now the Hungarian is in the morgue full of machine-gun bullets. Simple deduction, my dear Watson."

"You had Captain Gringo working for you one time, didn't you, Darling?"

"I suppose one might say that. Walker tends to be a free thinker and one just never knows how things will turn out. But what's all this sudden interest in a wandering gun thug, Pam? You don't know him, do you?"

The cool-looking blond rubbed herself hotter than Greystoke thought she should as she replied, "Can't say I have, but I did meet another spy who spent a night with him. She's still rather awed by the experience."

Greystoke grimaced, reached for a tie, and said, "No doubt. But I fear I'm sending you on another mission, Dear Girl. Try to think of it as a sacrifice for Queen and country, eh what?"

He chuckled as he knotted the tie and added, "I say, that *would* be something for the books, eh what? You seem to be insatiable and Dick Walker's said to be a sex maniac. Pity you'll never meet, eh what?"

"Don't be bitchy, Darling. A girl can't help her appetite and I told you you were quite nice. I'm not sure I'd enjoy this renegade American in any case. He sounds a bit uncouth and I do like manners in a lover, even if what that other girl told me about his anatomy could be true."

Mollified, Greystoke said, "Oh, Walker's as much a gentleman as those bloody yanks ever manage to produce. I rather *like* the chap—when we're not trying to kill one another. Have to go now, Pet. The admiral will have a fit when he hears Captain Gringo's in this game."

He was in a hurry, but Pamela was a curious profession-

al as well as a nymphomaniac, so she insisted. "Wait, there's something I don't understand about this business, Darling. You did say Dick Walker is a deserter from the American army, right?"

"Of course. It's in his dossier. He was a white cavalry officer with the colored U.S. Tenth, fighting Apache and all that rot, when he got in trouble with his superiors and had to leave the States one jump ahead of an army hangman. Some say he was brought up on a false charge by enemies, but that's neither here nor there now. He killed a fellow officer as he was escaping and so the fat's in the jolly fire if and when they ever catch him. Listen, Pam, this is all terribly interesting, but I have a bloody admiral waiting to fight a bloody war and ..."

"Stop and *think* a moment, Darling. No matter how interesting this Captain Gringo may be in or out of bed, he *can't* be here to work for the *other* side, this time, can he?"

Greystoke started to object, frowned, and spoke: "I say, you're right. The other side, here in Venezuela, is the bloody perishing *Yanks!* And the bloody perishing Yanks have a rather large reward on Captain Gringo's bloody head!"

Pamela laughed, "There, you see? He has to be on *our* side if he's on any side at all. Who was this Hungarian person, and why was he trying to kill Captain Gringo?"

Greystoke frowned. "The Hungarian was working for certain Venezuelan rebels against the established government who happen to feel they'd get a better shake living under the Union Jack."

"The Hungarian was trying to kill Walker for the Queen?"

"Not exactly, but close enough. Strictly between us, Venezuelan traitors, to give them their right name, heard Walker was coming and thought that all in all it might be best to eliminate him from the game no matter who he may be working for, see?"

"No, I don't see. I think it was rather rude as well as foolish. I think we might have been able to make a deal with him, since he's a soldier of fortune who'd worked for Britain in the past."

Greystoke shrugged and added, "I doubt he'd fight his own countrymen, bitter as he may be. But it's too late, now,

22

in any case. Walker has a bit of a temper. He'll never join the side that just tried to kill him. If he finds out they were tied in with British Intelligence, he'll no doubt be most annoyed with us, as well, and you can see how unsettling it can be to have Captain Gringo mad at you."

"Oh, dear, what do you intend to do about it, Darling?"

Greystoke shrugged. "Only thing I can do, I fear. We'll have to kill him ourselves."

"I hope you're not serious, Darling. It sounds rather beastly, if you ask me."

Sighing, Greystoke said, "Nobody's asking you, Pam. Nobody's even asking me. The lad's a wild card in a very serious game of power politics and you know very well that Whitehall would kill you or me, if it meant winning the Great Game."

As the capybara approached the tree-shaded hammock, Gaston reached for his pistol and observed, *"Regardez,* here comes the biggest rat on the face of the Earth, but it's our supper, anyway."

Captain Gringo grabbed Gaston's arm and said, "Hold your fire, damn it. It's not a rat, it's a capybara, and they're harmless vegetarians."

Gaston smiled and insisted, "But I am not, my old and rare. The overgrown rodent looks plump and juicy and I intend to have it for supper, as I said."

"It's early, yet. I don't want to build a fire out here on the open llano 'til we have a better idea who might be watching."

"Merde alors, I am hungry, Dick!"

"Oh, for Chrissake, it's not even three yet. Don't you ever think about anything but your Goddamn stomach?"

"Mais oui, I have other appetites as well, but that creature does not appeal to me as a sex partner, even if it was a bit larger. One must draw the line *somewhere,* hein?"

He started to raise the pistol as Captain Gringo shook

his own head and Gaston's arm as he said, "I mean it, Gaston. No shooting, no smoke, no nothing in this exposed position."

Gaston stared morosely around as he tucked his gun away, but observed, "You are becoming *très* wary, even for a man on the run, Dick. *Regardez*, we are in the middle of nowhere. There is nothing to be seen between us and the horizon on all sides. How far could the sound of a discreet shot carry across all this sawgrass, hein?"

Captain Gringo said, "Look again. It's not all open llano. There are other islands of trees, like this one, and your friendly neighborhood capybara just came out of that tangle of high reed, over to our left along the river bank. Isn't that more interesting than what the critter might taste like?"

Gaston's eyes narrowed thoughtfully as he traced an imaginary line from the stray rodent out in the open to the acre or so of twelve foot reeds it had come from. At about the same time the capybara became aware of the two men on the hammock and veered away, grunting like a suckling pig. Gaston shrugged and replied, "Perhaps it hoped for more shade here among our trees." But Captain Gringo shook his head and said, "It's an aquatic animal, Gaston. Capybara cool off in the river, not under a tree. Besides, there'd be plenty of shade among those reeds to anyone that short. Something spooked it out in the open."

The capybara had picked up their voices and was trotting toward another hammock a quarter mile away on its oddly deerlike legs. Gaston said, "Those reeds are not moving. Maybe a cayman wanted capybara for supper, too? How do you feel about roast cayman tail, Dick? Remember the time we had some in that Indian camp? It tasted quite acceptable, considering the source and crude preparation."

Captain Gringo shook his head with a weary smile. "Let's worry about supper when it's supper time. I want to get away from this damned river country before we build any fires." Then, before Gaston could reply, the tall American added, "Oh, oh, look at that spooked river rat."

Gaston did so, and said, "*Oui,* it does not seem to find that hammock over there to its liking, either. It's cutting back to the river bank. Perhaps it's just trotting about for exercise?"

"In this heat? It liked this hammock fine until it spotted

us here. It was making a beeline for that other one until it spotted something it didn't like over there, either!"

Gaston stared at the other tree clump, a rifle shot away, as he frowned and said, "I do not think so, Dick. Have you forgotten we were out in the open nearby, with our backs to those trees?"

"No, and it gave me one hell of a turn when I thought of it, too! There's something or somebody *over* there, Gaston!"

"Ridicule! Assuming some other people were already enjoying La Siesta when we arrived a short time ago, they most certainly must have seen us as we stood over there by the river bank, hein?"

"Yeah, makes you wonder, right?"

"Mais non! If they were bandits they would have ambushed us. If they are innocent travelers, they would have called out to us, *non?*"

Captain Gringo shook his head and said, "Why take chances? If anyone's over there, they don't know us, and this country gets sort of wild around the edges. You're right that out-and-out bastards would have opened up on us by now. Anyone else that may be over there is in our shoes. They don't know who we are and they see no reason to find out who we are, see?"

Gaston shrugged and asked, "What is your plan, then? Do we approach them waving our kerchiefs, or what?"

The tall American said, "I don't see any reason why we should. If people leave me alone, I leave them alone. They can't get at us without breaking cover. Why stick our own necks out?"

"But, Dick, they may have food, or even better, a boat to cross that damned flood channel!"

"We don't need to bum food. We've got guns and you just saw how good the hunting is with the flood waters high. If they had a boat, they'd be *going* somewhere in it, for Pete's sake! Would you drag a 'boat that far from the river to sit under a tree?"

Gaston pursed his lips and said, "You are right. Assuming someone's there in the first place. But how long does this Mexican standoff go on? If they are there, they do not have to guess about this hammock. They know we're here. Ergo they will not break cover until *we* do, hein?"

Captain Gringo glanced up at the sun and growled, "I

25

wish you hadn't brought that up. There's no point in trying to move on right now in any case, but once it starts to cool we have to think about crossing that damned flood channel."

Gaston reached over his own head to grasp a red barked tree limb as he explored the possibility of breaking it off. Captain Gringo asked, "What do you think you're doing now? They'll see the branches moving over here, Dammit!"

Gaston said, *"Merde alors,* we've agreed they know we're here in any case. While we wait each other out, it may be a good idea to consider how one is to build your triple titted raft without machetes, hein?"

"We can't use these trees, Gaston. They're gumbo-limbo and ironwood. Even if we could cut enough to matter with our damned pen knives, I doubt if anything we knocked together would float with us aboard it."

Gaston sighed. "That's what I meant. Don't ask me to *swim* that channel, either. Cayman and piranha both make me *très nervouse.*"

Captain Gringo didn't answer as he took out another cigar and gripped it, unlit, between his teeth. Gaston saw his bigger and younger friend was watching the other trees and said, "Dick? You *do* have *some* plans regarding that river, *non?*"

Captain Gringo shrugged and said, "Let's take it a step at a time. First we find out if anyone around here is likely to shoot at us while we're trying to cross the water. Then we figure out how to cross it."

"Eh, bien, perhaps they will come out for a chat as soon as things cool off a bit, hein. After all, they, too, must wish to resume their journey as the sun sinks to a more civilized angle."

Again Captain Gringo didn't answer. He knew that it was altogether possible there was nobody over there at all and that he was spooked over nothing more than an oddly behaving wild animal. But if he had no intention of breaking cover until he could be sure, how could he expect anyone who *knew* for sure to do as much? He sighed and said, "We have to wait until dark. I'll look dumb as hell if there's nobody over there, but I'd rather look dumb than dead."

Later that same afternoon a red-faced man in a soggy, white linen suit took advantage of the late siesta hours to slip in the back door of the American Consulate in Curiapo, another delta port sixty miles south-east of the provincial capital of Tucupita.

Without knocking, the American agent entered an office and sank wearily into a rattan chair across the map table from the two military attaches sticking pins in the charts spread between them. Neither the naval or army attache were in uniform, of course. The Venezuelan government in the capital was aware that their American allies were bending a few diplomatic rules, of course. Her Brittanic Majesty was bending a few others with a battle cruiser anchored in what Venezuela insisted was Venezuelan waters. So the civilian clothes were to fool the Brits, not the ruling military junta headed by General Juaquin Crespo of Venezuela.

The agent who'd just slipped in took out a cotton bandana, wiped his face, and marveled, "It must be a hundred in the shade out there. I just talked to my informant from the anti-Crespo faction. We got troubles, boys."

The less-wilted navy man at the table smiled wistfully. "I never would have guessed that, Rogers. Look where the fucking Lime Juicers have this battle cruiser, now. I get the distinct impression they're daring somebody to do something about it."

The Army attache growled, "They must think we're bluffing. What are you navy guys going to do about that British gunboat, Commander?"

The navy man grimaced and replied, "It's not a gunboat, it's a no-kidding battle cruiser with eight-inch guns. It's backed by some bigger, full-sized battleships with sixteen-inchers, just a few feet inside legal British boundaries to the south-east. They don't think we're bluffing, Gents. They *know* we're bluffing. We don't have anything in this neck of the woods that's about to take on such a boat."

The army man said, "Damn it, that trespassing cruiser's

27

between wooded banks all around. If we moved some field artillery in . . ."

"Why not ask the tooth fairy for coat artillery while we're at it, Colonel?" The navy man cut in, adding, "Assuming the Brits allowed us to land troops to the north, which is assuming one hell of a lot, there's just no way in hell that troops can move across the Orinoco Delta enough to matter. Look at the damned map. It's a maze of island, channel, and swamp. There's not a single road leading anywhere through the delta more than a country mile or so. If we have it out with them, here, it'll be an amphibious war, and, Gents, Queen Vickie *has* us on the *water!*"

"Guerrillas," cut in the florid field agent, flatly.

The two attaches looked blankly at him and he nodded. "That's what I came to tell you, damn it. There's a joker in the deck we just found out about. Somebody just imported a brace of outside mercenaries that neither Washington nor Caracas told us about. Guy called Captain Gringo's leading the outfit. He's supposed to be good."

The navy man looked blank. The army attache gasped, "Jesus, I know who he is. His real name's Richard Walker. He's wanted by the army on everything but child molesting and we're not too sure about that! He was posted as a first lieutenant on the Mexican border when he suddenly went crazy a while back. He sided with some Mexican rebels, against orders, and after his court martial he killed a guard officer busting out. He's supposed to be a small arms and machine-gun expert. Frankly, I think our little brown brothers overestimate him, but I guess they need outside help with anything more complicated than a muzzle loader, eh?"

The field agent said, "I hear it another way, Commander. This Walker guy's not your usual bush-league soldier of fortune. He's worked for the Brits and the Germans down here, as well as the unwashed locals. That's the part that's driving me nuts, trying to figure out."

The navy man shrugged and asked, "Isn't it obvious? If this renegade Yank works for the Brits, they must have hired him to add some woe to the troubles we already have right now, eh?"

Rogers shook his head and said, "Too easy. That's what *I* thought, too, when I heard he was in Venezuela. I told you I just picked up some stuff in the street. Walker and his

28

sidekick, Verrier, just blew the shit out of some guys we had down as hired-guns for British Intelligence. Happened this morning, up in Tucupita. An all-around bad guy called the Hungarian was all set to ambush this Captain Gringo when the renegade somehow turned the tables on him and his gang. Chopped the shit out of them with machine-gun fire and, get this, the Hungarian had a machine gun, too!"

The officers working the map table stared blankly at one another. The army man said, "Okay, so Walker's not over-estimated. But, what the hell can it mean? He can't be working for British Intelligence if he's swapping shots with them. But he sure as hell isn't working for *us!*"

The navy man asked, "Could he just be crazy, like you army guys say?"

Rogers, the field agent, shook his head. "I wouldn't know about his mental stability, but, up to now, he and Verrier have always worked for money. Walker's supposed to be a little quixotic and they say he'll shoot a bandit just because he's bothering somebody. But his French business partner's a dedicated cynic who only hires out for cold cash, to the highest bidder."

The navy man nodded and added, "Ergo, somebody here in Venezuela has offered these wildmen cold cash. But that takes us right back to *who,* doesn't it?"

Rogers said, "Yeah, some son-of-a-bitch is holding out on us. General Crespo and the ruling junta may be hedging their bets, since they don't know President Cleveland like we do. Try it this way: suppose Crespo's afraid we'll back down and leave him holding the Monroe Doctrine? That'd mean the Brits moving in, and the Venezuelans resisting as guerrillas in this green hell. If you're going into the guerrilla business, you need guys who know how it's done, right?"

There was a moment of silence. Then the army man said, "That has to be it. The fuckin' greasers don't *trust* us, after all we've tried to do for them!"

Rogers nodded. "That's the way I see it. I've never been too keen on this adventure anyway. I'll be damned if I see why one poor Yank should die down here for people who don't even like us. If it was up to me, the Venzies and Brits could fight it out between them for this soggy real estate. Who cares who owns the Orinoco Delta anyway?"

The navy commander suddenly looked older as he

sighed and said, "Our President and Commander-in-chief cares. I suppose it's what we get for electing a Fundamentalist; but whatever he is, Grover Cleveland is not bluffing. I wasn't supposed to mention this quite so soon, Gents, but both the Atlantic and Pacific fleets have been put on full alert and all leaves are cancelled until further notice for the United States Marines."

The army man frowned and demanded, "How come war wasn't informed of this, Commander? Are you goddam mop-jocks trying to hog this war?"

The navy man shook his head sadly and said, "I just told you Washington means to back Venezuela to the bitter end, and I assure you the navy won't try to fight the British Empire alone!"

"Yeah? So how come the army's not getting more of the action down here in the delta, Commander?"

"Two reasons. I just explained the opening campaigns will have to be amphibious. The second reason should be obvious: who's going to be defending three thousand miles of our border with *British Canada*, once the shooting starts down here?"

Out on the flooded llano, Gaston suddenly nudged Captain Gringo and said, "You were right, Dick. Did you just see that flash from over on that other hammock?"

The American nodded and answered, "Yeah. Looked like the sun glancing off gold. Must be a dame over there, or a guy with fancy taste. They know we're here, and they're trying to lie doggo, but somebody always moves, and when they're wearing gold bangles it can show."

Gaston looked up at the sun before he said, "I grow *très fatigué* with this game of hide and seek, Dick. They must know there are only two of us, and would have seen we have no rifles. They have to be a small party of *très nervous* travellers. Let me signal to them, hein?"

The American shook his head. "Don't. Nervous people shoot a lot. We'll wait until the sun goes down and nobody

gets hurt. We're almost due west of them. The sun will blind them from the horizon as we simply stroll out the back way. The moon won't rise for an hour or so and they'll likely run like hell through the darkness, too."

Gaston nodded, but said, "How droll, the lady wearing the gold whatever may be attractive, and now we shall never meet. You have no romance in your glacial Saxon soul, Dick, but, all in all, discretion may be our best bet."

Captain Gringo was about to say one thing, when he suddenly narrowed his eyes and muttered, "Oh, shit, look over there to the south-east!"

Gaston followed his younger friend's gaze, spotted the six horsemen coming over the grassy horizon, and whistled softly. "It is after three, so they've broken siesta, whoever they may be. They're not military, thank *Le Bon Dieu!* They look like vaqueros, non?"

Captain Gringo said, "You call 'em Llaneros down here, I think. I don't see 'em herding any cows, and they're packing a mess of hardware for run of the mill cow punchers."

Gaston studied the approaching riders with no further comment as they rode flashing and jingling in the afternoon sun. Each wore ammo bandoleers criss-crossed on his chest, and while they wore white cotton in place of the leather charro outfits of the northern vaquero, they'd sewn conchos along the seams of their tropic work pajamas and the leader's hat was a mass of gilt embroidery. A man riding at his left carried a red banner on a long bamboo staff. Gaston grunted and said, "The rather dramatic battle ensign would not seem to be the colors of Venezuela, Dick."

Captain Gringo agreed. "I noticed. I've never figured out why the gangs down here need private flags, but a lot of them seem to enjoy looking like soldados. Solid red's usually a rebel flag. Who do you suppose they think they're rebelling against?"

Gaston began to check his revolver's ammunition as he replied, "I have no great interest, but we might ask them, if they come this way."

Captain Gringo drew his own .38 and slipped an extra round in the usually empty sixth chamber as he said, "We're okay if they keep the same heading to the river. They should pass us by half a mile. Maybe this is a break. They're bee-lining. They may know a ford we missed."

31

The two soldiers of fortune hunkered down in the shade to watch as the armed band approached. Then, as if to make a liar of Captain Gringo, the man in the fancy hat spotted the water ahead and reined his pony to a slower walk as he considered this revolting development. Gaston murmured, "They must not have expected that flood channel to be filled, either. It must be a dry swale in less dramatic times, hein?"

"Just keep it down and watch, damn it! If that stream's really not supposed to be there, it might not be as deep as we supposed. If they know this country, they'll know where to ford it."

The six riders walked their mounts to the boggy bank that had stopped the two men on foot earlier. The one carrying the flag staff probed the muddy water with the butt, rode his mount knee deep in the current, then turned to rejoin his companions, shaking his head. Captain Gringo muttered, "Shit. They're as lost as we are!"

The mounted men seemed to be discussing their next move as they lounged in their saddles. The leader pointed east and it looked like they were about to ride off. Then one of them pointed at the mystery hammock Gaston and Captain Gringo had been worried about. He shouted to his comrades and even from a quarter mile away one could see the sudden tenseness in the mounted party. Captain Gringo said, "Oh oh, looks like somebody flashed a play pretty again."

"Better them than us." Gaston shrugged, adding, "If they attack the other party, all our problems are solved at once, hein?"

The mounted band didn't attack, exactly. All six dismounted and drew their guns at a safe distance before moving in a gingerly skirmish line toward the hammock in the near distance. The leader called out, loudly enough for Captain Gringo and Gaston to hear from their own hiding place: "Hey! Estupidos, we see you in those bushes! For why do you hide from honest men, eh? Come out and show yourselves. Let us see what you think you are hiding from El Ministro, eh?"

Captain Gringo expected the people hiding in the other cover to put up more fight. He knew he'd have started by blowing holes in that pretty hat if the sons-of-bitches tried that on *his* hammock. But a little black man in a white suit came out of the trees waving a kerchief, followed by two

women dressed in the white tropic habits of some religious order. As the sunlight flashed on the big gold cross one of them wore on the long skirt of her habit, Captain Gringo shook his head and said, "For God's sake, they're nuns! We've been pinned down sweating bullets over a couple of nuns all afternoon!"

The dismounted gang seemed amused, too, as they closed in, putting away their guns. From where he watched, Captain Gringo couldn't tell what the two frightened sisters looked like, but when one of the gang yanked her gold cross off her skirt he growled low in his throat and said, "Well, we know now. Those guys are bandits, and not very nice ones. A Hispanic Catholic who'd rob a nun would eat shit for breakfast."

Gaston said, "No doubt they suffered deprived youths. Stay out of it, Dick. I don't think they'll hurt those women, seriously."

The leader of the gang tossed his hat aside on the grass and reached for one of the nuns with a grin. The frightened nun cowered away and the old black man tried to get between her and the outlaw leader. The bandit backhanded him to the grass and when the spunky Negro gamely tried to rise, shouting something, the outlaw drew his revolver and shot him, like he was swatting a fly!

The nun he'd been pawing screamed and dropped to her knees by the dead or dying Negro in the grass. That was a tactical error. The outlaw leader jumped on her and proceeded to rip her habit off as they struggled in the grass.

The one who'd been wearing the gold cross tried running, but that didn't work much better for two of the bandits grabbed and threw her to the sod. Her naked legs looked strangely obscene as one of them proceeded to lift her skirts for his comrade. Captain Gringo muttered, "Okay, that's about enough of this shit!" as he rose to his feet, gun in hand, and started forward. Gaston pleaded, *"No,* Dick! The odds are *très* lousy and we owe these women nothing!"

Then Gaston shrugged and followed, muttering, "Sacre Goddamn, I thought you were a Protestant!"

There was no sneaky way to do it. So the outlaws spotted the two of them coming long before they were in pistol range. It seemed to take their mind off the women they'd been about to rape and the two nuns huddled on their

33

knees together near the fallen black man as all six of the outlaws lined up to face the two approaching strangers, more surprised than worried. The leader called out, "Hey, who are you hombres?" as Captain Gringo muttered to Gaston, "You start on the left and I'll start from the right, okay?"

"*Oui,* if we fail to meet in the middle, it's been nice knowing you." Captain Gringo didn't answer. He and Gaston both had their guns in hand, so, as he judged the distance about right, he started firing, not looking at the ones Gaston had selected to his left. There were six outlaws and the two soldiers of fortune had twelve rounds in their chambers. They each got off four, since after nailing the three men on either side of the leader in the middle, they each put a bullet in him at the same time. As one of the downed men rolled over and tried to rise, Gaston fired a round into his head and said, "How *anticlimactique!* Such obvious amateurs had no business taking up a life of crime, hein? *Merde alors,* not one of them got off a round at us!"

Captain Gringo ignored Gaston and the bodies stretched out on the grass in a long ragged line as he walked over to the two sobbing women by the gang's male victim. The little Negro lay on his back with a puzzled expression on his face. He was dead, anyone could see. Captain Gringo removed his hat and said, "I am called Ricardo Walker, Sisters. I'm sorry my friend and me were so far away when you needed help."

The older of the two women seemed a bit dazed and remained on her knees, staring mutely down at the dead man. The younger and prettier one rose to throw herself against Captain Gringo as she sobbed, "Oh, we thought you men were outlaws, too. How will we ever thank you? How can anyone repay such heroism?"

Captain Gringo was uncomfortably aware of firm and ample breasts against his chest as he absently placed his free hand around her to keep from losing his balance. She smelled good, too. Gaston came over, eyes twinkling, and said, "Eh, bien. I see everyone is on a friendly footing at last."

Captain Gringo moved away from the nun with a meaningless comment about reloading. As he did so she followed, not grabbing again but seemingly intent on staying close as possible to him. He introduced Gaston, not meeting the Frenchman's eyes, and the nun said, "Oh, forgive my man-

34

ners. I am Sister Dominica and this is my Mother Superior, The Reverend Mother Juana Maria. We shall ever be in your debt, Señores."

Captain Gringo wasn't sure how one said, "Shucks, 'twarn't nothing," in Spanish, so he didn't try. He was a Protestant, but everybody knew nuns weren't supposed to gush like that. It wasn't the words so much as the man-eating smile that went with them. He could see, despite her severe habit and whimple, that Sister Dominica was pretty as hell, with spitfire Spanish eyes. He supposed they'd put her in the convent before she'd learned what trouble a girl could get into by flashing them like that at a man.

Gaston was helping the older nun who'd worn the unfortunately visible gold cross. She still looked numb and hadn't missed the cross yet. Captain Gringo looked around and spotted it gleaming in the grass a few yards out. He tucked his reloaded gun away and headed for it. The young and pretty Sister Dominica joined him, hooking her arm through his as she said, "We were on our way to a new nursing mission when everything went wrong all at once. Poor José, our servant, let our team run off with our wagon when we camped last night. We were blocked on foot by that awful flood stream, there, and so were sheltered in those trees when we saw you and your friend approach. *I* thought you looked like gentlemen, but Mother Superior was afraid there were banditos about and . . ."

"Your mother superior was right." He cut in, adding, "I understand what's been going on, now. Aren't you, uh, ladies supposed to be a bit more shy around strange men, Sister Dominica?"

"Heavens, you and your brave little comrade are not strange men, you are our *saviors!* But call me Niqui, Ricardo. That's what the other girls call me."

He bent down, picked up the cross and its broken gold chain and said, "I'll call you Sis, if formalities bother you. You must have been sort of young when you joined up, eh?"

"Oh, yes, I was about fourteen when I took my first orders. Before that, I was an orphan at the mission, of course."

"You're starting to make sense. What do you mean, *about* fourteen? Don't you know how old you are?"

"Oh, I think I must be twenty or so. You see, I was a

35

foundling. They say I seemed to be two or three when I was left on the mission steps by someone. But what does it matter, how old I may be?"

He smiled crookedly down at her and said, "I guess it doesn't matter, Sis." Adding, under his breath, "Boy, what a waste!"

The older Mother Juana Maria had composed herself by the time they rejoined her and Gaston. Captain Gringo handed her the cross and said, "I'm sorry it's broken, but I'm sure it can be fixed."

"Those men will surely roast in Hell," Mother Juana Maria said grimly, as she took her cross back, saw it was now impossible to wear and put it away in some pocketlike fold of her habit.

Gaston looked up at the sun and said, "It will soon be cool enough to seriously consider moving on. Dick and me are on our way to the north coast. Might one ask where you sisters intend to spend the evening?"

The nuns looked blankly at one another and Mother Juana Maria said, rather imperiously, "You señores will of course have to see us to the nursing mission, two leagues to the north. I doubt if you would wish for to go much further. As you just learned, the llano is infested with banditos."

Sister Dominica added, "To the north of Los Llanos it gets worse between here and the Carribean. The hills along the coast are jungle covered."

"Infested with banditos, too?" asked Gaston, and the girl said, "No, wild Indians. Nobody goes into the jungle if they can possibly avoid it."

Gaston shot a look at Captain Gringo, who shrugged and said, "We can't possibly avoid it. But we'll get you ladies to your mission first."

Then he turned to Gaston and said, "We'd better round up those horses they left over there by the water, before they run off. Riding beats walking and they may have a shovel or two among their saddle gear."

"Shovel, Dick?"

"Come on, we can't just leave these guys laying here, can we?"

Gaston said, "I don't see why not." Then he winked at Mother Juana Maria and explained, "He takes his Christian duties *très* seriously, for a Protestant. But the ground is soft

after all that rain and what harm can it do to say a few words over them, hein?"

Mother Juana Maria drew herself up and snapped, "I will pray for poor José—but that is all. I have no intention of praying for the souls of men who tried to . . . never mind."

Gaston nodded, understandingly, and the two men ambled over to the six horses near the water's edge. One spooked and ran off nervously, but the other five didn't seem to care who rode them and, what the hell, they only needed four.

As they'd hoped, one of the dead bandits had a folding spade tied to his saddle. Gaston gathered the reins of the four best mounts and said, "I don't know how you do it, my old and rare. We left that steamboat on foot and alone. Now, we face the evening with spirited steeds and a couple of spirited women, if I'm any judge."

Captain Gringo muttered, "Don't talk dirty, you old goat. The dames are nuns, in case you didn't notice."

Gaston laughed and said, "True. But you seem to have the younger one eating out of your hand already and as for mine, well, what is romance if there is no *challenge*, hein?"

"You can't be serious. What kind of an asshole would make a play for a nun?"

"An asshole who likes women, perhaps? That is what they are, under all that camouflage, you know. Growing up in New England has left you at a certain disadvantage, my old and rare. I grew up close enough to Notre Dame to regard our faith with less awe than you Anglo Saxon types. We have had the church *très* domesticated in France for some time, you know."

"Screw France! Any man who fights with his feet and fucks with his mouth has to be a little confused about the facts of life. Those girls aren't French nuns, they're Spanish nuns, and the Spanish never invented the Grand Inquisition because they take a casual view of religion. For Chrissake, Gaston, you know how dangerous it can be down here to make a pass at a Spanish girl who's *not* a nun!"

"But of course, my old and rare. That is my point regarding these otherwise attractive women. Since it is so terribly easy to get killed down here over any woman at all, why not go after the ones that look attractive? Little Dominica is *très formidable*, and I noticed the older one's legs when those idiots were treating her so impolitely."

"Knock it off. We're getting close enough for them to hear you. And wipe that silly smirk off your face, too. We've got enough trouble facing us, and so help me, if you make a grab for either of those nuns I'm going to slap you silly!"

As they rejoined the nuns, Captain Gringo took the spade from its saddle mount and suggested they go back to the shade of the hammock while he and Gaston disposed of the dead. He didn't add that the next few minutes figured to be sort of ugly, but he could see by their stricken expressions that they didn't really want to watch.

Mother Juana Maria said, "I wish you would bury poor José well distant from those horrid bandits. Frankly, it is all the same to me if you just throw them in the stream and let the water carry them away."

She took her younger companion's arm and led her into the shade as the tall American shrugged and got to work. The sod was tough, but the red soil under the grass roots was soft as mellow cheese. Gaston offered to spell him after he'd worked a while. But the tall American said, "Hell with it. I'm hitting water, just a few inches down. Feeding them to the fish seems a little ornery, but I'm not going to plant 'em all that deep, so what the hell."

Gaston started going through the dead men's pockets as the American worked. As he saw Captain Gringo making short work of his mass shallow grave he hauled the leader over by the heels and said, "Again we would seem to be combining business and pleasure, Dick. Their guns are all old single action and *très* rusty, which accounts for a lot. But they would seem to have managed a bit of serious banditry with their quite ordinary weapons. I make it close to a thousand dollars, American, between a pocket here and a leather purse there."

"What about their ammo?"

"All .44s and .45s, alas. We can't use it."

"Somebody might. We'll drop all the weapons and ammo in the water when we head on out. You start rolling the outlaws in here and I'll scoop out a better place for the colored guy."

"Eh, bien. Rather an odd companion for nuns, non?"

"What are you talking about? Sister Dominica said he was their coachman."

"*Oui. Très* curious. The late José was not a member of

any religious order. Yet they were travelling alone with him."

"Oh, hell, Gaston, they had to have *somebody* driving them! Aren't nuns allowed to take cabs?"

Gaston shrugged and said, "Perhaps. Customs may not be as strict in this part of the world."

Captain Gringo snorted in annoyance and moved off a good fifty feet to dig José's lonelier grave. He dug deeper and neater as he wondered what the hell Gaston was getting at, now. The trouble with Gaston was that he never stopped talking and only made sense half the time. Sometimes the old goat was really on to something, though, so you couldn't simply ignore his chatter. He scooped a spadeful of semi-liquid red muck out, decided that would have to do, and stood the spade on its blade in the sod to rejoin Gaston as the Frenchman rolled the last dead bandit in the larger hole. The hole was a bit snug and the guy's rump rose above the level of the llano, but what the hell, they'd all settle down under the sod in a day or so, right?

Gaston stepped over to grab José by the heels and the American said, "Hey, let's carry him right, damn it. He's one of *our* guys!"

As he bent to pick up José's shoulders Gaston said, "One doubts José would know the difference, but I am also a man of sentiment. Sacre Goddamn, I am glad we are almost through with this silly business, though. Even with the sun at a more reasonable angle, I am sweating like the pig."

They got José to the grave and lowered him into the muddy water on the bottom. As Captain Gringo straightened up, Gaston started going through the dead man's pockets and the American snapped, "Knock it off, you fucking ghoul."

Then he saw the snub-nosed Webley revolver Gaston had found on the dead man and added, with a frown, "What the hell . . . ?"

Gaston smiled thinly and answered, "What the hell, indeed. A very curious weapon for an innocent coachman to be carrying, *non?* One does not need to mention, among friends, that this weapon is a favorite among British Intelligence circles, hein?"

"Oh, shit, you're not suggesting José was a British spy?"

"Why not? I don't think the British have any Jim Crow

39

laws forbidding it. Think what a formidable cover he had if he was working for the Queen! We know the Brits are up to something sneaky in this part of South America, *non?*"

"Oh, come on, next you'll be suggesting that those two nuns are really British spies, too!"

"Eh, bien, and again why not, Dick? *Their* cover would be even better! They were unfortunate enough to run into bandits of above average rudeness. But one can see that someone like our old friend, Greystoke, would assume very few men down here would trifle with two sisters of the cloth."

"Okay, put the gun away and let me cover this poor slob."

"You don't think my, how you say, hunch, is possible?"

"Anything's possible, but your hunch is wild as hell. What are we supposed to do, shake those two dames down for concealed weapons? If the women had been armed we wouldn't have had to *rescue* them, you chump!"

Gaston put the snub-nosed pistol in his coat pocket as Captain Gringo shoved sods over the corpse. He waited until Captain Gringo said something about getting the nuns before he nodded and said, *"Oui,* I will be *très* interested in the prayers they say over José. You know I no longer take much interest in such superstitions, but I was raised a Catholic."

"That was before you went nuts, right?"

"Oui. If José was their bodyguard, they might not have thought to carry weapons. On the other hand, it all happened so fast that José never had a chance to draw that weapon I found on him, and we know *he* was armed!"

Captain Gringo started to tell Gaston he was full of shit again. But as he thought back to the short savage scene they'd witnessed from a distance he couldn't honestly say neither of the women had been trying to get to a weapon under her habit. The outlaws had been all over them and, damn it, they *had* nailed José before the little Black could go for the weapon they knew he'd been packing!

The two women had been watching from the shade and as they tethered the mounts they'd selected for the night's journey, the nuns, if they were nuns, came out of the grove to join them.

Captain Gringo didn't look at Gaston as he pointed at the grave of José. The two women crossed themselves. Did

they make the proper sign of the cross? How the hell was a New England Yankee Calvinist to know?

He let Gaston pick up the investigation as he switched the good saddle on a poor horse to a better mount. The little Frenchman followed the nuns to where José had been planted. Captain Gringo finished his simple chore and walked over to them as they were finishing whatever they were supposed to be doing.

Sister Dominica asked her older companion about the other dead men and Mother Juana Maria sniffed and repeated her comment about leaving them to the devil. It struck Captain Gringo as a little uncharitable, but what did that prove? More than one ordained priest had ordered a heretic burned alive, and some respected Protestant ministers had treated the Salem witches a little rough, too. Calvin himself had executed people who argued religion with him, and nobody'd tried to rape him! Being mad at the dead bandits didn't make Mother Juana Maria a fake nun.

He shrugged and said, "Well, folks, the sun's going down and we'd better start thinking about fording that stream before dark."

Sister Dominica dimpled and said, "Poor José said there was a ford a kilometer to the east. After we lost our team and wagon he led us this far on foot and we were going to cross after dark, but . . ."

"We know what happened after that," the American cut in, adding, "I'd have guessed west, where it should be getting less soggy, but I suppose that's why you need guides in this delta country. So east it is. Do you, uh, ladies have anything over among the trees?"

Both of them shook their heads and Mother Juana Maria said, "That fool of a Negro let the horses run away with everything. We don't even have our bedrolls or a change of . . . never mind."

Captain Gringo looked at the mounts they'd just inherited and observed, "Well, there's a serape and ground cloth tied behind each saddle. If we don't make your mission by morning . . ."

"Don't be ridiculous!" Mother Juana Maria cut in. "In the first place we Sisters Of Mercy don't camp out with strange men, and in the second, those bedrolls are probably filthy and infested with lice!"

He knew she was probably right. He looked at the low sun and said, "Okay, let's be on our way. Gaston, help Mother Juana Maria mount the bay with the blaze. I'm putting Sister Dominica aboard this pinto mare."

The older nun insisted she was quite capable of mounting her own horse, which they noticed she intended to ride sidesaddle no matter how the saddle had been designed. Sister Dominica extended her hand to Captain Gringo with a Mona Lisa smile. He shook his head and laced his fingers together, saying, "You put your foot in my hands and I'll boost you up."

She nodded in understanding as he bent at the waist to offer her a leg-up. She raised her knee high as she grabbed the horn and cantle, keeping the reins in her left hand, of course. He noticed she had one trim ankle, despite the high button shoes. Did South American nuns wear expensive fashionable kid leather shoes? As he boosted her aboard, Sister Dominica forked her free leg over the saddle, like a man, and mounted astride, with her hitherto long skirts up around her thighs, exposing her bare knees. Mother Juana Maria gasped and said, "That is no way for any proper girl to sit a horse, Sister Dominica!"

But the younger nun laughed and said, "It's even more undignified to fall off, no? I was taught to ride this way, proper or not, and in any case it is almost dark."

Mother Juana Maria started to say something, but shrugged and told Gaston, "Lead on, my good man."

Gaston raised an eyebrow and asked, "Madame does not know how to guide her own mount?"

"I have never seen the need to learn. That's what servants are for." Gaston shrugged, forked himself aboard another horse with the older nun's reins in hand, and called out, "I shall take the lead, Dick."

Captain Gringo looked up at Dominica, who shook her head and said, "I can manage my own reins, thank you. I fear I was a bit of a tomboy before I joined the order."

He mounted his own chosen gelding with a thoughtful frown as Gaston headed east with the red sunset to his rear, along with Mother Juana Maria. Captain Gringo was anxious to talk to Gaston alone. Aside from any slips the Catholic Frenchman might have noticed, Sister Dominica had just made a *lulu!*

42

She'd told him two stories, now, about her childhood.

First she'd said she'd been left on the convent doorstep as an infant. Now she said she'd been a tomboy who rode like a llanero before joining up. Either story could be true, but he couldn't see how *both* of them could!

He waved the younger nun forward, saying he'd guard the rear, and he did, in fact, looking back every once in a while. But he wasn't as worried about the empty sea of grass behind them in the sunset as he was about the mysterious women they'd picked up.

Captain Gringo wasn't as cynical as Gaston. Nobody could be. But he'd learned the hard way not to trust people blindly, and the more he thought about the nuns they'd just met, the less he trusted them.

It was true that any woman could slip into a nun's habit and it did make a swell cover in a savage but devout neck of the woods. Those outlaws had been a lot nastier than your run-of-the-mill Catholic bandit. Had he *missed* something back there? What if the band hadn't just stumbled over two innocent nuns and a servant? What if they'd been *looking* for them, and known they weren't really nuns? Rebel bands didn't just ride around out in the middle of the llano hoping to meet attractive victims. That flag they'd carried could indicate they were part of some faction in the pending war. The Brits were mixed up in it and, yeah, the Brits did issue Webley snub-noses and Sister Dominica's shoes looked a lot more Bond Street than Village Shoemaker! He wondered if she packed a Webley.

But how was he going to find out?

How did a guy go about feeling up a nun?

In the capital city of Caracas, far to the north-west, a recently purchased house of Spanish Colonial architecture had been gutted and converted, inside, to a degenerate's dream of a Persian whorehouse. The owner was indulging his limitless lust, and almost unlimited wealth and power, in what had been the master bedroom when Earth People lived there.

you to, Child. Don't worry. You'll enjoy it. While you're sucking Pedro, here, I'll be screwing your nice wet little box, eh?"

The girl started to cry. Sir Basil laughed. That was the nice thing about having orgies with children. They were never blasé about unusual positions. He knew his two young victims were confused, frightened, and filled with conflicting desire and shame. It made him feel much bigger, even though he was shorter than the black boy and almost as small as the young girl, when everyone was standing up.

He grabbed Pedro's slim brown buttocks and thrust home deeper as the boy whimpered with a mouthful of what he really wanted. A telephone rang on the nearby marble topped table. Sir Basil frowned and reached out for it, trying not to break the rhythm.

Sir Basil prided himself on his self-control, too, and business came before pleasure, when one's business was Death.

The voice at the other end snapped like a whip in Sir Basil's ear as it said, "All right, you little bastard, just what do you think you're up to, now?"

"They're named Pedro and Celestina, I believe. Is this Greystoke?"

"You know damned well it is, you sneaky Turkish whoremaster!"

Sir Basil chuckled and said, "Temper, temper. I'm a British subject of Turkish heritage in the first place, and I deal in arms, not whores, in the second. What's made you so surly, Dear Boy?"

The British Intelligence man at the other end of the long distance line said, *"You,* you oriental cocksucker! I suppose you're going to tell me you know nothing about Captain Gringo being in Venezuela, right?"

Sir Basil blinked and blanched, withdrawing from the sodomized black as his uneasy erection dropped to half mast. He said, "As Allah is my witness I hadn't heard! What's Dick Walker doing in this country, Greystoke?"

"That's what I called to find out, you two-faced little child molester."

Sir Basil glanced over at the bed, where the black Pedro had mounted Celestina to relieve their mutual tension. The boy had overstepped himself and would have to be punished,

45

but it was rather interesting to watch his brown rump bouncing like that between the girl's cream white thighs. Sir Basil asked, "Have you been spying on me again, Greystoke? My private life is none of your business. I'm a Peer of the Realm and I lunch with His Highness, as you found out the last time you tried to put me out of business."

His caller growled, "Yes, I suppose His Highness likes to be sucked off like your other friends in High Places. Let's get back to Captain Gringo. I happen to know he's worked for you in the past."

"As he has for you, Dear Boy. Soldiers of fortune tend to work for the highest bidder. But I assure you I had no idea he was in Venezuela."

"I think you're full of it, but since you won't tell me the truth when the truth is in your favor, what the devil *is* your game in Caracas?"

"Haven't your spies told you? I said his name is Pedro and she's called Celestina and at the moment they're screwing like minks, on my time, so if you don't mind . . ."

"Hang up on me and I'll send a company of Royal Marines after you, you treacherous Turk! I just asked you a question. I'm waiting for an answer!"

Sir Basil hesitated as he stared down at the children rutting on the bed. For a girl who seemed to look down on Negroes, Celestina had gotten quite friendly indeed with her fellow love toy. He'd teach her how it felt to be dominated by a grown man in a moment. Greystoke was one of those disgusting civil servants who took his duties seriously. You couldn't buy him and he wasn't as respectful of his social betters as he should have been. The prince had warned him, the last time he'd tried to get Greystoke fired, that there were some blokes working out of Whitehall that even the crown had to be careful of. Greystoke had enough on half the peers of the empire to bring down the government in scandal. Hence, it seemed more prudent to have him working for the government than against it. When Sir Basil had suggested assassination, His Highness had seemed shocked. That was the trouble with the British. They were only half-hearted degenerates with an unfortunate streak of decency when it came to more serious fun and games. Sir Basil sighed and said, "Very well, to save your agents a lot of work I may as

well tell you I'm here on my usual business. I sell things that go bump in the night."

"I know you're a stockholder in Krupp as well as Vickers Armstrong and a dozen other arms combines, Hakim. But your tale won't wash if you're suggesting you came to peddle guns in Venezuela. We're not about to have the usual banana revolution; we're getting ready to have a war between the Empire and the stubborn Yanks. The Yanks buy all their weapons from people like Colt and Remington. The Royal Navy and Marines bring their own, too. And before you feed me a lot of twaddle about arming Venezuela, I've just confirmed that Washington is shipping more weapons, free, than all the forces of Venezuela would ever be able to use."

Sir Basil shrugged and said, "True. I don't think President Cleveland is bluffing, this time. You and he have a lot in common, Greystoke. You idealistic chaps tend to be stiff necked about honor and all that rot."

"Never mind who's bluffing whom. Get to where *you* come in. If you can't sell arms to Britain, the States, or the legal government of Venezuela, who's left?"

"The illegal government, Dear Boy?"

Greystoke hesitated, then snapped, "You're mad. General Crespo's been firm in the saddle for some time in Venezuela. That's why the perishing Yanks are backing him. They have this thing about stable dictatorships."

"Quite. Makes it easier for Wall Street when a country doesn't have a revolution every few months. It's true the Crespo junta has been running things rather well down here for the past few years and it's true no rebel faction would have much chance of unseating Crespo, under normal circumstances. But we live in uncertain times, Dear Boy. This pending British invasion has everyone here in Caracas in a bit of a flap. The friends of one Cipriano Castro seem to feel a stronger hand may be needed at the helm if Venezuela is to survive this alarming confrontation between major powers, eh what?"

Greystoke asked, "Are you talking about the only crook in town that can hold a candle to you, Hakim? The Yanks would never back Cipriano Castro and his bunch. Hell, *we* wouldn't want the oily bastard running Venezuela, either!

47

He's an unscrupulous greedy political adventurer nobody in his right mind would want to do business with. I can't see Washington *or* Whitehall dealing with him!"

Sir Basil nodded and said, "You're right. Fortunately, I demand cash in advance for my wares, so he can't stick *me*."

"Good Lord! You don't mean you're running guns to the Castro faction?"

"Well, somebody has to. They have no friends in the U.S. or U.K."

"Listen, Basil, no shit, you've got to stop! Things are starting to fall in place, now. It's obvious that the rebels are hiring soldiers of fortune like Captain Gringo to go with the goodies you've been selling them! The minute we and the Yanks get into it, Castro's bunch will pull their own power play. God knows where it will lead if this thing turns into a three-sided war!"

Sir Basil shrugged again and said, "I'm an honest merchant who doesn't worry about my wares, once I sell them. I don't see why Whitehall's worried. I should think a spot of civil war here in Caracas would make things simpler, down there in the delta, eh what? Castro's gang wants to run things here where it's more civilized. They couldn't very well stop the Royal Navy, once the Yanks pull out, as they will if a band of unwashed bandits takes over the country." He sniffed and added, "One may say I'm acting as British patriot, in my own way."

Greystoke snorted at the other end of the line and said, "Listen, you oily son-of-a-bitch, I'm not *asking* you to stop playing with fire for your own good. I'm *ordering* you, in the name of the *queen!* This ruddy row with the Yanks is complicated enough, without *you* throwing eggs at the fan!"

Hakim laughed and said, "I know. Whitehall's rather counting on Morgan money and DuPont explosives when and if they have to teach the new young Kaiser a lesson, eh what? If you want my opinion, it's *you* chaps who've been casting eggs in odd places. If I were running Whitehall, I'd back off and let the ruddy Yanks and their little brown brothers *keep* the flaming delta of the flaming Orinoco."

"Nobody's asking you, you faggy Turk!"

"I know. That's why I'll tend my store and let you tend yours, and, between us girls, I wouldn't be so free with my

accusations about who may be a fag and who might be the fagee. I've heard some very odd stories about that class of yours at Eton, eh what?"

Before Greystoke could reply with more than a strangled gasp, Sir Basil hung up and said, "Move over, children. Father is coming to show you how it's done. I think you'd better suck me, Pedro. I found that business call rather distracting."

Out on the llano, the moon was rising as Captain Gringo reined in and called out, "Gaston?"

There was no answer. He and Sister Dominica seemed to be alone on the moonlit swampy prairie. The girl chimed in to shout, "Mother Superior?" and he said, "Not so loud. We seem to have gotten separated in the dark but they can't have strayed far, and we don't want to meet anyone else."

"Oh, do you think there may be more banditos on this side of the river?"

"Don't know. Let's not find out if we don't have to. How far is this nursing mission of yours supposed to be?"

"I'm not sure. Mother Juana Maria said two leagues from where you rescued us. José knew the way, but since he is dead . . ."

Captain Gringo nodded grimly, as he looked up at the stars to get his bearings. A league was about twenty statute miles—so two made forty and forty miles was a long ride when you weren't sure where the hell you were trying to go. The dead-flat soggy llano was dotted with other islands of trees all around, but presented no particular problem as long as they didn't hit another floodwater stream. He said, "Well, we could do it two ways. By now Gaston must be missing us. So if we stopped and built a fire, he'd be able to find us muy pronto if he circled back the way he and Mother Juana Maria drifted."

"But, Dick, what if someone else should see our fire?"

"I said there were two ways. Gaston's more nervous than I am, so he won't build a campfire and he'd probably be

49

surprised if I did. Putting myself in his saddle, I think I'd ride on with Mother Juana Maria and hope to spot us on the horizon, come sunrise."

The girl looked uneasily around at the silvery grass that faded into blackness well short of any horizon and said, "I am frightened, Dick. What if we get lost? What if we pass the mission in the dark?"

He shook his head and said, "Impossible. Our mounts won't carry us that far before morning. We can't risk a faster pace than a trot in this light and of course we'll have to rest them once an hour or so. If we're lucky we'll be a little more than half way there by the time it's light enough to see. If we're very lucky indeed, we should make the mission before it gets too hot for the mounts to carry us. We may have to siesta on some hammock, but . . ."

"Dick, I am a Bride of Jesus, and we are alone together," she cut in.

He grimaced and said, "Hey, let's not get *silly!* Gaston and me risked our necks to save your honor back there, remember?"

She looked away and said, "You are right, and I am sorry. I don't know why I spoke like that, just now. I didn't feel awkward around you as long as the others were with us, but now . . . never mind, shall we ride on?"

He nodded and clucked his mount forward, taking a bearing on the big dipper. He'd set a course due north. Gaston would probably do the same. When and if they stumbled over one another again they could dope out just where the damned mission might be, if there *was* a damned mission and these two dames weren't trying to pull something over on them.

Captain Gringo had been on the run too long to trust a stranger just because she was young and pretty and said she liked him. He'd never been led into an ambush by anyone dressed as a nun before, but there was always a first time. And she sure wore fancy shoes for an orphaned peon girl. He switched to English as he pointed at the sky and said, "The tail of the dipper's below the horizon, but that's the north star, there, and it never drops out of sight, even this far south."

She answered, *"Por favor, no hablo la lengua inglesa."*

50

So she hadn't bit, if she spoke English. But what good British spy would fall for such a bush league trick, right?

He said, in Spanish, "I said we'd better watch where we're going. The ground's starting to get mushy. Hear how our hoofbeats splash?"

She didn't fall into that trap, either. She said, "Oh, what are we to do if we come to more floodwater, Dick?"

It was a good question. He knew the footing was too uncertain to risk even a trot and sunrise was sure as hell fixing to catch them out in the open with one pistol between them, assuming he was packing the only one around here. He said, "I'm surprised you and Mother Juana Maria didn't think to bring along any weapons, Dominica."

"José had a shotgun in the wagon, but we lost it," she replied.

Okay, if she'd been issued a Webley she wasn't ready to announce it, even given a graceful chance.

He tried to tell himself it didn't *matter* if she and the older woman were travelling under false colors. Assuming the worst, they'd been on some dumb mission of their own, not out to trap him and Gaston some way. They were all strangers who'd met by chance, whoever anybody might be. Even if Dominica was some sort of secret agent, she wasn't interested in any secret *he* might have. What the hell did he care if she kept some of her own? He just wanted to get rid of her and be on his way, damn it!

He saw a blur of moonlit motion ahead and reined in to call out, "Hey, Gaston?"

There was no answer. He glanced over at the nun, sitting her own mount quietly, and said, "Wait here. I'll scout ahead and call back if it's all right."

"What if somebody shoots you, Dick?"

"Ride like hell. Meanwhile, just sit tight. I don't want to lose track of you, too."

He clucked his mount forward. It acted shy about going, but he heeled it hard and insisted. He started missing Dominica before he'd gone far enough to matter. He saw the motion again, low and just ahead. He reined in and swore softly. It was moonlight on running water, damn it to hell! He studied the slough for a time, called out again to Gaston, then turned to ride back to where he'd left the nun. He said,

51

"We're cut off by another flood channel. I don't understand this at all. We're only five miles or so from that last place we forded. Gaston and Mother Juana Maria have to be on this side of the creek ahead. So where the hell *are* they?"

He started to reach for his gun. The girl said, "Oh, no, if you fire your gun for Gaston, and someone else hears it . . ."

"You're right." He grimaced, putting the .38 back in its holster.

She asked, "What if they did not see the water in time? Sometimes there are cayman or piranha even in the temporary streams and . . ."

"Hey, *both* of them? One or the other would have been riding ahead. Would you follow me if I took a dive on horseback into a river, Sister Dominica?"

She laughed, relieved, and said, "Oh, you're right. And I told you to call me Niqui, Dick."

He noticed she didn't pronounce his name Deek, the way most Spanish speakers did. He didn't comment on this as he answered, "Niqui it is, then. I thought it made you nervous to be alone with a man like this?"

She sighed and said, *"Es verdad.* Right now my heart is pounding and I don't know why, but I wish for you to call me Niqui anyway. What are we going to do now, Dick?"

He assumed she meant travel plans. He said, "Well, we can't risk trying to ford strange waters in the dark and it's sort of silly just sitting here in the saddle. Let's find some high ground and cover. I think it's safe to build a small fire, in the brush. The clown who used to ride this gelding had some coffee in his saddle bags, along with a mess kit and what I sincerely hope is refritos. We'll rest our mounts while we put something in our stomachs and wait for some light on the subject."

He led them back the way they'd just ridden. As they passed the tree-covered hammock nearest the river ahead she asked, "Why do we not stop here, Dick?" and he explained, "You and your friends already made that mistake, remember? We'll be safer further from where everybody passing has to stop, and the next hammock should be drier, too."

She said, "Oh, you are so wise. I never would have thought of that. What sort of business are you and Gaston in, Dick?"

"We're sort of travelling salesmen."

"Oh, dear, I've heard dreadful stories about you travelling salesmen."

"That's all right. You're not a farmer's daughter."

He reined in at a likely island of trees and dismounted, handing his reins up to the nun as he said, "I'd better check and see if any snakes made for high ground. Wait here."

He drew his revolver and struck a match as he entered the tangle. He saw they were in luck. The tree-shaded ground under the trees was sandy and dry. A screen of brush grew all around like a privet hedge. Nobody passing would be likely to spot a modest campfire in a sandy hole he could easily scoop with the spade he'd brought along.

He got the nun and the horses. He tethered the mounts to the outer twigs of the brush, leaving them free to graze, and invisible in the dark in any case. As Niqui sat on the dry sand, he scooped out a shallow fire pit, filled it with kindling and dry branches, and lit a little blaze an Apache would have approved of. The pretty little nun looked even less nunnish as the ruddy glow illuminated her features. He noticed her whimple was pushed back and that her hair was a dark shade of red. He waited 'til he'd put the coffee pot on to boil before he commented: "I thought you girls shaved your heads."

Niqui laughed and said, "Heavens, we're a nursing order." Then she removed the cowl entirely, tossed it aside, and ran her fingers through her luxurious red mop, adding, "Oh, that feels good. My head's been itchy all day."

He frowned and worked on the tin of refritos or whatever as he asked, "You mean different orders of nuns have different rules, Niqui?"

"Of course," she said. "Our order spends less time counting our beads, if that's what you mean. We have a mission to care for the bodies of the poor, and that keeps us busy enough. We let the Sisters Of Carmel worry about their souls."

He filled a pan with the contents of the food cannister he'd found in the bandit's gear. Had Mother Juana Maria said they were Sisters of Mercy or had she mentioned some other order? What the hell difference did it make to a Protestant, anyway? He didn't know what the rules were in *any* order, but Niqui sure seemed casual, considering.

As he put the food on the fire she sniffed and asked, "What are you cooking, Dick?" and he said, "Hard to say. It

53

looks like refritos, with some sort of herbs mixed up with the bean paste. Almost anything helps, when you start with mushy beans."

"It smells delicious."

"Yeah, we're both hungry. There's no sugar for the coffee, but that's starting to smell right, too."

Niqui moved closer as he poked at the refritos. He hadn't realized how much he needed a warm meal until just now. Hadn't realized how long it had been since he'd had a woman, either, until he caught another whiff of her perfume. Did nuns wear perfume? He supposed an order that allowed long hair wouldn't be stuffy about other small luxuries.

It was still pretty stupid to be getting an erection at a time like this, so he said, "I guess the stuff's warmed up enough," and proceeded to fill the mess kit for her, adding that he'd eat from the pot. He poured two tin cans full of coffee and warned, "Careful, don't burn yourself," as their fingers touched. Damn that Gaston! This was no time to be alone with a pretty lady, nun or not. He knew he'd never be tempted to flirt with Niqui as long as Gaston was watching with his all-knowing eyes. He knew his temptation was an exercise in futility, too, if Niqui was really what she claimed to be. And how the hell was he to find out if she wasn't? The odds were fifty-fifty, and he didn't want to make a mistake!

Niqui sat back and took a spoonful of the insipid looking bean paste, washing it down with coffee before she opined, "My, it's quite good."

He tried some himself. It wasn't bad. The herbs or whatever seemed to make the beans more interesting and he was hungrier than he'd thought. They both settled down to consume the modest meal as the little fire winked between them. The flames sure looked pretty, purple and green.

What the hell kind of wood burned purple and green? He took a swallow of black coffee, repressed a belch, and then, as the fumes came out his nose, he laughed and said, "I'll be damned, it's marijuana! That's what they mixed in the refritos!"

Niqui looked owlishly at him and asked, "Who is Maria Juana? Mother Superior is called Juana Maria."

He laughed again, wilder than he'd intended, and said, "You'd better not eat any more of that stuff, Honey. You look like it's already hitting you."

54

The little nun frowned and said, "Nobody had better hit me," as she took another heroic swallow of the cannibas-laced bean paste, belched discreetly, and added, "Wheeeeee!"

He said, "Jesus," and she brightened and said, "Oh, that's my husband. I'm a bride of Jesus, you know."

"I know, and you're getting stoned. We'd better stop eating this stuff, Niqui. I've got forty or more pounds on you and *I* can feel it."

"Oh, do you feel like flying, too, Dick?"

"No, I've just got a hell of a hard-on and ... did *I* say that? Sorry."

Niqui swallowed the last of the drugged refritos in her mess kit and asked if there was any more. He shook his head and said, "There's a little left, but I don't think you ought to have any more. It's full of dope. Strong as hell, too. Might have something worse than marijuana in it. Botany sure gets wild down here."

"Am I drunk, Dick? I don't feel drunk. I feel ... let me see, I feel like taking my clothes off."

"I sure wish you wouldn't do that, Niqui. I'm a little mixed up, too, but I seem to remember reading something somewhere about it being naughty to fuck a nun. Did I say fuck a nun? Strike that from the record. Jesus, what on Earth did they put in those beans?"

Niqui said, "I wish you wouldn't keep talking about my husband. I'm feeling a little cross with Jesus, tonight. You see, our marriage has never been consummated and they told me it was a sin to relieve myself with my hand, but, damn it, a girl has *feelings!*"

Captain Gringo was having feelings, too, but he was still fighting them when Niqui slipped her habit off over her head, placed it on the ground, and reclined stark naked atop the folded cloth to ask him, with an inviting smile, "Would you like to consummate me, Dick?"

He shook his head to clear it. It wouldn't clear. But his pecker was going to explode like a bomb if he didn't do some damned thing with it, and it sure seemed silly jerking off in front of a nun.

The fire was subsiding to glowing coals, filling the clearing with ruby light and purple shadows as he wondered why he was taking his own clothes off. It wasn't really that hot, but that strange lady over there was naked, so what the

hell, a guy had to be polite. Niqui laughed as he gravely folded his pants in a neat pile. She said, "I see your privates. Does it always wave around like that?"

He took a bearing on her, crawled soberly over on his hands and knees, and said, 'Hi there, I'm Dick Walker. Who the hell are you?"

She rolled on her back, opening her firm thighs to welcome him as she husked, "I forget who I am. Let's consummate."

That sounded reasonable, so he lowered himself a mile or so until her turgid breasts cushioned his fall and, below the waists, their bodies greeted one another like old friends. He was barely clear headed to notice how easy it was to enter her, although, once she clamped down and embraced him with her thighs she was tight and lovely to explode inside. She laughed and asked, "Did you just come?" and he said, "I think so. Want to try it again?"

She sobbed and said, "Oh, shut up and consummate me, you silly!" So he did. They were going at it hot and heavy when she suddenly gave a startled gasp and said, "My God, I'm being raped!"

He stopped, leaving everything in place, and muttered, "That's the trouble with cheap dope. I'm starting to remember who we are, too."

Her vaginal muscles contracted sensually around his shaft as she sobbed, "This is terrible. My order would never approve. What will I ever tell Mother Superior?"

"That you enjoyed it? Why tell her anything, Niqui?"

She started to shove him away, moved her hips experimentally, and held him closer as she sighed, "Oh, we're probably going to hell, anyway, and I do remember how good it felt when you consummated me before."

He decided she might be ready for some more consummation and began to move his hips, gently. The little nun arched her back to take it deeper as she sighed and said, "Well, I'm going to have a terrible time at Confession in any case. Could you move a little faster? It couldn't feel *that* good with my head starting to clear but ... oh, my God, it feels even *better!* Don't stop, Dick, don't ever stop!"

He tried to kiss her as he pounded harder. But when their lips met she rolled her head aside and protested, "Please, don't, it seems so wicked to go all the way."

56

"Are you serious? We're about to come together, Baby!"

"I know. I have no control down there, but don't you think kissing, too, would be wicked?"

He said, "Let's try," and this time she let him, returning his passion with a resigned sigh as he tongued her, pounded her, and felt her shudder in orgasm as he came deep inside her.

He braced himself for some screaming and scratching as he felt her relaxing inside around his shaft. But she said, "Oh, that was lovely. Do we have to stop, now?"

"Not if you don't want to, Niqui."

"I don't want to. I know I should. We've committed a terrible sin, but I've never been so happy. Do you suppose I'm in love with you, Dick?"

He certainly hoped not, but this seemed a cruel time to say so. He answered with silent thrusts until he could tell by the way she was responding that words were the last thing she had in mind. Now that she'd gotten over what must have been quite a shock to her, Niqui settled down to some good old-fashioned barnyard rutting and he noticed she moved like she'd done it before. That reminded him of his earlier suspicions. She still had her high button shoes on, but she hadn't been wearing a stitch under her modest habit. They lay on top of her clothes in the soft sand, so it was easy enough to explore for concealed weapons with his free hand. He cupped a palm under her buttocks and she giggled and said it felt naughty but nice when he fingered her anus while feeling for a gun with the back of his wrist. He didn't find any gun, but she asked if it was true that some bad girls took it down there. He said he'd heard rumors to that effect and she purred, "I want to try everything, tonight, Dick. You've no idea how often I've wondered what this would be like, and now that I'm ruined as a nun anyway . . ."

He frowned and said, "Oh? How do you figure you're ruined, Niqui?"

"Silly, you're inside me even as you ask such a question!"

"I thought you could go to Confession or something."

"Oh, I shall. I have to. But naturally I can't remain with my order after breaking my vows so marvelously. I'm sure Mother Superior will release me, once I tell her I'm going away with you to be your woman forever."

There was absolutely no way to answer that without looking like a shit, so he didn't try. He rolled part way off, rolled her on her side, and tried a new angle. She laughed and said, "Oh, it feels nice this way, too. But when do you wish for to put it in my rear, Dear?"

He said, "I don't think we'd better. I might hurt you," as he started moving fast enough to distract her. He didn't know if she'd like it Greek or not. He was afraid to find out. It was going to be one bitch of a mess, now that she'd gotten used to taking it old-fashioned! He'd have kicked himself if it had been possible. Damn his suspicions and damn that dead bandit who made such funny refritos! He seemed to be stuck with a lapsed nun, who enjoyed being lapsed and expected him to do something more honorable in the near future. How the hell did you explain to such an innocent kid that a soldier of fortune had no business getting married to *anyone?* He'd had a couple of *whores* cry when it was time to ride on!

She came again and since he'd gotten past passion into showing off he called a smoke break. Niqui said she wasn't allowed to smoke. He didn't want to start her on any more bad habits, so he nodded and smoked a solo cigar while she snuggled against him. The fire was almost out. He kicked a stick into the pit and she said, "Oh, let it get dark. I'd die if anyone saw us like this."

"We'll be bitten to death by mosquitoes or jaguars if we don't keep some sort of smudge going, Honey. Are you tired enough to sleep? I'll spread a blanket for you."

But as he started to move she ran a hand over his flesh and crooned, "Don't move. This is perfect. Do you suppose it will always be like this between us, Dick?"

"I guess it will, as long as it lasts."

"Oh, won't we be together forever, Darling?"

He let some smoke out before he said, "Nothing is forever, Niqui. Let's stick with tonight, for now."

"Do you wish for to consummate some more?"

"Hey, let me finish this smoke and get my second wind, huh? It's early and we've got all night, Doll."

She began to fondle his limp flesh as she sighed and said, "I'm so glad. Finish your cigar while I get this one ready to go crazy inside me again!"

He frowned and asked, "Aren't you getting a little, well, sore? You are, or were a virgin, right?"

She didn't answer. He smiled crookedly and insisted, "Niqui?"

She sighed and said, "I don't think *candles* count, do you?"

"Depends on where you burn them, I guess. Are you saying you've been, well, practicing with a candle when the lights were low?"

She giggled and said, "I told you a girl has feelings. It's all very well to be the bride of Jesus, but when Jesus never seems to want to sleep with you . . . I have never done this with a man before, though. My worst sin, up to meeting *you*, was with a rather large and wicked cucumber."

He laughed and said, "I'm sorry if I disappointed you," even as he felt a warning tingle in his groin that told him he'd be ready for more in a moment. She felt his growing erection, too, and squeezed to assure him, "I think I like the real thing much better. It's not quite what I expected, but it feels nicer. Are other men as small as you, Dick?"

He started to protest he'd never been accused of being underdeveloped before. But then he reconsidered his options and said, "Well, I may not be hung as well as some hombres, but that's not my fault, is it?"

She began to stroke him as she soothed, "Oh, no, you have a sweet little thing. It's bigger than a candle and I suppose one the size of a cucumber would be asking too much, eh?"

"Oh, I don't know. I've seen men with things as large."

"Is that possible, Dick? I have often wondered what it would be like to make love to a man with a huge erection like that."

"You've been giving the matter some thought, eh?"

"Well, I never thought I'd really get to *do* it, but perhaps, alone in the night at the convent, one does get carried away. We are seldom allowed to see male patients naked, but one time I did see this man in the ward, and it was most unsettling. He wasn't as big as a cucumber. Maybe only a little bigger than you, but that night, when I was alone in bed . . ."

"I get the picture. Everybody's been alone in bed. Funny, I never thought about a scene like that in a convent, but it makes sense, when you consider how young some folks are when they join up. That reminds me. You said you were left

as a foundling. Then you said you'd learned to ride astride, like a tomboy. Am I missing other secrets, Niqui?"

She laughed and said, "If I have any secrets from you, it's only because you're shy about exploring my body, you terrible man. I was a foundling. I was a tomboy, too. They used to let us play at the convent orphanage, of course, and I liked to play with the boys. We had a pony for to ride and..."

"Never mind, I've got a better grasp on things, now. I'd tell you what I thought you might be, but you'd laugh like hell."

Niqui fell silent a moment. Then she stammered, "How did you know about Mother Juana Maria and me, Dick?"

He started to say he had no idea what she was talking about. But then he did. So he said, "Oh, I noticed she indulged you in things like nicer shoes and that French perfume. She gets to be the *boy* a lot, right?"

Niqui grimaced and said, "Well, *she* has feelings, too. She said it is not sinful for the brides of Jesus to consummate one another, as long as they are discreet about it. But I don't think I like it with another woman the way I like it with you, Dick. What's the matter? Why are you laughing?"

He said, "You wouldn't understand. You still want to try some Greek loving?"

"You mean, in the back way? Oh, yes, I tried that with a candle one night, when Mother Superior was eating me from the front. Your thing is as big as a candle and ... oh, my, it seems to be getting even bigger."

Despite the fun and games out on the llano and in Sir Basil's nearby quarters in Caracas, the rather satanic looking man they called Sortilego was too worried to screw. So he sat playing chess with himself by the telephone in his study, waiting for it to ring and not too sure he wanted it to.

El Sortilego wasn't called The Fortune Teller because he could see into the future with tarot cards or a crystal ball. El Sortilego's clients paid him to make the future turn out the

way they wanted it to. Up until a short while ago, the future had been coming along just fine, but now everything seemed to be getting fucked-up and El Sortilego's customers could get nasty as hell when predictions they'd paid for didn't come true.

There was a knock on the door. El Sortilego moved a knight on his chess board and said, "Entrada" in a voice as friendly as a spitting cobra. A burly man whose linen suit bulged under the left armpit came in and sank wearily down across from the prophet for hire. El Sortilego moved another pawn and asked, "Well?"

The other said, "Hakim's in town, all right. But he's locked up with some kids he's screwing, and none of his people are on the street. Our man in customs checked out that so-called farm machinery he landed last Friday, legally."

"And?"

"It's farm machinery. I don't know what the hell anyone in Venezuela is going to do with a wheat combine, but that's what he shipped in from New Orleans, disassembled in a mess of crates. The Turk must be crazy."

El Sortilego moved his knight again and said, "Ah, I have the black bishop in a knight's cross. Basil Hakim is only mad when it comes to sex. The farm machinery is obviously junk he never intends to claim from the docks."

"Our man in customs said it was pretty rusty. But why send scrap metal all the way from New Orleans, for God's sake?"

"He didn't send it for God's sake. He sent it for the sake of the American customs officials in New Orleans. He needed an export license and the Yanqui government is interested in any shipments to Venezuela these days, thanks to the current crisis."

"Sure, Boss, but the stuff he sent was just rusty junk."

"You're not paying attention. He took out an export license and had the crates loaded aboard ship. Then he used the same license to load another ship at another time. U.S. Customs can be rather casual about such matters, once you have some papers to wave at them. They don't take much interest in shipments *leaving* New Orleans, since no duty is owed on them."

The street agent started to ask another dumb question, saw how it could have worked, and nodded to say, instead,

"Then the arms he sent from the States hasn't arrived yet, right?"

"Wrong. Hakim will have landed his arms at another and less well policed port by now. He anticipated that British Intelligence would try to put a crimp in his operations, too. Even a man who drinks with the Prince of Wales would raise a few eyebrows if he shipped British-made arms to a country the Royal Navy was about to invade. That's why he sent American-made arms from the factory he has an interest in, there."

El Sortilego moved the knight and took the bishop as the gun thug growled, "If you ask me, that damned Turk is causing everybody a lot of trouble." El Sortilego nodded and replied, "That's the business he's in. Who buys arms when there's no trouble?"

The phone rang. El Sortilego picked up and said, *"Presentar un informe!"* He didn't ask who it was. Nobody had the number unless they were working for him. The informant at the other end reported on the current situation in distant Tucupita and El Sortilego hung up without thanking him. He sighed and said, "Not a sign of Captain Gringo anywhere in the delta towns."

"The delta is a big place, Boss. Besides, nobody knows for sure the big Yanqui really shot those chumps on the roof."

El Sortilego shrugged and said, "We know Captain Gringo was spotted going down the river. We know those men were waiting for him in ambush. We know they were machine gunned. We know Captain Gringo is a machinegun expert. We know Basil Hakim deals in machineguns and that Captain Gringo has worked for him in the past."

"Sure, but Sir Basil's here in Caracas, Boss."

"Idiot! The Turk *runs* guns. He doesn't *shoot* them! He's sent his Captain Gringo to meet the people landing the guns and show them how to set them up. Hakim knows everyone is watching him, here in Caracas. That is why he's laughing so much as he molests those children across town."

The gunthug shrugged and said, "I don't see why we couldn't knock the little Turk off. It ought to simplify things a little, no?"

El Sortilego grimaced and said, "It would simplify things to knock off the Pope, too. And it wouldn't be as dangerous.

There are one or two countries the Jesuits might have trouble reaching you. Basil Hakim has agents everywhere. Besides, the big boys have a gentleman's agreement about assassination."

"Is Sir Basil that big a boy, Boss?"

"What would you call a man who drinks with the Prince of Wales and yachts with Der Kaiser? I don't think that story about him and the Czarina is really true, but he has been a house guest at St. Petersberg often enough to make one think twice about murdering him. We already have all the secret agents and hired assassins we need in Venezuela right now, so let's not worry about knocking off Sir Basil. Get out on the streets and find Captain Gringo. He has no friends at all in high places, and I want his head on a pole within forty-eight hours."

"That's cutting it sort of short, considering we don't know where the bastard is, Boss."

"Find out where he is, then. He has to be somewhere in Venezuela and the balloon's about to go up. I want him dead before the war starts, damn it. So find him. Find him if you have to look for him in a convent!"

The medical mission wasn't a convent. It was a ramshackle cluster of tin roofed houses set on stilts along another stream running over the llano toward the even soggier delta country to the east. Captain Gringo and Sister Dominica rode in the afternoon after they'd been such good friends alone on the hammock. She was wearing her habit again, of course, and putting it back on had apparently reminded her she was a nun because he noticed she'd stopped talking about running off with him. He was relieved albeit a little insulted as he considered her possible reasons. She'd made some rather disparaging remarks about the size of his tool the last time he'd used it on her. He knew he was hung as well or weller than most growing boys, but that was the trouble with letting a girl break in with cucumbers and fantasy. When she said something about maybe giving religion another chance, he

63

assumed, sadly, that she meant to hold out for somebody hung like a stallion. She was likely to be sort of disappointed with the future, but a lot of guys in times to come were sure going to be happily surprised.

They found Gaston waiting for them on the veranda of the main building. The little nun went inside to report to her Mother Superior while Gaston filled Captain Gringo in with a silly story about getting lost in the dark with the other nun. Captain Gringo said, "Cut the bullshit. Was Mother Juana Maria packing a gun or not?"

Gaston chuckled and said, "Ah, you got to search yours?"

"That's for damned sure. Are you saying Mother Juana Maria puts out, too?"

"Mais oui. Why do you think we got lost? She was *très formidable.* But she was not carrying anything more dangerous than her astonishing body under that modest habit."

Captain Gringo frowned, gazed over toward the tepid brown river to the north, and said, "Okay. So they're not nuns. What the hell do you suppose they *are,* Gaston?"

The Frenchman shrugged and replied, "It is hard to say. Juana tells me this is a medical mission of the Sisters of The Society of Jesus. And that we are welcome to stay here as long as we like. She must like me. On the other hand, there seem to be no sick people that would call for all this medication, and there are no female Jesuits, as far as *I* know."

"You mean The Society of Jesus might not know about this place at all?"

"Not unless they have been recruiting female Jesuits since I last took any interest in such matters, and not unless the Jesuits have started setting up hospitals where nobody seems to need any. The Jesuits are not a medical order in the first place and, as you can see, we are out in the middle of nowhere, surrounded by a fair imitation of your Florida Everglades. I can see an occasional hunter or fisherman dropping by with a splinter in his toe, but enough patients to justify a medical mission, here?"

Captain Gringo nodded and said, "Yeah, I thought I was being conned, too. I'll buy one horny nun, but two are a little much and Niqui keeps changing her story. Where'd you leave your horse, Gaston?"

The Frenchman said, "The corrals are over beyond that big corrugated iron building. But what of it? You must have noticed how soft the ground was, getting here. The far side of the river is worse. That is not *wheat* you see waving across the water at us, my old and rare. It is saw-grass and water-reed, and if you climb higher you can see it extends all the way to the horizon north of here."

"Okay, if we can't *ride* out, how the hell *do* we get out?"

"I have been pondering this as I waited for you, my overactive child. There are some native dugouts under this building. We could see if one would float long enough to take us down stream somewhere, hein?"

"Shit, that'd put us back in the delta, Gaston."

"*Oui.* I don't see why that would be more uncomfortable than wading through all those soggy reeds across the way. We could always stay here and play house with our new friends, I suppose."

"That sounds more dangerous than running through the delta. We don't know who we might meet in the delta, but these fake nuns are starting to make me nervous. While you were snooping around under the housing, I don't suppose you saw anything that might give us a line on what the fuck they're up to?"

"*Mais non,* fucking is all I managed to get out of Mother Juana Maria. They have a telephone or telegraph line running east, on the ground in a droll attempt to conceal it. It seems obvious this is some sort of a headquarters, for someone very sneaky. More than that, I cannot tell you."

Sister Dominica came back out, eyes downcast, and murmured, "Mother Juana Maria wishes for to speak with you, Dick."

Captain Gringo shot Gaston a thoughtful look, got no suggestions, and decided to see what the older whatever wanted. He'd seen a couple of men and women dressed as peon servants as they moved about the compound at a discreet distance. But aside from the two maybe nuns, nobody else on the premises looked all that religious.

He went inside to find Mother Juana Maria seated severely behind a flat topped desk. There was a telephone nearby on the wall. So that answered what the wire Gaston had noticed was all about. It also meant that by now the lady

in charge had had time to make some calls. How long would it take a steam launch to get here from the other end of that mystery wire, assuming she'd called anyone about them and assuming she had any reason? After all, neither he nor Gaston had told the women that they were flying under false colors, too.

Mother Juana Maria indicated a seat across from her and as he perched on the bentwood chair, she smiled and said, "Your friend, Dear Gaston, said he didn't know how long the two of you might be staying here, Señor Walker."

He said, "Well, we told you we were on our way to the north coast when we ran into you, uh, Mother."

"You may call me Juana, since we're all such good friends, Dick. You two dear boys can't get much further north from here, but there will be a river boat going upstream in a day or so and, meanwhile, we do owe you our very lives. I'm sure we'll be able to make you comfortable."

He kept his face blank as he realized she'd made that call, all right. No real nun would be about to invite strange laymen to shack up with them. Fakes up to something else would be glad to see the last of them, if they intended to let them ride out alive and possibly report this weird out-of-the-way "mission" in even casual conversation.

He shrugged and said, "We'll think about it. We wouldn't want to be a bother. Do you have, uh, guest quarters or something?"

Mother Juana Maria smiled sort of sneaky and said, "Of course. You didn't think you could sleep in the nuns' quarters, did you?"

"Of course not. By the way, I haven't seen any other sisters since we got here."

"The others haven't arrived yet. Sister Dominica and I were on our way to establish this mission when we met those terrible men and you saved us."

Again he nodded and again he wondered if she could really think he was that dumb. Those nun costumes had made them both overconfident. He supposed they hadn't been doing this sort of thing long, whoever in hell they really were.

The older whatever got to her feet and said, "It's settled, then. I'll show you to your quarters if you'll walk this way."

He followed as she led him out another doorway and

deeper into the building. For an older woman in a nun's habit she walked sort of sexy. He knew she was putting it on, too. What he couldn't figure was why.

She opened the door to a small room with a big brass bedstead and said, "Here's where you can stay as long as you like. Why don't you take your clothes off and get some sleep, Dear Boy? You must be tired after all that riding, no?"

He frowned at the jalosied window's sunny slats and said, "It's way too early to go to bed, for Pete's sake."

Mother Juana Maria sat on the mattress and sighed, "Oh, dear, that naughty Dominica has been fibbing to me again. She says you rode all night while you were lost."

He looked at the window slats some more and chose his words as he replied, "Yeah, you could say we rode a lot. But I'm not tired and it's early. Why don't you ladies go on missioning or something and Gaston and me will find some way to amuse ourselves, huh?"

She reached out, took his hand, and said, "Will you tell me something, Dick? Do I have your word you were not wicked with poor little Niqui when you had her alone in your power?"

He muttered, "Oh, hell, ask the girl, and whatever she says is all right with me."

"She swears you were a gentleman, but I know she's wavered from the path in the past, Dick. I wish I could be sure she wasn't sinning again."

The dame was stalling him with all this garbage. If they were lesbian lovers as well as partners in whatever, they'd compared notes by now and who did she think she was kidding? But any number can play the same game, so he shrugged and said, "Well, I don't see how I could convince you, if you want to have a wicked mind, uh, Juana."

She moved his hand to the front of her habit and said, "There is one way. I'm not sure the church would approve, but we have to make sacrifices in the cause of the truth, I fear."

She had bigger knockers than her younger companion in whatever and the nipple against his wrist was already turgid. He sat down beside her and said, "I'll go along with any test that doesn't hurt."

So she laughed and reached for his fly as he proceeded to feel her up. She felt his growing erection and said, "My,

67

you don't *feel* like you've been wicked with any woman recently. There certainly is a lot of you, isn't there, Dear Boy?"

He muttered, "Oh, Bullshit!" and rolled her on her back to hoist her long skirts as she unbuttoned his pants. She wasn't wearing anything under the skirts. So he let his pants drop half way down his own thighs as he rolled aboard her and settled into the saddle. She was laughing dirty and it *looked* dirty as hell with her still dressed in her nun's habit as he proceeded to give her what she was asking for. Her legs were more padded than Niqui's and her face was middle-aged as she smiled up at him, eyes closed and lips parted sensuously, but her love box was as tight as Niqui's rectum and she groaned with mingled delight and discomfort when he entered her and hit bottom. As he started to work she moaned, "Please start more gently, Dearest. I'm not used to this sort of sacrifice, you know."

"Yeah, I understand you nuns don't get much of this."

"Don't talk dirty. Just *do* it! I'm only allowing you to abuse me like this as a test of Niqui's faith."

The game she was playing sounded stupid as hell, and he'd played some stupid games in his time, but the way she moved her body made up for the dumb things coming out of her mouth. So he let himself go, bracing his feet against the floor boards as he pounded her. He didn't care if she enjoyed it or not. He figured she was just trying to keep him lulled and unwary until somebody she'd called on that office phone arrived. But she must have enjoyed it, some, for after he'd come in her she sighed and said, "Oh, that was almost perfect. But let's take our clothes off and do it right."

He hesitated, decided there was time, and shucked his own clothes as she beat him to it by slipping out of her habit and tossing it to the foot of the bed. She had a surprisingly nice body as he took her in his arms again. She said she wanted to get on top, so he let her. The sunlight through the window slats painted tiger stripes on her passion-warmed flesh as she moved up and down on him, saying dumb things about not telling Sister Dominica. He promised he'd never tell as he wondered how Gaston was enjoying the change in partners. The crazy dames were out to screw them both to sleep, were they? Okay, that meant they didn't expect anyone

68

to get here for a while, and he could think of a lot of lousier ways to spend an afternoon.

This time Mother Juana Maria came, herself, and it seemed to knock some of the starch out of her. She rolled off, weakly, and marvelled, "Oh, God, that was fantastic!" as he rolled over to remount her, growling, "Yeah, I'm getting my second wind, too!"

"Wait, can't we rest a bit, Dear?"

"No. I'm mad with desire. What's the matter, Baby? Why'd you start this if you didn't want to screw?"

"Oh, I do, you know I do, you naughty boy! But, heavens, let me get my breath between times."

He laughed, pulled her knees up and hooked one over each of his elbows as he started hitting bottom on every stroke and she gasped with awe and protested, "Not so deep! Not so hard! You're killing me, you brute!"

But her rollicking rump made a liar out of her as she started rising to meet his thrusts, moaning and rolling her head from side to side as he chewed her collar bone and joined her in a primitive orgasm. She went limp and sighed, "Oh, yes, I needed that. But let's rest a bit, now."

He shook his head, withdrew, and rolled her over to mount her dog style while he still had it up. She realized what he was doing as her head began to clear again and protested, "Not that way, you maniac! You're trying to put it in the wrong hole!"

"Whaddayah mean *trying?*" he laughed as he felt it enter her quivering rectum, to the roots. She sobbed, "Stop! You're splitting me! It's too big that way!" And then, as he'd expected, she arched her spine to take it that way. Dames who went in for unusual sex usually did. He'd already figured that a woman who took the dominant role with other women enjoyed being submissive with a man, if they went for men at all. And Mother Juana Maria proved he was right as she wrung his shaft out with her anal muscles, protesting like hell all the while that he was hurting her. He wanted to hurt her, not just because he was sure, now, she'd set them up to be taken, but to wear her out so thoroughly that she wouldn't be in shape to try and stop him when he and Gaston lit out.

Women tended to think they had a monopoly when it came to using sex as a weapon. Most of the time they were

right. Few men ever thought about faking an orgasm or pretended passion they didn't feel. But Captain Gringo had been on the run long enough to use every weapon there was, and he was a whalebone and whipcord young giant in his prime. So he managed to keep it up just by moving it while he managed not to exhaust his ammo by thinking of something else every time he started to come. It wasn't hard to distract himself. The two fake nuns were pulling something more naughty than simple fornication, so wondering about it as he pounded her lent an almost mechanical detachment to his lovemaking, although, in all fairness to Mother Juana Maria, it sure beat chopping wood as a pastime.

She rolled her face from side to side on the mattress as he cornholed her. She moaned and groaned that he was killing her. Then she put both hands down between her braced thighs and began to play with his balls as she masterbated. He didn't think she could do what she was obviously out to try, but he moved closer, leaving it deep with her spread buttocks pressed to his hip bones while her one hand massaged her own clit and the other attempted to stick his dangling scrotum up her open gushing vagina. He was intrigued by the idea, too, and found himself rising to new heights in her rear entrance as she popped one ball after another in and out of her larger opening. It was obvious they wouldn't both fit at once and painful to contemplate if she ever made it, since she was contracting pretty good down there. He decided he'd better quit while he was ahead. So he withdrew and rolled her over without warning and dropped on her heavily to finish old-fashioned albeit tall-in-the-saddle. Her breath wooshed out of her as his shaft entered her and she gasped for air as she came with a wide-eyed look of little-girl surprise on her forty-year-old face.

He could tell from her contractions and the pink flush of her breasts that he had her on a plateau, so he announced he was coming, too, and proceeded to pound her harder. She closed her eyes and groaned, "Stop it! You'll kill us both! Nobody can keep going like this without having a stroke and . . . oh, yes, stroke me some more, I'm coming again!"

So he screwed her into the ground, giving her orgasm after orgasm as he paced himself by counting silently. He'd slam her hard for a hundred, and then take a break, moving slowly and sensuously as he smothered her with kisses and

love-lies, then, recovering his wind, he'd say something like, "Oh, Jesus, you're driving me nuts!" and methodically banged her a hundred more good bumps and grinds. He was starting to go soft, despite his best efforts, when she suddenly went limp in his arms and he saw she'd fainted or simply passed out from exhaustion. The helpless condition of the treacherous bitch intrigued him, and, since he no longer found what he was doing a chore, he allowed himself to enjoy it. His abused organ responded by gushing with held-back vigor as soon as he allowed it to. *He* almost passed out in the saddle and it would have been the perfect ending for a lovely ride if he'd been in safer company. But he shook his head to clear it and gently withdrew, whispering, "Are you all right, Honey?"

Mother Juana Maria didn't answer as she lay legs apart with a gentle smile on her face, absently fondling her own crotch in her sleep.

Later, when she awoke, she was coming again and for a moment she thought they were still at it. Then, as she stared up at the blank ceiling, running her passion-wet fingers in and out, she blinked in dismay, finished her orgasm, and sat up, cursing.

Still nude, Mother Juana Maria rolled stiffly out of bed and tottered out to her office. She spotted the note and some Brazilian money on her desk. She was reading the note, red-faced, when Sister Dominica came in from another room, wearing a bemused expression and nothing else as she marvelled, "Jesus, that Frenchman had a long tongue for such a little man! Where are the boys? What's that you're reading, Juanita?"

The older woman crumpled the note Captain Gringo had left her and said, "They've left in one of our dugouts! The big one left me this money to pay for it, the sneaky son-of-a-bitch!"

She stepped over to the wall phone and began to crank it. Her younger companion asked who she was calling and Mother Juana Maria snapped, "Our confederates down the river, of course. How far can they get in an Indian dugout? I don't think they have more than an hour's lead and if our launches are signalled from the shore a few miles down . . ."

Niqui frowned and said, "That seems sort of mean, Juanita. Those boys did save our lives and they were both very nice in bed, don't you think?"

The older woman said, "All's fair in Love and War, Niqui. The loving is over and we have to get back to the war. I don't think they figured out who we really were, but I'm pretty sure who *they* were!" She gave the crank another twist and sighed, "Damn, the line is dead. They must have cut it before they left in one of the canoes under the house. That settles it. They were the British agents Hakim warned us about. We'd better get dressed. The launches are due any minute and I'm really not up to servicing any more soldiers of fortune for a while!"

The two women barely had time to shower and dress before a peon came up on the veranda to announce steamboat plumes down the river. Mother Juana Maria said, "We're expecting some, ah, medical supplies, Antonio. By the way, would you look under the building and see which canoe our recent, ah, visitors took?"

As the peon left them alone for a moment, Sister Dominica giggled and said, "I'm glad they got away. My God, my poor little twat is still tingling! Between the way Dick sensitized it and the way Gaston licked it . . ." But Mother Juana Maria snapped, "Shut up. We're supposed to be nuns. Try and look holy, you little slut!"

They were standing primly when the peon came out from under the house to announce the larger of the dugouts had been dragged out and down to the water's edge. He added, "Nobody saw them leave because it was La Siesta, Madre Santa. I would have been watching, had anyone told me to."

Mother Juana Maria pasted a saintly smile across her face and murmured, "It's all right, Antonio. I confess I was in bed during La Siesta, too."

This struck Niqui's funny bone and she started to giggle. Mother Juana Maria muttered, "Stop it, you little idiot. The launches are putting in. Most of those gun runners think we're really nuns."

"How come they don't question our reasons for having so many weapons on hand, Juanita?"

"I told you. These are unsettled times. It's only logical a Catholic mission might feel the need for certain precautions with Protestant ruffians about to invade the country, right?"

Sister Dominica saw the launches had put in at the river landing and a tall well-dressed man was leading others up the

bank toward the mission. She nudged her older sister in sin and said, "He's cute. Is that General Castro?"

"Don't be silly, Niqui. Cipriano Castro's not about to show his hand before the time is ripe. He's sitting out the invasion in Caracas, as a member of the Loyal Opposition. When the Brits start to beat the current government the Castroistas will save the day with the modern weapons from Hakim's combine and, of course, wind up running the country they've just saved, see?"

Niqui sighed and said, "It's all so complicated. Men do everything but sex the complicated way. I don't see why Cipriano Castro doesn't just stage a revolt and . . ."

"Just keep your mouth shut and your legs crossed, damn it," the older woman cut in. "It's not all that complicated. Castro can't take over until the popular Crespo government is shattered by outside forces. Let me do the talking when those men approaching ask about storage and so forth. I'll bet you told Dick and Gaston everything you knew, eh?"

"I did not! I only told them I was a naughty nun." She giggled and added, "As a matter of fact, neither one of them seemed interested in anything but my body. How did *you* make out, Dear?"

The older woman permitted herself a smug smile as she returned the wave of the approaching gunrunner. And then all hell broke loose.

Captain Gringo and Gaston hadn't left in the dugout they'd dragged from under the mission. They'd hauled it down to the river and then, seeing nobody was watching, they'd simply cast it adrift on the water and taken cover under the stilts of a storage shed near the landing. The two whaleboat-sized steam launches had been left with their fires going, bows against the bank. One crew member had remained aboard each launch as the others disembarked, of course, but that was *their* problem, not Captain Gringo's.

As he and Gaston popped out from under the shed and leaped in the nearest launch, he shot the man at the tiller and then, for good measure, put a round in the startled man in the other launch alongside while Gaston threw the engine in reverse and cracked open the throttle to churn them backward off the bank!

As the members of the gang on shore turned, swearing, to slap leather and make other rude gestures, Captain Gringo

made his way forward over the crates piled in the launch. He'd noticed the machine gun mounted in the bows of the launch he'd chosen. As he armed it the men on shore saw what he had in mind and proceeded to scatter like quail. So Captain Gringo muttered, "Spoilsports" and held his fire until Gaston had them out in midstream and swung around to tear down the river as fast as the little steamcraft would go.

The view to the east, where they seemed to be heading, consisted of little more than reed-grown banks and a gently winding channel of tea-brown water. So Captain Gringo headed back to join Gaston in the stern, where the action seemed to be. As he climbed over a crate marked "Smith Brothers Cough Drops" he found himself wondering if it were possible the people in the tropics caught that many colds. He took out his jack knife, pried up a board, and noticed the Brothers Smith seemed to make 30–30 ammo, too. As he joined Gaston in the stern he saw the other steamlaunch had put out from the fake mission to give chase. He commented on this to Gaston, who shrugged and said, "I noticed. Some species of idiots just never know enough to quit while they are ahead. Where are we going, my old and rare? You were not very conversational as we crouched under that shed back there a million years, hein?"

Captain Gringo shrugged and said, "The first things first. We have to get out of sight before we find a side channel and ditch this launch. We might blow it up. It's loaded with ammo and other goodies, so . . ."

"*Merde alors*, all those crates are filled with *arms*, Dick?"

"Yeah, I suspect our old friend, Hakim of Woodbine Arms, has a finger in this pie. A couple of nymphomaniacs posing as nuns sure sounds like old Basil's style."

Gaston started to object that Sir Basil was a British subject who could get in trouble supplying arms to people opposed to the March of Empire. But then he remembered a couple of other times they'd tangled with the tiny Turk and decided not to say something stupid after all.

Up the channel behind them a machine gun cleared its steel throat with a woodpecker's gargle, and as spouts of white water began to tap dance on the brown surface between the boats, Gaston said, "I hope this is only my imagination,

74

Dick. But those camel suckers seem to be gaining on us, *non?*"

Captain Gringo nodded and moved forward to get their own machine gun. As he tried to lift it from its bow mount, he saw why the others were so confident. The gunrunner's Maxims were jury rigged to Spandau mounts. Some silly son of a bitch had drilled new holes and used rivets instead of nuts and bolts to hold the mess together. He figured he could remove the machine gun from its mount, given tools and a little time. But he had no tools but his knife, and time was running out!

He called back to Gaston, "Give her hard right rudder, *now!*" and the little Frenchman called back, *"Merde alors!* You will put us broadside to them, with our bows headed for dry land, you maniac!"

But then, since he'd worked with his younger comrade before, and the rounds from the other craft were getting the range too close for comfort in any case, Gaston did as he was told.

Aboard the other boat, a cheer rang out as they saw the fugitive launch yaw and head for the bank. Gaston ducked below the bulwarks to avoid their fire and, if possible, to encourage their idea that he'd been hit by a lucky shot. It was well he did so, for the launch in pursuit came in for the kill, a bone in its teeth and machine guns chattering as Gaston, face down on the duckboards, muttered, "Species of idiots! You will blow your own ammunition sky high, any moment, with your wild fire!"

A couple of rounds tore through the rail above Gaston, spattering him with slivers as he wondered how far he might just be below the water line, and if there were any cayman near enough to matter when the boat sank under him. Then the duckboards tingled as Captain Gringo in the bow opened up with their own machine gun!

The two craft were less than three hundred yards apart, now, so he blew the gun crew in the other bow to hash with plunging fire before elevating still further to rake the other launch from stem to stern. He couldn't tell, as the other boat yawed broadside, whether he'd hit the helmsman or if they'd decided to turn upstream where things were quieter. A couple of his rounds had holed the steam boiler over there and the

enemy craft vanished in its own cloud of hissing white steam and screams. He lowered his elevation and proceeded to hose 30–30 slugs into the cloud at what he hoped was a belt buckle level. A man dove over the side, swam a few yards, and went under in a sinister swirl of brown as a cayman's tail stirred the surface like a wooden spoon in a soup bowl. Nobody else went over the side. Nobody else got the chance. One of Captain Gringo's rounds hit something right, and the interior of the steam cloud blossomed into a big orange fireball as the ammo aboard the other launch exploded!

Captain Gringo glimpsed planking, rag doll bodies, and other debris scattered like confetti against the sky above the steam and flame before he ducked below the bulwarks to let the shockwave sweep over and through the place he'd just been. Things thunked into the boat he and Gaston were in. When he felt something wet, he looked up to see a human leg outlined by the sunlight as it lay on the canvas awning over them. The blood was oozing through a vent in the canvas. Gingerly, he rose, punched the leg from the bottom of the canvas and sent it flying to the cayman and other meat-eaters in the water all around. He called back, "Let's get out of here!" and that's when he noticed Gaston had already thrown the screw in reverse and they were moving out to mid-channel again. By the time he rejoined Gaston at the stern, they were rounding a bend downstream and the widening pool of bloody foam behind them was settling down to a feeding frenzy under thinning clouds. Captain Gringo sighed and said, "I'll bet they heard that back at the mission. But with the wire cut, what the hell. We'll put a few miles between ourselves and those weird sisters before we look for another landing."

Gaston frowned and asked, *"Eh, bien,* why do you insist on doing everything the hard way, my overactive youth? This east-bound river channel obviously intends to take us to the Atlantic, hein?"

"I don't want to go to any fucking Atlantic. I want to head for the Caribbean. This country is starting to blow apart under us and the damned fool war is starting on the Atlantic side, right?"

Gaston nodded, but said, "You are not *thinking,* my glandulour friend. Consider a moment, hein? We *tried* to make a discreet exit across the llano. As you saw, the troubles

76

have brought all species of insects out into the light. It is no safer, and a lot farther, across the open grasslands to any safe port we can find, if such a thing be possible in a country at war. We would have been in Tucupita and possibly aboard a tramp steamer by this time, had not you insisted on being so *très fatigué!*"

"Bullshit. We might have made it to Tucupita if we'd stayed aboard that river boat, but I doubt like hell we'd have found a tramp to take us out. That dame on the riverboat was probably going to turn us in to her side, whichever side that was, and any cops ask questions of strangers in a war zone. Tucupita might be close, but it's too big a boo, Gaston!"

Again the Frenchman shook his head as he insisted, *"Mais non,* you have the *idée fixé* about a little river port you have never seen, Dick. I agree it may be dangerous to go there. But when have we recently visited a place that was *not* dangerous, hein? Consider that nobody knows us in the delta country. Consider that if your suspicions regarding Bubbles were true, she will by now have reported you leaving the boat and heading off across the llano, *non?"*

Captain Gringo started to say something, but Gaston snapped, "Wait, I have not finished! It gets more interesting, if anyone at all is really interested in us! We left the river over to the south. We shot up a gang of somebody. We have left a noisy trail as far as that *très* strange mission up the river. We *told* those crazy nuns we were heading for the north, remember?"

Captain Gringo sighed and said, "When you're right you're right. I guess we're as likely to have people laying for us on the open llanos as anywhere, and the delta swamps are easier to hide in on short notice. But, Jesus, we'll never be able to board a ship out with both the British and American fleets patrolling just off shore!"

Gaston said, "I know. We'd better try and make friends when we get to the delta, hein?"

Captain Gringo swore softly and said, "Call me sentimental, but the side I'm rooting for is the U.S. backed Venezuelan army and navy. We can't join *them!* Aside from Uncle Sam having a hard-on for me, Venezuela might be a little sore about that time we sided with those Brazilians in a border brush you may have forgotten."

Gaston shrugged and said, "I doubt it would be wise to volunteer for that side, too. But one must be *practique*. There are many sides and we do have this boatload of arms to trade with the natives, hein?"

"You asshole! I'd never help Queen Victoria out with one bullet, if I thought she might use it on a U.S. Marine!"

"*Merde alors*, you know the Brits do not buy smuggled arms, Dick. Did I say anything about joining the British Navy? *Sacre* Goddamn! They serve terrible food and piss in the bilges besides!"

Mollified but puzzled, Captain Gringo asked, "Okay, if we can't join the U.S.-backed Venezuelan regulars and don't want to join the invading Brits, who'd be left?"

"The Venezuelan *irregulars*, of course. These guns we just highjacked must have been going to some rebel faction. There is always a rebel faction in these odd countries, hein? I think I told you about Cipriano Castro and those men trying to stop the so-called nuns could not have been on their side, whichever one it may be. So, when we hide this boatload of presents near Tucupita and stroll into town, I, Gaston, shall ask some *très* discreet questions and find out who might be the highest bidder."

Captain Gringo took a claro from his shirt pocket and lit up as he gathered his thoughts. Then he said, "Well, it's going to take a lot of money to bribe our way out of this mess, and it would be sort of wasteful to just ditch all this stuff. You realize, of course, that anyone who buys arms on the black market has to be a treacherous sneaky son-of-a-bitch?"

"But of course, Dick. Who else in Venezuela could we deal with, hein?"

Captain Gringo grinned, despite his mixed emotions, and moved forward, cigar gripped between his teeth, to have a look at the "medical supplies." He doubted it could all be small arms ammo, after seeing the way that other launch had blown up. But the first box he opened was also filled with 30–30 rounds, albeit in machine-gun belting and labeled cough syrup. He pried open another box. It seemed to be filled with wooden shavings. He took the cigar out of his mouth and placed it on a thwart at a discreet distance before plunging an arm into the packing. He felt steel and gave a

heave. It heaved hard. So he put his back into it and pulled out the plum. Then he whistled softly and lowered the shark-nosed artillery round gently back into its nest. He picked up the smouldering cigar and tossed it overboard, saying, "The smoking lamp just went out, Gaston. We seem to be carrying .155 Howitzer shells, too. There has to be some cordite powder bags among this stuff That's what I hit in the other boat! This isn't ammo for a guerrilla band. It was meant for a heavy weapons outfit."

Gaston shrugged and said, *"Eh bien,* now all we need to find is some plucky lad who owns a *cannon,* hein?"

Tucupita was the provincial capital of Delta Amacuro. So it tried to look impressive. But like every other town on the lower reaches of the Orinoco, it had to stand on stilts to keep its feet dry. The delta land had a habit of bobbing up and down like a cake of soap in a tepid washtub, depending on rain upcountry and tides from the sea. The "streets" of Tucupita were steaming muddy lanes, or canals, depending, so the wrap around verandas of the buildings doubled as boat landings as the occasion demanded. The poorer classes lived in what looked like grass huts perched on fishing poles. The more imposing framed buildings looked more like steamboats converted to giant bird houses as they stood eight or ten feet off the mucky ground, shallow water, or whatever happened to be under them at the moment. Along the main "streets" the verandas were connected one to the other by a series of catwalks and/or what looked like Japanese bridges. So once one got to the odd giddy "ground level" of the main drag, one could walk about normally. But it was a bad town for drunks and jaywalkers. Many a stranger, stepping between two drinking spas to take a leak, had broken his neck in the resultant fall.

The water level was low when Captain Gringo and Gaston walked into town along a jungle pathway they'd come to after hiding their stolen launch in a reedy cove. They

couldn't leave it there, of course. Even camouflaged with branches it was likely to be stumbled over by some kids or fishermen. But they had to get the lay of the land before they found a safer place to hide it. Gaston had been through, once before, and vaguely remembered boat houses along the main channel where ocean going ships put in to anchor offshore.

As they approached the outskirts of town, they noticed little patches of garden, set higher behind basketwork retaining walls. Gaston pointed with his chin and said, "Milpa agriculture, as around Mexico City, non?"

"If you say so. We passed through Mexico City in a hail of gunfire as I recall, so I never got into the local farming methods all that much. But I can see how it works. They fence in an acre or so, haul muck inside, and create a little high ground. Must be back-breaking labor, in this heat. I can see why the locals don't like the idea of giving it to Queen Victoria, now."

"Oui," Gaston said. "There is more dry land around here, now, than there was when I last came through. Give the Venezuelans a few hundred years and they will have created dry land, here, like the Dutch. How curious that the British feel they need to save these people from their own sloth and ignorance, hein?"

"I thought you didn't care who won, Gaston."

"I confess I have not been losing sleep over this particular land grab, but one does find the Widow of Windsor's pious greed a bit tedious. I know what it means to be poor, and these delta peasants have nothing that even the most vicious Paris Apache would fatigue himself with stealing. Why do you suppose your *own* countrymen are interested in this squishy part of the world, Dick?"

Captain Gringo shrugged as a monkey cursed them from the branches overhead. He said, "Beats me. I guess President Cleveland takes the Monroe Doctrine seriously. Nobody in the States could *want* this swamp."

Gaston said, "Both sides want it. Or, at least, they want to control it. Nobody fights for ideals anymore, if they ever did."

Before Captain Gringo could come up with anything new, they saw the main drag ahead and he said, "Let's pick it up. It's almost dark and it looks like rain."

"That pink wedding cake on stilts, ahead, is the best hotel as I remember. Regard how they have been piling cinders along the streets of late. If they continue like this, the town will soon sit on dry land *all* the time, *non?*"

"I doubt if it'll be in our time, Gaston. Listen, I'm not sure about a big hotel in the center of town. We've both gotten sort of ragged and stinky and . . ."

"*Merde alors,* it is a ragged and stinky country. Who will notice? Everything and everybody is *très* wilted in the delta, Dick. We are both wearing hats and boots. We are both white men. It would attract *more* attention if we put in at some little *pasada* in the native quarter, *comprenez?* Come, we are prosperous tourists, a bit soggy from our travels. Once we show them we have money, and force them to disclose the location of the bathing facilities . . ."

So Captain Gringo followed Gaston up the rather alarming stairway to the wide and solidly built veranda wrapped around the pink hotel like a ballerina's tutu. A sign over the doorway announced in greenish gilt lettering that they were entering the Hotel Flamingo. Offhand, Captain Gringo couldn't think of a better name for it.

Inside, the lobby looked even more like the interior of a Mississippi steamboat, with whorehouse overtones afforded by fake gilt Louis XV furniture and a cut glass chandelier with naked Edison bulbs screwed into it. A mestizo room-clerk, busting a gut trying to look like a Frenchman, stared at them with a snooty attitude until he saw the color of their money, then began to treat them like visiting royalty. They asked for adjoining rooms with perhaps a bath. The clerk said there was a bath on their floor, which was the best he could do, and asked if they wanted any women. When they said they didn't, he looked them over understandingly and said he preferred boys, too. He dinged a bell and a tall sad Negro in a uniform two sizes too small came to take up their bags. When they said they had no luggage, he said he'd carry their keys. So they let him, and gave him a tip large enough to keep him from bitching and small enough to keep him from bragging.

Gaston won the toss of a coin and headed for the bath as Captain Gringo cased their quarters. There was a lousy lock on the door between their adjoining rooms. The ones leading

81

out to the hall were little better, but there were barrel bolts on the inside, so what the hell. He went to the window and opened the jalousies. They were on the second floor of the Flamingo, but the nice thing about buildings on stilts was that it put them three stories above the muddy ground below and there were no trees close enough to matter. There was an awning over the wrap-around veranda, so he considered somebody moving along the side of the building from one window to another. But then he poked a finger through the rotten canvas and decided they were safe from anybody heavier than a monkey.

Burglary was the least of their worries in any case. They had nothing on them they'd be leaving in the rooms when they went out and the local burglars probably had some arrangement with the hotel help in any case. Nobody else was going to waste time pussy-footing in from outside. Anybody with an official interest in them would just kick in the thin mildewed doors, right?

Gaston returned to report the water was reasonably hot and the soap more suitable for a Chinese laundry. So Captain Gringo picked the towel from the foot of his brass bed and said he'd soak a while. Gaston said to meet him, later, in the hotel bar downstairs. He'd seen all there was to see up here but he was beginning to remember his way about town and thought he'd check into a better place for their stolen boat.

Captain Gringo went down the hall to the bathroom. The door was closed. He turned the knob and a feminine voice protested in English, "I'm in the tub. I'll be out in a few moments, whoever you may be."

Captain Gringo shrugged and went back to the room to have a smoke. The sound of English had surprised him. The voice had seemed vaguely familiar. The woman had spoken with a New England accent—that was probably it. He lit a claro and tried not to dwell on how long it had been since he'd spoken to girls who pronounced the letter R like that. He told himself not to wonder who she might be and what she might be doing down here. With the current unrest it seemed obvious enough that other Americans should be in Venezuela. The idea was to *avoid* them, not to ask questions. He wasn't about to address any strangers in English. So, if the mystery lady in the bath spoke no Spanish, that was a problem be

didn't have to worry about. He wondered what she looked like, as he pictured a naked lady in a tub. Nobody could look *that* good! He wondered why his mental picture was so lewd. The woman he'd caught bathing had sounded simply embarrassed and annoyed, not dirty.

Jesus H. Christ, it wasn't as if he had any reason to paint dirty pictures of her in his head. He'd just had a couple of women the other day, Goddamn it. He and Gaston hadn't taken two full nights on the river getting here. He'd been sure, when he climbed off Mother Juana Maria, that he wouldn't be up to another orgy like that for at least a month, right?

He paced the room, smoking furiously, as he wondered where Gaston was and if it wouldn't make more sense to just go down dirty and forget the damned bath. Who'd notice, now? It was almost dark outside and artificial light kept a lot of secrets daylight wouldn't.

But as he ran a nail along the stubble of his jaw he knew he'd be more comfortable once he got cleaned up and had a shave. He'd about killed the claro. He snuffed it out in a copper tray and decided to see if the dame was finished down the hall.

As he approached the door again it opened and a vision of improper beauty came out, wrapped in a red silk kimono with her black hair pinned high. She had cameo features, wearing an attractive blush as she spotted him in the dim lit hallway and tried, without much success, to hide more of her freshly scrubbed flesh inside the flimsy thin silk she shouldn't have ducked outside her room in. He stopped where he was, putting a hand to the brim of his battered straw hat as he waited for her to move away, pass him, or whatever. He was in luck. Her room had to be on the other side of his. She lowered her long lashes demurely and tried to edge past. Then she stopped, looked up at him, and suddenly laughed, saying "Why, of all people! What are *you* doing down here in Venezuela, Dick?"

He felt a large fuzzy something turn over in his gut as he stared soberly down at the familiar but not *that* familiar face. He knew he was supposed to say something, so he said, "I know we've met before, Ma'am, and I'd be a liar if I said you had the sort of face a gent forgets, but . . ."

"Silly Dick," she cut in, still smiling, "you know perfect-

ly well you never looked at me when I sat next to you in algebra at Jefferson High. I'm Nancy Dorman. The skinny one with glasses, remember me now?"

He ran his eyes down her barely concealed curves as he smiled crookedly and said, "Oh, yeah, *Nan!* I guess I didn't recognize you without your, uh, glasses."

She laughed again and said, "Yes, I'm rather pleased the way I filled out, too. But I must say you still look much the same as when you were the big man on the campus. I'm down here with my husband, Dick. We're with the U.S. Consulate. But we just got in and had to check into this odd little hotel. I'll bet they didn't have room for you, either, eh?"

Wishing she'd go away, he nodded and said, "Something like that." The last thing he wanted to meet was a lady from the U.S. State Department, with or without a husband!

"Well," she said, "I'd better get back to our room and put some clothes on. Would you like to come along and meet my husband, Bruce, while I dress for dinner?"

He shook his head and said, "Later, maybe. I've got to get cleaned up myself and, uh, I'm meeting someone."

Nancy dimpled and said, "If I know you, she's pretty. Maybe we can all get together later this evening, eh? Bruce and I are in Room 207 and, by the way, my married name is Gordon. What room are you in, Dick?"

"Uh, gee, I never looked, Nan. I'll try and remember the next time we run into each other, right? It's been swell talking to you again!"

She looked a little puzzled, perhaps a little hurt, as he tugged his hat brim again and edged around her to lock himself in the bathroom. He thought about some sensible moves as he ran the water. It was coming back to him, now. There *had* been a skinny little brunette next to him in that algebra class back home and, boy, she sure had filled out nicely! But if she was from the old crowd, she had to know about his midadventures out west. It had been in all the hometown papers. "Local Boy Bakes Bad" was probably the way they'd carried the story of his busting out of that army guardhouse near the border.

He peeled and got in the tub. It felt good, but his mind wasn't in it. Damn that Gaston, where was he? They had to get the hell out of here before Nan remembered and told her damned husband! It was amazing she hadn't remembered

84

right off. Could she be that blind without her glasses? No, if she hadn't been able to see him she'd have never called him Dick. Okay, let's say she remembered a guy named Dick from school and hadn't connected the face with the story of his disgrace? That was it. He'd known her without remembering her last name. Few people remember the details about old school chums and he hadn't even been that chummy with little Nan Dorman. He hadn't remembered her name was Dorman, as far as that went. But it could pop in place any minute in Nan's pretty little head. And she'd said her hubby was with the U.S. Government!

Captain Gringo rose from the tub pronto, spilling water on the tiles. He patted himself dry and risked a quick shave, cutting himself twice with the razor before he forced himself to slow down. The nicks weren't bad and he stuck toilet paper to them as he dressed again, aware, now, how much he needed a fresh shirt. Scooping up the towel from his room, he cracked the door open, saw the hall was empty, and ducked back down the hall to see if Gaston had returned. Gaston hadn't. He swore, checked the chambers of his .38, and put the room key in his pocket after locking up. They were out the price of the rooms, but that was the nice thing about travelling light. A guy could move out fast when he had to, and right now it sure looked like they had to. Gaston would be over by the waterfront. The town was small. All he had to do was find a shadowy vantage point between the river and this fucking Flamingo and . . .

"Yoo hoo, Dick!" a feminine voice trilled as he tried to cross the lobby looking six inches tall. He managed not to grimace as he turned to see Nancy in a doorway sporting a feathered hat and a pudgy pink man in a rumpled linen suit. The man wasn't yelling for the cops, so Nancy hadn't made the connection yet. It didn't seem possible, but the Shantung beige dress she was wearing now revealed more curves than the kimono had upstairs. Maybe the brighter lights accounted for it.

Not knowing what else to do, Captain Gringo removed his hat and walked over to them. Nancy introduced him to her husband, who said, "We were just about to dine. Would you join us, Mister, ah . . . ?"

Captain Gringo said, "Marvin. Dick Marvin!" grabbing a vaguely familiar name out of midair. Nancy nodded and

said, "Oh, I remember, now. You must be related to the minister at the Calvinist Church, right, Dick?"

"I think my folks mentioned he was a distant cousin or something."

Nancy dimpled and squeezed her husband's arm as she confided, "I was so embarrassed, Dear. I went all through high school with Dick and I was *sure* I knew his last name until it came time for me to *say* it! Aren't I the silly?"

"Happens to everyone, My Dear," Bruce Gordon said smugly. "But let's all sit down, shall we? Nancy tells me you're with the U.S. Military, Dick."

Captain Gringo muttered something non-committal as he followed them into the dining room and found a seat with his back to the wall, adding something about just having a spot of tea with them before he had to leave. Gordon nodded and said, "Nan said you had a date. Forgive me if I order coffee. This is no time for Americans to be drinking *tea,* but everyone to his own taste, I suppose."

Captain Gringo said coffee would be jake with him, adding with a thin smile that the tea down here was home grown in the first place.

Bruce Gordon laughed drily and added, "I doubt if anybody would ever take you for a damned lime juicer, anyway, Dick. You didn't say what you were doing down here for our army."

Captain Gringo looked down at the silver, noted his fork had egg stuck to the tines, and said, "I'm, uh, not supposed to tell people I'm with the army these days, Bruce."

Gordon nodded owlishly and replied, "Oh, I get it. Military Intelligence, right? Nan said she'd heard you'd been given a scholarship to West Point after the two of you graduated from high school together."

His younger and far prettier wife gushed, "Oh, yes, Miss Pruett, the dean of girls told me all about it. Jefferson High was so proud of a boy from our school being chosen." Then, as the waiter came over to take their orders, she looked puzzled and added, "Was there another boy in our class at West Point, Dick?"

He sensed where her thoughts were taking her. He nodded quickly and said, "Yes, there was, as a matter of fact. I forget his name. We were in different classes at The Point."

Nancy said, "It's coming back to me, now. He got in trouble in the army after the two of you graduated, right?"

"I heard something about it, Nan. I don't remember the details."

Her husband, Bruce, had finished ordering just in time to chime in, "I do. The chap's name was Walker. His first name was Richard, too, by an odd coincidence."

Nan looked puzzled and asked, "How did you know that, Dear? You didn't go to Jefferson High with us."

Gordon smiled and said, "Hardly. But everyone in the diplomatic service down here had heard of Dick Walker. They call him Captain Gringo and he's been raising pure Ned since he disgraced himself as an officer and had to leave the States."

Then he smiled at Captain Gringo and added, "It's sure a small world, isn't it, Marvin? I confess that when Nan first told me she'd met an old school chum named Dick, who used to be in the army, it gave me a bit of a turn. I knew this Dick Walker had come from Nan's home town, of course, so . . ."

Captain Gringo managed a hearty laugh as his stomach filled with buzzing bees. Nancy looked puzzled, blinked, and joined the laughter as she gasped, "Oh, Bruce, you never! Why, the Marvins are one of the oldest and most respectable families in Connecticut and, now that I think back, I do remember that awful Walker boy. His name was Richard, too. They were right about that. But they didn't call him Dick, in school. I think they called him Richie. Isn't that right, Dick?"

Captain Gringo frowned and said, "I really can't say, Nan. I hardly knew the chap." Was she making another mistake? Had she mixed him up with another guy named Richard, or was she *covering* for him, and, if so, *why?*

The waiter brought coffee for Captain Gringo and the first course for the Gordons. Nan dipped her spoon in her turtle soup but didn't taste it as she nodded, thoughtfully, and said, "Yes, it's all coming back to me, now. Richie Walker was one of those big men on campus and I never liked him. He spent all his time playing football and showing off. He wasn't as scholarly as Dick Marvin, here. Do you remember how you helped me cram for that algebra test that time, Dick?"

He nodded, knowing she was full of shit. He'd barely

noticed the shy little brunette next to him in that class and he'd sure as hell never helped her with her homework! Her husband was looking at his soup a little pensively, now. Was she trying to make him jealous?

Bruce Gordon tried to change the subject by bringing up the current international crisis and Captain Gringo knew Nan was either scatter-brained or a hell of a psychologist. Gordon obviously didn't want to talk or even think about her high school days and/or any crushes she might have had on anyone in the past. Nan wasn't mixed up. Nan *knew!* She might not have made the connection as they met outside her bath. But somewhere between blurting to her husband that she'd met an old school chum down the hall and here, she'd put the loose ends together and now she was helping him out, damned cleverly. But why? She didn't owe him any loyalty. They'd never been close friends in school.

Captain Gringo finished half his cup and said something about having to meet someone as he excused himself. Gordon nodded and said something in turn about having to get down to the U.S. Consulate, adding that they'd probably meet there, later. Captain Gringo didn't answer that one. He smiled himself away from the table and went out to look for that fucking little Frenchman! He had to find Gaston and tell him it was time to light out for parts unknown, *poco tiempo!*

But, as he walked along the odd skyway fronting on the main drag of Tucupita he began to wonder about that. *Did* they have to light out for parts unknown, now that at least two people connected with the local U.S. Consulate could seem ready to vouch for him as an innocent military attache or whatever? Gordon, of course, was laboring under a sincere mistake. Nan could blow the whistle any minute she felt like it. But she didn't seem to feel like it, and as long as she wanted to play it that way he was safer here than anywhere else he could think of! He lit another smoke and enjoyed a dry chuckle as he thought of being arrested by the local cops and demanding to see his friend, Bruce, at the U.S. Consulate! Jesus, if Nan could get him some blank passports or diplomatic visas ... but why the hell would she want to? What *did* Nan want? She wanted *something*. Everybody wanted something.

He found himself on the veranda of a closed general store. There was no light behind him as he lounged up there,

watching the barely visible figures moving all around over the bridges and catwalks. It was a good position to watch for Gaston. He knew the little Frenchman's movements, even in semi-darkness. He took a drag of smoke and settled down to sweat Gaston out. He didn't have anyplace better to go, right now.

He heard clumping boot heels as someone came along the catwalks from the direction of the Flamingo. He turned and saw it was Bruce Gordon. The other American recognized him at the same time and said cheerfully, "Ah, so here you are. Nan thinks you're meeting a woman, but we know better, eh?"

"I am sort of waiting for a man," said Captain Gringo, cautiously. "I figured as much," nodded Gordon and said "We'll never be able to stand the lime juicers off unless we get some help from the local greasers. How does it look, Marvin? Think the little brown monkeys will fight for their own country, or do they expect *us* to do it all for them?"

"I think the Venezuelans will fight, if they get the right backing."

"Well, you know more about the military aspects. Frankly, I expected Washington to send more help to us down here, if they really expect us to hold the Royal Navy off. I don't like to bluff when I play poker and, Goddamn it, we sure hold a piss-poor hand down here."

"Yeah, I'd like to see a few Yankee battleships standing off shore in case the Brits think we're bluffing, too. But we might have a few aces up our sleeves. By the way, Gordon, I'd sure feel better about my mission if I had your word it was confidential between us."

"Oh, sure, mum's the word, Dick. I won't blab all over town about you being here to organize the greasers for Grover Cleveland. There could be British spies right in our hotel, right?"

"I figured you'd spent some time at the Great Game, Bruce. That black hallporter has a Jamaican accent, now that I think about it."

Gordon nodded and moved on, feeling important. Captain Gringo settled down to wait some more. Then a couple of bedraggled-looking whores came along the high walkway and gave him the eye. He passed on both of them, but he saw the local paseo was starting and a man standing still during

the nightly flirtation walk stood out like a sore thumb. He cursed Gaston roundly, tossed the butt of his smoke to the wet mud far below, and headed back to the hotel. Gordon hadn't looked like he was running anywhere to call the law. There were telephones at the hotel if either of the Gordons planned to betray him. He decided he'd be as safe in his room as anywhere. So he went back to it.

He had second thoughts about the safety of his room when he saw the slit of light under the door. Someone was inside, waiting for him. It could be Gaston, if Gaston had returned by some less obvious route. On the other hand, it could be somebody else. Anybody else.

He eased to Gaston's door, next to his down the hall. The key to his own room wasn't supposed to fit and it didn't, exactly. But they were both cheap locks and as he'd hoped, it only took a little fiddling to get Gaston's latch to quietly open.

He stepped into Gaston's room, moved to the connecting door on the balls of his feet, and opened it as he drew his revolver, coming in at whomsoever at a hopefully unexpected angle of attack.

Nancy Gordon nee Dorman sat up in bed and gasped, "Oh, you startled me!"

She startled him, too. Nan wasn't wearing a stitch and hadn't bothered to pull the covers up enough to matter, her clothes and feathered hat were on a chair near the dresser. He spotted himself in the mirror above, looking sort of dumb as he stood there holding a gun on a lady. He tucked it away as he bolted the door behind him. Then he moved over to sit gingerly on the edge of the bed. Nan leaned back on one elbow, breasts pointed at him like a brace of six guns as she dimpled and asked, "Don't you want to take your clothes off, Darling?"

He said, "Very much. I just spoke to your husband and he still thinks my name is Marvin for some reason."

Nan reached out, took one of his hands, and placed it on her firm but fleshier than remembered stomach as she said, bluntly, "I had to lie for an old schoolmate, didn't I?"

As she started to move his hand down, he said, "You *did* remember, huh, Nan?"

She moved his hand between her thighs, closed them on

90

it, and as his fingers parted the moist trembling flesh between her legs she husked, "I remember everything, Dick! My God, I had such a crush on you, all through school!" She moved his wrist, wriggling to meet the thrust of his fingers on her turgid clit as she added, "I had to do this to myself after school, you brute. You never knew how much I wanted you inside me, did you, Dick?"

"Hell, no, I thought you were a shy little virgin, Honey!"

"I was, then, but I'm not anymore and, for God's sake, are you still going to sit in class beside me like a big dope or are we going to make up for lost time at last?"

As he half rose, he said, "I'll get the light." But she insisted, "No. I want to watch us in the mirror over there as you make my dreams come true, Dick Walker. My God, if you only knew the positions I've had you in, in my secret world . . ."

He pulled his hand out and popped a button shucking his duds as he grinned and said, "Let's try 'em *all,* then. I'd forgotten some of the dirty thoughts I used to have about *you* in algebra, Nan."

As he rolled atop her she purred, "Oh, did you want me, too?" and then as she spread her thighs in welcome and felt him entering her, she gasped, "Oh, my, you *must* have! It's even bigger and harder than I imagined and . . . oh, yes, Darling, this is the way I dreamed it would be, only better!"

He pounded her old-fashioned style, to get their bodies used to one another before they settled down to the orgy she obviously had planned for some time. As she came the first time she started to cry about wasted years and made him repeat that he'd wanted her, too, back when the world was younger and less complicated. He lied gallantly, for in truth he'd never even thought about making the skinny little kid in the next seat over. As he rolled her on her hands and knees he shoved it to her dog-style and said, "This is how I used to picture doing it to you when you walked ahead of me down the hall."

She arched her back and thrust her now fuller rump up to meet his thrusts as she crooned, "Oh, did you really, Dick? I used to put padding under my Dolly Varden, because I had such a skinny little behind, but . . ."

"I used to go crazy watching your Dolly sway back and

forth when you walked, Nan. I used to wonder if you wore anything under it and how it would be to catch you like this, bending over."

He caught himself in the mirror and tried not to laugh. What the hell was he talking about? The girl with the great ass at Jefferson High had been Molly Brady, the redhead in biology! Jesus, there'd been no doubts about *her* round rollicking rump under that thin skirt she wore, and he'd often pictured her naked from the rear, with the red fuzz winking as she walked, and that gave him an even bigger erection so that the once skinny Nancy got the full fruits of Molly Brady's teasing walk. Nancy enjoyed every inch of it. As she moaned she was coming, he fell forward with her across the mattress and put a hand under her to finger her as he slid in and out of her prone quivering body. He let her enjoy it. Then rolled her over to enter her frontally again, deeper, as he pounded his own enjoyment into her semi-sated and sensitized flesh. She pressed her thighs tightly together as he worked on her with his own legs spread outside hers and it felt almost painfully tight. She gasped, "Oh, that's lovely, that way, when a man is long enough. Do you like it that way, Dick?"

He answered by exploding inside her, collapsing long enough to recover his breath, and growling in her ear, "That was great foreplay. Now, let's get down to some serious fucking!"

She laughed like a naughty child as he raised her knees high enough to hook one over either elbow. As he started moving again, hitting bottom with every stroke, she matched his lust with bumps and grinds as bawdy, saying, "Oh, you're just as awful as I hoped you'd be. Did you really kill that officer out in Texas, Dick?"

"For God's sake, do you want to discuss manslaughter or do you want to fuck, Baby?"

"Both. I like to talk dirty, Dick. Did you know Bruce makes love in his nightgown, with the lights out?"

"I figured he might. That's *really* talking dirty, Nan! You don't have to tell me your husband's no good in bed. I had that part figured out already, and I'm sort of old-fashioned about sharing twat with other guys. I'm not dumb enough to insist on virginity, but I like to pretend I'm the only guy using a particular cunt, if it's all the same with you."

92

She began to bounce to meet him, saying, "Oh, use it all you *want*, then! I swear it feels like I'm losing my cherry to you, you marvelous brute. God, if you'd really been there when I was playing with myself as a teenager, I think you'd have killed me. Did you ever see that statue of David, without the fig leaf, Dick?"

"I've seen photographs of it in art books. Why?"

"I used to picture making love to you and that's what you looked like in my dream. I mean, cock and all. I didn't know cocks came bigger than poor little David's, Dick. If I'd really seen you, naked, I'd have fainted dead away, I'll bet."

"Yeah, well, statues are supposed to be more artistic. You've got more between your legs than any marble Venus, now that I study it."

"Can I get on top, Dear? I told you I wanted to try it every way with you."

That seemed pretty obvious, but there was something funny going on, here. He withdrew and rolled on his back to let her mount him like a witch on a broomstick. She was obviously enjoying it and it seemed reasonable that a lady with a chance to realize an old sexual fantasy might take advantage of a chance meeting far from home to do so. But she was working too hard, like a whore trying to please a customer. Since he wasn't paying her in cash and she had all the cock in her a love sick school girl ever could have imagined, there had to be something else in her pretty little head. Sooner or later they'd get to it. Meanwhile, she was one hell of a lay and his own distraction, by prolonging his orgasms, made him a great one for her, too. Her mouth pursed into a little rosebud as she closed her eyes and gasped, "Oh, God, it's happening again and I was just doing this to get us hot again!"

He knew what she meant. He rolled her half off so he could move his own hips faster and as they went at it side-by-side she grinned roguishly at him and said, "Oh, yes, this is the best way to make it last! Where did you learn to screw so good, Dick?"

"Same place you did, I guess. For a gal with a lukewarm hubby you sure have practiced pretty good with somebody, Nan."

She laughed suggestively, thrust her pubis forward to

envelope him to the roots and purred, "I cheat on the poor little simp every chance I get. But I must say you're the best, so far. Roll on top of me, Dick, I'm ready to come again and I want it deep when I do!"

That sounded reasonable and he rolled over to help her out with what he assumed was another old-fashioned orgasm. But Nan drew her legs up to lock her ankles across the nape of his neck as she swallowed him alive, reaching down to grasp his scrotum as she whipped it back and forth across her anus and then tried to stuff him in the front way, balls and all. He said, "It's no use, Doll, it won't work that way." And then he felt her open wider as his testes joined the rest of him inside and he gasped, "That's impossible. Nobody, ever, took it that deep! Where the hell is it all going, Nan?"

She moaned and replied, "Out my mouth, if we can manage. Give it to me harder, Dick!"

"Jesus, take it easy. You'll rupture something!"

But she didn't take it easy and since she damned near ruined him when she clamped down in a long shuddering orgasm, it obviously hadn't hurt her as much as it had him. He grimaced as she rolled off and she said, "Oh, did I hurt em balzy-walzy? Momma kiss em and make em all better."

She did that good, too. He stared at the overhead light as he tried to figure out how she'd developed herself so amazingly since school and, more important, what she *wanted!* The freak show had surprised him more than it had satisfied him, so she was able to arouse him again with oral sex and when he protested he was ready to put it in her again she shook her head, with her mouth full, and swallowed hard as he exploded deep between her tonsils. She had him ready to pass out as she slithered her moist curves up his overheated flesh to snuggle against him like a contented love toy, or perhaps a boa constrictor. She buried her face in the crook of his neck and collar bone and asked, softly, "Was that as nice for you as it was for me, Dick?"

He said, "Better. But how long can you stay, Nan? We must have been at it for hours and . . ."

"Poor old Bruce said the meeting at the consulate would last half the night. He won't catch me here with you in any case. He doesn't know your room number, even if he suspected."

"Yeah, but he could find out easily enough if he asked at the desk, and he might, if he comes home to find you missing."

"He won't. I told you I've done this sort of thing before. But, by the way, what name did you register under, Darling?"

"Oh, Jesus, I just remembered! I didn't use Walker, of course, but I didn't use Marvin, either. I generally use a Spanish name when I travel. Saves problems when the local cops check registers, see?"

"Don't the room clerks suspect you're not Spanish, Dick?"

"Sure, but what do *they* care? Nobody ever checks into a hotel under their own name anyway, unless they're sissies."

She laughed and toyed with the hair on his belly as she said, "Oh, well, we told Bruce you're some sort of secret agent. But he'll never look for me here. I always know when Bruce comes home. He wanders about calling my name in the halls. There are certain advantages to staying in hotels with the toilet facilities scattered about the premises."

"Oh, I get it. You just nip back and tell him you were pissing someplace else, eh? He must be sort of dumb, if you do that often."

"He is, Dear. I manage to satisfy him easily enough, whenever he can manage to get his little thing up. So he never suspects I've just been with anybody else, and *anybody* else is *better!*"

Captain Gringo grimaced and said, "You somehow give the impression your marriage is not a happy one, Nan. Why don't you leave Bruce if he's such a pain?"

She began to fondle his genitals again as she said, matter of factly, "I've thought about it. But my parents arranged our marriage and my father would disown me. That wouldn't be so bad if my poor father wasn't rather well-off. More important, Bruce has a lot of money, too. I've given the clod too many of my best years to let him off that easily. He wouldn't have to give me a thin dime if I simply left him."

Captain Gringo didn't think it would be gallant to suggest she had a modest fortune between her legs, considering how freely she gave it away. So he shrugged and patted her rump, silently.

Nancy began to stroke his shaft fondly as she asked, quietly, "Dick, would you do me a little favor?"

"If I'm up to it, Nan," he said. "What have we left out? What do you want me to do for you now?"

"Would you be a dear and kill my husband for me, Dick?"

He blinked himself wide awake and said, "Come again?"

"I'd love to. But let's talk about Bruce, first. I've been trying to come up with a fool proof way to get rid of him, so when I met you again and remembered how you liked to kill people . . .'"

"Stop right there," he cut in. "Nobody likes to kill people. Nobody normal, anyway."

She snuggled closer and gripped his shaft harder as she nodded and said, "I know it's harder than it looks, Dick. I've started to murder Bruce a couple of times and I've always lost my nerve at the last minute. But you're *good* at killing people, if half of what they say about you is true. They'd suspect *me*, of course, between his insurance and a little gossip about us in certain circles. But if *you* killed him, nobody would ever know. You could do it when I had a . . . a what do you call it?"

"You mean an alibi, Nan. And stop talking like little goody two shoes. We're discussing cold blooded murder for gain, Doll Face!"

She began to stroke him harder as she giggled and replied, "I know. Isn't it exciting? Nobody would ever suspect you, Dick. Nobody would ever connect you with his death and I've got it all figured out. We could make it look like some Venezuelan rebels assassinated him!"

He started to tell her she was full of shit and probably crazy, too, but this was no time to have a crazy lady mad at him, and there were some odd angles to this mad proposition that might be worth thinking about.

He said, "Knocking off a Yankee diplomat could bring this crisis to a head, Nan. If Washington thought the Brits were behind it they might stop screwing around and just declare war on England."

"Pooh," she said, "what do we care? You and I don't have to fight the war. Besides, I don't think Bruce is important enough. His family bought him his job with the State

96

Department because he didn't have the brains to graduate from Harvard Law."

"Oh? What does he do at the consulate, Nan? Could either of you get to the files and rubber stamps?"

"Heavens, no. Bruce is just a messenger boy. Why do you think we're staying in this rinky-tink hotel instead of inside the compound? Bruce travels about delivering things and taking things back to Washington. That's where we live, most of the time. We have a home in Fairfax County, but we're hardly ever there."

He tried to ignore her finger as she shoved it up his rectum and added something about going sixty nine. He said, "Later. Let's not get our sins mixed up. Are you saying Bruce is a diplomatic courier? I thought those guys travelled alone with their sealed attache cases."

She began to finger-fuck him with his testes cradled in her palm as she replied, "Most of the *younger* couriers do, I can report with some pleasure. Couriers get terribly hard up away from home for weeks or months at a time. Bruce says that some day couriers may be able to travel anywhere in the world in a few days. He reads H.G. Wells and Verne a lot. Meanwhile, he takes me along on his silly missions, spending his own money. I don't think he likes variety as much as I do."

"I thought you said he wasn't very passionate."

"Oh, we make love almost every night." She grimaced, adding, "At least, *he* does. The silly fat thing poops out just about the time I'm starting to get hot. Honestly, Dick, if you had any idea how many nights I've had to satisfy myself in some dingly little port of call!"

She moved her hand teasingly and her voice got really dirty as she said, "I've often day-dreamed about our school days and one night in Rio you and some wax fruit I improvised with had an astounding fuck. I had a hell of a time getting that wax banana out after it was all the way in, but it was worth it. You don't have any candles or ivory-handled hair brushes in here, do you?"

"Not that I've noticed. Why?"

"Oh, I thought it would be fun if we did it with both my holes nicely stuffed. You may have noticed I'm built sort of, well, roomy."

He grimaced and said, "I've no complaints when you

97

clamp down. But you ought to stick to smaller toys if you don't want to stretch things out of shape. I met a lady one time who'd been trying on all sorts of things for size, and by the time she got to where she could screw a milk bottle, no man on earth could satisfy her."

Nancy laughed and said, "I'll bet I could take a milk bottle, if I put my mind to it. But we were talking about killing Bruce."

His dawning erection went limp as her hand suddenly felt like reptiles hissing between his legs. He didn't owe Bruce Gordon. He didn't even *like* Bruce Gordon, but as a fellow human being he couldn't help feeling a bit sorry for any man married to this little she-monster. He was glad he hadn't known she was a nymphomaniac with a crush on him, back in his schoolboy hard-on days. As a jerk-off kid he'd have been putty in her hands. As a grown man, she was starting to disgust him. But he said, "Okay, let's think about how we get away after."

She said, "I told you it would be easy, Dick. I have a motive, but I can always be having coffee and cake at the consulate when you kill him. Nobody has any reason to connect *you* with the deed and everybody knows the natives down here are wild and crazy."

"Sure they do. There'd still be an all out flap if almost any Yank was assassinated in the middle of a diplomatic crisis. To clear themselves, even the Brits and various Venezuelan factions would cooperate in any all out investigation. The local police would turn this town upside down and question everybody, including yours truly. You know I'm wanted on other charges and the papers I carry wouldn't stand up to a real check out by some wise-ass cop with a long distance telephone at his disposal."

Her nails dug thoughtfully into his scrotum as she murmured, coldly, "Oh? Are you saying you won't do it for me, Dick? I thought as old school chums we had a certain understanding."

So there it was, like vomit on the rug. She wasn't asking him to murder her husband. She was ordering him. One word from Nan and he'd be on his way back to the States in irons!

Stalling for time, he placed his own free hand in her lap and soothed, "I never said I wouldn't do it, Honey. I said I

98

have to do it right. You have to remember that if *I* get caught, *you* get caught."

"You'd *tell* on me, Dicky-Wicky?"

"Wouldn't have to. The hotel help have seen us together. I wouldn't count on them not knowing about you slipping in here tonight. I've heard a couple of people pass my door since you've been here and you do come sort of noisy. It's only a fifty-fifty chance that anyone on the staff knows we're in here screwing and plotting, but fifty-fifty are lousy odds."

"Oh, Dear, couldn't you just kill him and sort of run away, Dick?"

"No. Not if anyone knows we've been playing slap and tickle behind your husband's back. But there is a way."

Her hand between his legs went soft and gentle as she purred, "Oh, I knew a professional would find a way. How many people have you killed, Dear Dicky-Bird?"

"Who counts? How many people have we kissed between us? The idea is not how many guys I may have knocked off in the past, but how we get away with the murder you're interested in. First of all, I need my own alibi. Can you get me into those coffee and cake orgies at the consulate by introducing me as the innocent Major Marvin you went to school with and know in Washington?"

"I suppose so. But how will you be able to kill Bruce if you're with me at a party, Dick?"

"I have friends in low places. My sidekick, who shall be nameless, was knifing people before either of us were born. You've got to understand that *killing* people is *easy*. *Getting away with it* is the part that takes a little thought."

She giggled and said, "Oh, I see, it's a lot like adultery. But don't you think it might be dangerous for you to meet the consulate crowd here in Tucupita, considering who you really are?"

He shook his head and said, "Not as dangerous as appearing to avoid them. There's an old saying in the army: *when in doubt, move toward the sound of the guns*. The last place anyone would look for an American outlaw would be the U.S. Consulate."

"What if you run into someone there who remembers you from the army?"

"I'll be embarrassed as hell. But that's a chance worth taking. In a town this size any American is going to be

pointed out to any other. I served in the Indian Fighting Army. Most of my troopers were black. I doubt like hell any of the good old boys I chased Apache with have been transferred to the State Department. You saw how easy it was to fool your husband, once he'd been introduced formally by someone he already knew. Nobody at the consulate is likely to ask to see the papers of a guest introduced by the wife of a diplomatic courier and, as you may have noticed, I lie pretty good on my feet. Let me get in with the local American Colony and the rest will be easy."

"Oh, you're so smart. How soon will you have your friend kill my mean old husband, Dicky-Wicky?"

Captain Gringo had no intention of asking Gaston any such thing, even though he knew Gaston was capable of being "practique" if it meant them getting at the visa blanks and rubber stamps he meant to look for at the consulate, if and when they accepted him. He began to fondle Nancy's clit as he said, "I think I ought to make a couple of visits, first. When are you two planning to leave Venezuela, Doll?"

"This coming weekend. Bruce brought some secret papers down from Washington and when the consulate finishes a situation report for him to take back, we'll be boarding a north bound steamer. But do we have to wait that long, Darling? Think of the fun we could have if we didn't have to meet on the sly like this."

He said, "We'll have to be even more sly, after. Recent widows are supposed to cry a little before they start screwing openly. Let me work it out, Nan. It's better if you don't know the details. That way your surprise will seem genuine and you can fake the grief."

She relaxed and parted her thighs as he worked her hotter. He didn't really want her again. He'd had more than enough of Nan, even before he'd known she was a moral monster. He figured he'd make her come with his hand and send her back to her rightful room. But she seemed to have other plans. She threw one thigh over him, opened wide, and pleaded, "Put your hand in all the way, Dick. Give it to me with your fist."

He laughed and said, "That's not likely, Honey. I've got big hands."

"That's all right, I've got a big cunt. Come on, two fingers are just teasing me. I want it all!"

He shrugged and worked his ring finger and pinkie in, driving all four to the knuckles as she started to gush. He started to say he'd told her so. Then, to his surprise, she gave a little grunt and his knuckles were inside. He found himself rising to the occasion as his fingertips fondled her cervex, deep inside as she pleaded, "Deeper! Put your thumb in, too!"

He insisted, "No way, Honey!" as he drove his hand up into her until the web of his thumb was rubbing her clit as she started bouncing up and down, teasing his erection with the muscular hemispheres of her athletic derriere. She giggled and said, "Oh, that's nice." He thought she meant his hand until she arched her spine, reached in back of her, and grasped his turgid shaft to guide it into her anal opening. She got the tip in and then settled down, legs impossibly spread, with his wrist pinned to his belly, his hand almost fully inside, and his shaft up her rear. He could feel his own tool sliding over the knuckles of his hand through the fleshy partition between her openings. She seemed to like it, too, for she went sort of crazy. She had him pinned to the mattress but moved enough for any three people, from side to side as well as up and down. It was wild as hell. Then it got wilder. She reached down and grabbed his thumb. Then she folded it and tried to force it inside with the rest of his fist. He didn't resist, but he didn't think she could do it, either, until she did. His eyes opened wide with wonder as he felt his *wrist* filling her opening, with his fingers inside folded into a fist by her internal contractions as she began to come in a series of multiple orgasms. He was coming, too, as she moved her mad rump up and down in a corkscrew motion. It was a long and teasing orgasm because of his mingled desire and disgust. As she loomed above him in the harsh electric light, Nan was a vision of lovely well-bred womanhood. But he knew the brain behind that cameo face was filled with worms, and from the waist down she was a freak of nature. Almost a freak of nature, at any rate. Nan's astounding capacity was more the result of self-abuse with anything she could stuff inside her insatiable love maw.

Captain Gringo exploded lustfully in Nan's rectum as, at the same time, Nan's husband exploded through the door, shouting, "So, I've caught you at last!"

Captain Gringo muttered, "Oh, shit!" as Nan popped off

his shaft but hung on to his good right hand by clamping tightly on his wrist in surprise and embarrassment. As she rolled away and groped for some sheets to cover herself, Captain Gringo tried to pull his fist out of her. He needed it. Bruce had slammed the door behind himself, leaped on the bed with them, and was beating the shit out of everybody and everything in sight!

"Hey, take it easy!" grunted Captain Gringo as the outraged husband bounced a pudgy fist off his skull while the younger and stronger American tried to fend him off with his left elbow. Bruce was sobbing stupid things you expected husbands to sob at times like these and Captain Gringo had to agree he had a point or two, but the silly bastard's punches stung pretty good when he landed. Bruce threw his fists like a girl throws rocks and Captain Gringo could have licked him with one hand tied behind his back, if it had been his *left* hand. But his *right* hand was hung up like a hound's pecker inside Nan's crazy twat and she didn't help at all by rolling around moaning and groaning like that. Captain Gringo back handed her husband off the bed with his left and tried to sit up, saying, "All right, let's all simmer down and talk this over, huh?"

But Nan was hysterical and wouldn't or couldn't relax enough to let him pull his fist out of her, and the damned fool Bruce was getting up and reaching in his pants for something as he said rude things about them both. Captain Gringo tugged in vain as Bruce pulled out a jack knife and said, "I'll cut your balls off for this, Marvin!"

He must have meant it for he dove headfirst across the bed and stabbed down hard with a knife as he landed atop them both. Captain Gringo grabbed Bruce by the nuts with his free left hand and squeezed hard. The outraged husband gave a gargled gasp of agony and pounded fist and knife wildly as Captain Gringo tried to tear his crotch out by the roots. He felt Nan's vaginal muscles relax and pulled his fist out with a magnum cork pop. He grabbed Bruce by the hair with the wet hand and rolled him off his chest as he rose, starting to feel thoroughly annoyed. Bruce wound up on the floor again as Captain Gringo swung his feet to the rug and leaped from the bed to land in a boxing stance. Bruce came in for another try with the knife, crouching low. Captain Gringo muttered, "Some guys just never learn," as he grabbed the

102

knife wrist with his left and drove a right cross into the pudgy man's face. Bruce must not have had as many boxing lessons as he should have: he didn't roll with the punch, but took it like a sucker. The blow straightened him up for a lovely left hook. So Captain Gringo threw it, and felt something snap as the smaller man staggered back to the wall, slid down it, and lay limp on his side.

Captain Gringo rubbed his tingling knuckles and muttered, "That's more like it. You okay, Nan?"

Nan didn't answer. She couldn't. When he turned to stare soberly down at her she lay spread-eagle across the bed, eyes open and a faint little smile on her saucy face. He could see, now, why she'd let go of his wrist like that. Bruce had stabbed her smack in the bread basket. Most of the bleeding had been internal, but a hell of a lot had oozed out of the little hole between her breasts to run down and ruin his bedding. He noticed some brown streaks he'd have trouble explaining to the chamber maid, too. He sighed, stepped over to the bed, and wiped his stained penis off on a corner of the sheet while he was at it. Then he turned and said, "Okay, Bruce. We'd better figure out a good story for the cops."

Bruce didn't answer. Captain Gringo went over, knelt, and felt the side of Gordon's neck. Then somebody poured ice water down his naked spine. The poor chump was dead, too. That snap he'd felt had been Bruce's *neck!*

Captain Gringo muttered, "Oboy!" as he cast a nervous glance at the silent and fortunately shut door leading to the hallway. Apparently they hadn't made enough noise to be heard in the lobby, so he had at least a minute or two to get his ass out of there.

He moved Nan's feet out of the way as he sat on the bed and started hauling on the clothes he'd dropped beside it under friendlier conditions.

How the hell had Bruce gotten through that locked door like that? Oh, yeah, now he remembered. He hadn't *tried* the door when he spotted light under it. He'd assumed it was locked, but Nan had let herself in with some jiggle-jiggle of her own and then simply waited for him, with the door unlocked in welcome. Old Bruce had come home to find his own bed empty, gone exploring, and who could miss the noise of a lady who came as enthusiastically as the late Nancy Gordon?

He shot her corpse a sad disgusted look as he muttered, "Well, he had to catch you sooner or later, Doll. But you two sure picked a hell of a place for the last act of Hamlet!"

He checked the time and chambers of his gun. The night was young; his gun was still loaded; the name he'd given downstairs was a fake. He'd just leave quietly and see if he could find Gaston and . . .

And if he didn't find Gaston, Gaston would be wandering back to find *him*, about the time this place was crawling with cops!

Okay, how much time did they have? None of the help would enter any of the rooms up here before it was time to change the linens in the morning. If anyone had heard the fight they'd be knocking on doors by now. So, if he just sat tight, until Gaston got back . . .

He stood up, stared around the shambles, and muttered, "Oboy, this figures to be one long cheerful night! In this heat you kiddies will both be sort of rank by sunrise. So they'll find you before noon even if I hang up the 'Don't Disturb' sign. Gaston and me will have a short lead and it'll be broad daylight and . . . Jesus, Nan, I sure wish you'd taken geometry instead of algebra at good old Jefferson High!"

He heard footsteps out in the hall and stiffened warily. Whoever it was passed by without breaking step, probably on their way to take a crap. He took out a cigar and lit it, too keyed up to sit down as he paced, considering his options. He knew Gaston would have cut out by this time. He knew Gaston would think he was a jerk to stay. But he knew he had to wait for Gaston, and if Gaston didn't get back soon, they'd both be nailed, anyway.

He saw that a random stream of Nan's sluggishly wandering blood was almost to the edge of the mattress. So he folded the sheet back to keep it from dripping on the rug. The rug was still clean. Aside from Bruce over there in the corner, most of the debris seemed to be confined to the bed they'd all been romping together on.

He wondered if the dead man had soiled himself. He went over and rolled Bruce over. The corpse was still limp and Bruce flopped on his face like a wet dishrag. His linen pants were a little brown in the seat, but nothing much had soaked into the rug. Captain Gringo hauled the dead man over to the bed and shoved him on the soiled sheets beside his

messy bride. Then he stared soberly down at the loving couple and muttered, "Now, why did I do that?"

He blew a thoughtful smoke ring as he stared around the rest of the room. Except for the God awful mess in his bed it seemed neat as a pin.

He nodded and reached in the purse Nan had dropped near the foot of the bed. Yeah, her room key was inside and the number on the tag said it was just down the hall. There was nothing else of interest in her purse but the half-empty tube of vaginal jelly. He'd been wondering about that.

The footsteps returned and faded away. The coast was clear outside. At this hour few guests would be in bed. He turned out the overhead light and carefully cracked the door open. The hall was darkly deserted. Somewhere in the night a ballroom combo was playing a two step. There was a dance or something going on downstairs.

He closed the door behind him and locked it. Then he moved down to the Gordons's room and unlocked it. He stepped inside and flicked on the light. Their room was almost a mirror image of his, but the bed looked a lot neater. It had the same spread his had, and it hadn't been slept in. Moving quickly and smoothly, Captain Gringo got to the bed, unmade it, and rolled up bedding and mattress cover in a neat bundle. He switched off the light, checked the hall, and scooted back to his own room with the clean bedding. He tossed it in a corner for now. Then he said, "Ladies first," as he proceeded to roll Nan's body in the messed up covers of his own bed. He had no idea how he'd explain a mad desire to deliver laundry at this hour if he met anyone, but he didn't meet anyone as he carried Nan to her own room and sat her down, still bundled, and muttered, "Don't go 'way. I'll be right back."

Bruce was a lot heavier, but not as messy. Captain Gringo delivered him in the sheet with the shit smears on it and left him next to Nan while he went back for the rest of his ruined bedding.

Nan's blood had soaked into the quilted mattress cover, but the mattress under it was okay, save for a little piss. He turned his mattress over, damp side down, and remade his bed. Everybody pissed in bed once in a while, if any maid ever noticed the stain, once it dried.

He made it back to the Gordons's room without incident

105

and placed the bloody mattress cover on their own bed. Then he rolled them out of the other bedding and tossed it loosely aboard. As he got Nan back in bed her corpse farted, loudly. It was amazing how anything he'd been having so much fun with a few minutes ago could seem so unpleasant to handle. He'd heard there were guys who enjoyed making love to dead women. They had to be sick.

He started to put Bruce to bed. Then he reconsidered. Nan looked natural in bed. Bruce was fully clothed, so what the hell would he be doing in bed, right? It was best to leave him there on the floor like that. Let's see, the guy had come in as somebody was knifing his wife à la Jack The Ripper. They'd struggled, and he'd been killed, too. Where the hell was the chump's knife?

That could wait. Captain Gringo took the purse and clothing Nan had worn and hung it neatly on wall hooks across the room. He studied her and decided she looked like she'd gone to bed as usual. The bedding was a mess, but what the hell, the killer had been raping her when the husband came in, see?

He tried to think like a sex maniac and decided robbery called for fewer artistic touches. He knelt by Bruce and started going through his pockets. He kept all the coins and bills he found and tossed everything else across the rug, carelessly. Unlike himself and Gaston, the couple had checked in with luggage. It was locked. Bruce had a ring of keys, but Captain Gringo took out his own knife and slashed open the leather luggage to toss the contents around. There didn't seem to be much worth stealing, but the cops would figure the thieves had taken anything of value. It was sort of funny that Nan hadn't had any jewelry until he remembered the hotel safe, downstairs. He straightened up, took a last look, and decided he'd set the stage artfully enough for most small town cops. As he made ready to leave he spotted an attache case in a corner that he'd overlooked. That gave him another idea. He put it on the dresser and forced the lock. It was filled with typed papers. He folded them, put them in his side pocket, and tossed the case out the window. They'd find it in the mud, some day, and a diplomatic courier's missing case might give them a few more red herrings to sniff at.

He went back to his own room, switched on the light, and got down on his hands and knees to look for the missing

knife. He found it under the bed where it had been kicked in the fight. The blade was still bloody but there didn't seem to be any visible stains on the rug. He left it open as he switched off the light again and tossed it out the window at an angle, to land as far out of line as possible. Now all he had to do was get rid of the diplomatic dispatches and there'd be nothing to connect him with the people down the hall.

He decided he may as well read them before he flushed them down the drains down the hall. So he switched on the light, pulled the shade, and sat on the bed to go over the latest gossip from the delta. He was still reading when he heard a light tap on the door between his room and Gaston's. He called, "Entrada" and Gaston came in, saying, "I see you are alone. You're slipping, Dick. What's that you're reading?"

"Diplomatic pouch. They don't have a magazine stand downstairs. Hey, did you know Uncle Sam was serious about this Monroe Doctrine shit? They say here that they want to send a raiding party into British Guiana to show the Brits they're not bluffing."

Gaston pulled up a chair and sat down, saying, "I don't need to read other people's mail to tell you that, Dick. I just came from the waterfront. Everybody in the cantinas expects the Americans to back Venezuela. Everybody but the British, that is. It looks as if that big war everyone has been arming for for so long is about to start in this odd little corner of the world. I would have placed my money on the Balkans, but we live and learn. Where did you steal those papers, anyway?"

"It's a long story. Hang on to your hat." Captain Gringo sighed as he folded the papers and proceeded to bring Gaston up to date. When he'd finished, Gaston sighed and said, *"Merde alors,* that's what I get for leaving children alone and unsupervised. I had a few nibbles on our boat load of arms, but I imagine our best bet, now, would be to see how fast she travels, hein?"

"Damn it, Gaston, we have no place to go that's any safer. Tell me about your nibbles. Who's in the market for heavy weapons these days?"

Gaston shrugged. "I don't know about the cannon shells, but 30-30 rounds are going for a dollar a dozen on the open market, no questions asked. The price should rise in a day or so. Meanwhile, I ran across an old comrade who owns a

boathouse where we can hide our launch. He asks no questions, either, but the species of insect demands a dollar a day."

Captain Gringo consulted his watch, saying, "That sounds reasonable. But do you think we can make it to the boat and back before daylight?"

Gaston nodded and said, *"Oui,* if we leave at once and run into no river patrols. Washington has just loaned the Venezuelans some old monitors and they seem anxious to try the gun turrets out. Fortunately the old tubs are slow and how often can one hit anything in the dark, hein?"

"You don't *have* to hit anything *often!* You just have to hit it once, if we're talking about big guns. Are we talking about those monitor class gunboats left over from the Civil War? I didn't think they were still around. The guns must have rusted solid by now."

"Mais non," Gaston said. "The hulls and engines have been reconditioned. The guns are new. Six-inch breech loaders, I have heard. But, as I said, the craft are slow and deep draft. Come, we have some marching to do, *non?"*

Captain Gringo nodded and started to rise when he heard a woman scream like a banshee out in the hall. He looked at Gaston, who put a finger to his nose and murmured, "Perhaps we march another time?"

Captain Gringo went to the door and opened it for a glance down the hall. A sobbing chambermaid was on her knees by the open doorway of the Gordons' room. Male staff members were either milling around down there or appearing in increasing numbers on the stairs. He spotted a couple of police uniforms and shut the door, muttering, "Shit. We're not going anywhere. Let's get rid of these papers while we make up a damned good story."

All the guests the police could find on the premises were herded into the downstairs dining room for questioning. Captain Gringo and Gaston chose a corner table so they were able to listen in as a rather officious fat police captain took

108

earlier statements from the staff and guests. It was a break, in a way, that the puffed up little bastard seemed to suspect everybody.

He really gave the maid who'd discovered the bodies a hard time. Captain Gringo had wondered what the hell she'd unlocked the door for at that hour, too, but he could see she was a simple peon girl and her story made sense, to him.

The maid said she'd been sent up to La Señora's room to return an earring the busboy here in the dining room had found when they were cleaning up. She said Nan had mentioned losing it at the desk, so when an earring answering the description was found, she'd gone up with it. She'd knocked and, getting no answer, assumed La Señora was out. She'd unlocked the door with her pass key to put it on the dresser. The rest was hysterical history.

The police captain couldn't seem to understand this, or maybe he enjoyed seeing the girl cry. She was sort of pretty as well as simple. Some grim-lipped guys wearing American haircuts and linen suits came in as the police were badgering the maid. They said something to the police captain, who pointed at the girl and said, "It is true two of your people were murdered here tonight, Señor Consulado. But I think we have the murderess, here."

The peon girl wailed and covered her face with her apron. One of the Americans, to his credit, looked dubiously at her and asked the cop why he thought she'd done the deed.

The cop repeated her story in a sarcastic tone, adding, "She lies, of course. The tale of missing jewelry was simply an excuse to let herself into the poor woman's room. When La Señora surprised her in the act, she killed her and then her husband and . . ."

"Bullshit," said Captain Gringo, rising to his feet as Gaston tugged at his sleeve and muttered, "For God's *sake*, Dick!"

The tall American knew Gaston was right, but enough was enough, and he knew sooner or later they'd connect him with having dinner here with the dead Americans in any case. So he advanced on the guns by stepping over beside the maid and saying, "Look at the size of this kid. Look at her clean apron. Does she look like she just cut up two grown adults with a knife?"

The cop said, "Only the American woman was stabbed. The man died of a broken neck." Then, as Captain Gringo grinned at him, the cop saw how dumb he'd been talking, and blustered, "Who are you? Are you a detective?"

Captain Gringo felt pretty slick about that deliberate mistake about the cause of death, but he was painfully aware of the Americans from the consulate staring at him as he shook his head and said, "No, my name is Marvin. Major Richard Marvin, Retired. I knew the Gordons. Had coffee with them in this very room tonight, as a matter of fact, and I do remember poor Nancy mentioning a missing earring." He turned to the maid and asked her, "Do you have it, Señorita?"

The maid shot him a grateful look and took a small piece of costume jewelry from her apron's pocket. The cop took it from her with a scowl and said, "I am impounding this as evidence."

Captain Gringo looked at one of the other Americans, turned to the police captain, and said, "Bullshit. That's American property, Sonny! I told you I was with the Gordons earlier this evening and I remember she was wearing earrings like that. If you think this girl stole it, why don't you ask the busboy if he really found it?"

A timid looking Negro stepped forward and said, *"Es verdad, Señores!* I, Gomez, found it under that table over there when I changed the linens. I gave it to Rosario at the desk, who gave it to Camelia, here!"

"In that case you are a suspect, too!" snapped the police captain. Captain Gringo sidled up to the American consulate man who looked most disgusted and murmured, "I don't know about you guys, but this moron is sure throwing his weight around and he's pretty stupid, besides. Don't we have anybody at the consulate who we could turn this investigation over to?"

The American nodded and said, "Great minds run in the same channels. I remember you, now. Gordon mentioned running into you down here. What's the score? Military Intelligence?"

"Let's say I'm just a retired officer, officially."

"Oh, right, lots of majors retire young as you. I know the rules of the game, Major Marvin. Who do you think assassinated Bruce Gordon?"

Captain Gringo shrugged and said, "Beats me. I didn't

ask him what he and old Nan were doing down here, either. They probably weren't after *her,* poor thing, but you'd know more than me about what they might have been after."

The one he was talking to suddenly paled, turned to his companion and snapped, "Jesus, I just remembered! He left the consulate tonight with dispatches! Go up and check his room, Simmons!"

The other man nodded grimly, and started to elbow his way for the stairs. The police captain protested, "See here, I am conducting this investigation, Señores!"

The boss from the consulate smiled grimly across his bows at Captain Gringo as he said, "Like the man says, bullshit. You and your cops just run along, okay? The man they murdered was a diplomatic courier on a mission for both our countries. If you want to *keep* your dumb little country, you'd better stand aside and let the big boys do it right!"

"I am insulted!" protested the officious little cop. The bigger American snapped, "Oh, shut up and go play with your jacks. You've already fucked around enough. If you get in our way again I'll call El Presidente Crespo long distance and have you cutting sugar cane by this time mañana!"

"But Señor . . ."

"But me no buts. Just butt out," snapped the American. He nodded at the frightened maid and said, "You can go back to your duties, Miss. The U.S. Government thanks you for your co-operation and we'll call on you if we have any further questions. Marvin, what can *you* tell us about this mess? You were here when it happened, right?"

"Wrong. I met them here in this room, earlier. I met Bruce outside, later, as he was on his way to the consulate. I just got back to the hotel a few moments ago. So they must have been dead when I passed their door. Sort of spooky, now that I think of it."

The man who'd run upstairs ran back to rejoin them, saying, "It's gone. They tried to make it look like robbery, but they must have been after his diplomatic pouch like you figured, Chief. They haven't moved the bodies, yet. I'd say they were killed a couple of hours ago if I remember my last war right."

The boss from the consulate nodded at Captain Gringo and said, "Okay, I didn't think you did it anyway. But I'm going to have to write some reports and for the record, it

111

might look better if we could be neater in pinning down the time you came back. Did you pick up your key at the desk, Marvin?"

"No, damn it. I had it in my pocket. But somebody must have seen me in the lobby."

The little maid touched the suspicious consulate man's sleeve shyly and said, "Por favor, Señor. I remember this Señor and his friend coming up the stairs just as I was about to go to the room with the dead people in it."

Captain Gringo didn't know whether he wanted to kiss her or kick her. The two American diplomats looked past him at Gaston. The one in obvious command said, "That's that then. Is this other gent with you, Major Marvin?"

Captain Gringo tried to look sneaky as he winked and said, "M'sieu DuVal is, uh, with the French. Get it?"

"Oh, right. Heard the French were offering to act as go betweens down here. One hand washes the other and we don't need a statement from him in any case. It looks like that goddamn Greystoke wants to read other people's mail pretty bad."

Captain Gringo nodded and scored another goal by saying, "Yeah, I heard British Intelligence plays pretty rough."

"Oh, you know who Greystoke is?"

"Sure, doesn't everybody?"

The consulate man smiled thinly and said, "Yeah, you're with Army G2, all right, but nobody will hear it from us. Is there anything State can help you with, unofficially, of course?"

Captain Gringo started to shake his head. Then he decided to go for broke while the dice seemed hotter than usual. He said, "Well, I don't know if I ought to tell you this, but I had a reason for looking up Bruce when I heard he was down here. We're neighbors up in Fairfax County, you know. But asking a friend is one thing. I wouldn't want to put you boys in a spot."

"Hey, Bruce was *our* friend, too! What were you two working on?"

"I think Greystoke and the Brits may have gotten a line on my cover. I guess I don't have to tell a pro like you my name's not really Marvin, right?"

"Of course not. Only sissies put their right names down on travel visas. Was Bruce going to get you some new identity papers from us?"

"Well, he said he'd try."

"Hell, Major, *that's* no problem. Drop by the consulate in the morning and we'll rubber stamp you off the Brit's organizational charts. I'm getting tired of that Limey bastard making problems for our agents, too!"

It started to rain just after midnight. As the sun came up it was coming down cats and dogs and the river was rising, too. The soggy ground the town stilt-walked across vanished under ankle deep water, brushed silver by wind and rain. Gaston had been thinking about their hidden boat upstream. With the visibility on the river so lousy it seemed like a good time to run their stolen arms into town. But with the jungle trails under water, it seemed impossible to get back to where they'd hidden the launch. He suggested taking a couple of his local confederate's peons to fetch the launch while Captain Gringo fetched their new documentation from the consulate across town. Captain Gringo pointed out that nobody was likely to stumble over the hidden cove in this kind of weather unless they were part duck. Meanwhile, Gaston said he'd go over to the waterfront and see if he could find any customers. He didn't want to hang around the hotel while the killings were under investigation and he most certainly didn't feel up to entering the U.S. Consulate with or without Captain Gringo. It was Gaston's considered opinion that his younger friend should quit while he was ahead. "You are sticking your head into the jaws of the lion," Gaston insisted. Captain Gringo smiled crookedly and remarked, "The British consulate would be the lion's jaws. I think I'm going into the eagle's nest. I know it's risky, but so would ignoring the offer. Those guys are expecting me to show. They'll wonder why if I don't."

Gaston grimaced. "I tried to shut you up last night. Why

113

on earth did you ask them for forged papers in the first place, Dick? Don't you know they have a cable connection to Washington?"

"Sure I do. And they'll use it *faster*, if they get *suspicious!* I told them I was travelling under a false I.D., so they have no name to check on. Frankly, I figured they'd brush me off when I said I'd asked Gordon for help from State. How the hell was I to know they'd lose sight of interservice rivalry with the Brits about to invade? We've never had a big war in my time. Army's never been able to get shit out of State before."

"Oui, that sounds like my old government, Dick. But I still don't see why you asked any favors in the first place."

"Hell, they knew I'd been cozy with the Gordons. What the hell was I *supposed* to tell them I wanted?—A piece of Nancy's tail? The girl was screwing around. Somebody at the consulate's going to remember that as they run out of leads. I don't want them wondering how well I knew *her*. I want them to think of me as his old Washington buddy, see?"

Gaston shrugged and said, *"Oui,* one can see the advantages of glossing over one's knowledge of the lady's alarming appetites. But all this sudden familiarity with a government that wishes to hang you is making me *très* nervous. Listen, Dick, if we sloshed our merry way back to the launch and simply, as you say, lit out . . ."

"Oh, shit, Gaston, where would we go? We don't know our way around this delta in the first place and it's crawling with opposing gunboats in the second. Our best bet is to sell the arms, take the money, and run. We can board any damned boat out with the papers I'll be picking up."

"Assuming it is not a trap, you mean."

Captain Gringo thought that over before he shook his head and said, "I doubt that. They had the hotel crawling with cops last night if they'd wanted to arrest us. They couldn't have suspected a thing."

"Perhaps not, in the first act of this drama, my old and rare, but consider that they've had all night to reconsider and this dawn is cold and gray indeed. Our Yankee friends were in a flap over the missing papers and had a mental picture of the secret agents they suspected. But by now they must be reconsidering their options, since nobody has been arrested in or around the town, hein?"

Captain Gringo started to say it seemed obvious the secret agents or whatever had run off into the surrounding swamps. But Gaston had a point. He'd done some military police thinking in his time. So he knew that when the obvious leads failed to pan out, the routine called for going back over everybody's story again, as many times as need be.

Gringo said, "That little maid seems to think we came in together. So, where the hell were we last night?"

Gaston said, "One could hardly tell the truth. Why don't we say we were at El Gato Negro?"

"Swell. What's El Gato Negro?"

"Cantina cum whorehouse. The largest such establishment in town. As I recall, you had a wonderful time with Lolita, or was it Conchita?"

The American started to object. Then he nodded and said, "Right. Nobody would say he'd spent the night whoring unless he had it sort of forced out of him. I'll go with you as far as the waterfront and you can show me where I got in so much trouble. I'd be up shit creek if I couldn't describe the place. Is it open at this hour?"

"Oui, El Gato Negro never closes. Maybe, this time, we'll really screw somebody, non?"

Captain Gringo couldn't think of a thing he needed less, right now, than a roll in the sack with some down at the heels waterfront whore. But what the hell, they could kid around with the girls and buy a few drinks in case anyone ever asked if they remembered them.

They left the Flamingo to walk, or wade, toward the waterfront over the high cat walks serving as sidewalks in the delta town. Most of the walkways had awnings or corrugated overhangs, but they still got soaked by the time Gaston dragged Captain Gringo into what looked like a big red barn on stilts and announced, "Regardez, the hub of Tucupita's social whirl. Trés chic, non?"

The cavernous interior was dark and dank as the hold of Noah's Ark and smelled sort of like a zoo, too. The air reeked of tobacco, marijuana, cheap rum, vomited rum, and unwashed cunt. The dance floor was covered with sawdust as damp and rotten as jungle mold. There were empty tables around three walls. The third wall was covered with filthy pictures behind a long plank bar. A trio of bedraggled whores in short fandango skirts lounged dully against the bar. As the

115

two men walked over to join them, Captain Gringo was hard pressed to decide which was the ugliest. The bleached blond with Indian features was built like a nail keg. The Negress next to her had a nice figure, but her face was scarred by smallpox and the armies that had marched over her. The one with European features and black hair, gray at the roots, might have been pretty, thirty or forty years back. She looked like a Halloween witch dressed up like a Spanish dancer for some odd reason.

Captain Gringo nodded to the mulatto barkeeper and ordered drinks for everybody. Then he nudged Gaston and muttered, in English, "Where are the cribs? Upstairs or out back?"

"Are you serious, Dick? I'd rather make love to a reasonably clean pig."

"That makes two of us, but I might want to brag a little about the nicer one I met last night. Where the fuck did I take her?"

"Out back. And if you fucked anybody from around here, stay away from me. I have heard one can catch a dose from the seat of a toilet, hein?"

The thick-waisted Indian girl came over to link her arm through Captain Gringo's as the barkeeper served her colored water. She smiled, exposing a gold tooth, and said, "Hey, you are most generous. But you look like a brute to me. Do you like for to make brutal love, handsome one?"

"Not this early." He sighed, adding, "We just dropped by for a drink. Maybe we'll come back later, when it livens up a bit, eh?"

The whore shrugged and said, "I am better before I have been had by anyone. But ask for me anyway. I am called Goldy Locks, and, for a friend, I can be persuaded to take it all three ways."

The black girl sipped her own sucker-drink and confided, "Hey, don't listen to her, handsome. Ask for me, Ebonia. I am the only girl here that a man does not have to tie a board across his ass for to avoid falling in."

Goldy Locks looked at her listlessly and said, "It is true you have a tight pussy. It is all filled with scabs from the loathsome illness your father gave you."

Ebonia poured her drink down the front of Goldy Locks

116

with an amazing lack of enthusiasm as she said, in a bored tone, "At least I had a father, you filthy little Indian. Your mother was too ugly for any man to trifle with, so she had you by a crocodile, who later died for shame."

The barkeeper stared at the darkness overhead as he muttered, "Hey, ladies, let's not fight, eh?" and Gaston said, "I think we've seen this floorshow before, *non*?" He turned as the older of the trio was reaching for his hip pocket and chided, "I don't keep my money there, M'selle, but it was a nice try. Shall we go, Dick?"

Captain Gringo nodded and they headed for the door as, behind them, one of the whores called, wistfully, "Hey, Caballeros, come back and we'll be good, eh?"

"Gee, that sure was a neat place, Gaston," Captain Gringo said as they got outside. Then he asked, "What the hell were you and I doing in there last night, anyway?"

Gaston shrugged and replied, "It is a good place to do business. Who watches the tables when the whores are dancing naked on the bar, hein?"

"Gotcha. If things go sour and I can't meet you at the Flamingo, I'll meet you later in that dive." Then he frowned and said, "Wait, that won't work, if I'm going to tell people I hang out in places like that."

Gaston took his arm and led him around the corner toward the waterfront. He pointed with his chin at a corrugated iron building standing on stilts over the water and said, "That is the boathouse of my old legion buddy. His quarters are on the far side. A green houseboat tied alongside the warehouse, *comprenez?*"

"Right. What's his name?"

"Who knows? Call him the Dutchman. That's the only name I know him by."

"Is he a Dutchman?"

"But of course not. He is French, like me. You must understand something about the French Foreign Legion, Dick. Most of the men dumb enough to join it are French, but, since they are wanted by the law, they say they are from some other country. I never asked the Dutchman, but it is my understanding he was the victim of a crime of passion in the old country."

"The *victim*, you say?"

"*Oui*. He killed his woman in a fit of passion and the police found out about it. Fortunately, the legion accepted his droll tale of being a deserter from the German army."

"That sounds reasonable. But what's he doing here in South America?"

"*Merde alors*, he deserted as soon as he got the chance, of course. The Dutchman is a murderer, not an idiot. I think he deserted from French Guiana a few years ago. One understands that sometimes it is not wise to ask people such details, hein?"

"If you say so. But how do you know you can trust this guy? He sounds pretty wild, to me."

"*Oui*, have you ever heard the stories they tell of the *trés* savage murderer, Captain Gringo?"

"Touché, but damn it, I never murdered any goddamn wife, and before you say it, I didn't kill Nancy Gordon, her fucking husband did!"

"True, but would you like to explain that to any judge, Dick? One must not be hasty in judging one's fellow soldiers of fortune, Dick. To the world at large, we are all scum. Don't worry about the Dutchman. I know him and, more important, he knows me. Deserting the legion is no great undertaking. Getting away from *me* would be a problem I do not feel the Dutchman would feel up to."

"The Dutchman's your problem," Captain Gringo said. "My problem's finding the goddamn U.S. Consulate before I drown. Do you know where it is, Gaston?"

"*Oui*. Everything of importance is on the little high ground they manage in these parts. I, Gaston, your faithful native guide, shall conduct you to the nearest catwalk leading inland. Then, forgive me if we, how you say, split up? There is a French legation as well as others in the droll neighborhood and I find this flirting with polite society *trés fatigué*."

Gaston led Captain Gringo upstream along the waterfront and while the rain seemed to be letting up it didn't help much. They were both soaking wet. Out on the river a ship's bell chimed and Captain Gringo glanced over to see a squat dull gray vessel at anchor between two lighters. He grimaced at the monitor and said, "They were right. It does look like a cheese box on a raft. You didn't pick up any poop about more serious gunboats coming down from the States, did you?"

Gaston said, *"Mais non.* But a monitor class gunboat is *très formidable* in these waters, if you ask me."

"Nobody's asking you, Gaston. I don't know what the Brits have just down the coast, but H.M.S. Anything is going to laugh like hell when it meets that old Civil War tub! Look how it's sitting in the water, for Chrissake! They've removed all the ballast and the top blade of the screw is sticking out of the river!"

Gaston nodded. "True, but let us be just to the so-called Venezuelan Navy. To operate in shallow waters one must have the shallow draft, *non?* That old gunboat was designed for open seas. There are channels in this delta where the water is only knee deep. Even with her ballast tanks pumped dry she threatens to run aground in this maze of land and water."

"That's the least of her problems, if she's not a complete bluff. If they ever have to fire those turret guns they'd *better* be in a shallow channel! She was designed to fire smaller guns with her decks almost awash. The recoil from either of those six-inchers would flip her over on her back like a turtle!"

"Eh bien, perhaps the British are less familiar with American ordinance, Dick."

"Oh, sure, nobody in the Royal Navy reads. Jesus, I'm an old *army* man and I can see from here that tub's a bluff."

They'd come to a dog-leg where another catwalk forked off between a pair of barn-like warehouses. Gaston pointed with his chin and said, "I shall leave you here, Petit Chapeau Rouge. If you meet any wolves on the way to Grandmother's house don't say I did not warn you."

Captain Gringo said they'd meet either at the Flamingo or the Dutchman's, depending, and stepped between the buildings.

The sky fell in on him, or, rather, six or eight guys did! Captain Gringo was borne to the wet planks by sheer weight of numbers as he tried to get his gun out without much luck. The gang was grunting and punching with the silence of serious professional thugs and the only thing that kept them from kicking the shit out of him on the way down was that there were so many of them they got in each other's way!

Gaston had better luck as the gang concentrated on what they thought was the tougher of the two soldiers of fortune.

119

The gang was right about Captain Gringo being stronger, but they made an awful mistake in dismissing the small dapper Frenchman as less mean. While the main attack concentrated on Captain Gringo, a mere trio went after Gaston. Two from the front and one from the rear. As the one behind grabbed Gaston and pinned his elbows to his sides, Gaston muttered, *"Merde,* surely you jest!" as he sent one in front of him over the catwalk rail with a high kick many a ballet dancer would have envied! The man he'd kicked in the head bit the mud eight feet below with a soggy thud and the other boring in to punch out what he'd taken to be a helpless victim paused to reconsider while the one holding Gaston grunted, *"Take* him, damn it! He's stronger than he looks!"

Gaston took advantage of the moment by reaching between the legs of the man holding him, grabbing a fistful of assorted sex organs, and twisting viciously. The man trying to hold him screamed in agony and let go as his comrade came in, swinging, to the rescue. But again Gaston's right foot whipped up and as his boot heel connected with the thug's breast bone the attacker sat down with a glazed expression. The one Gaston had by the nuts was back against the railing, pleading, "Let go, I give! I've had enough!"

Gaston smiled pleasantly and said, *"Mais non,* I, Gaston, shall say when you have had enough!"

Then, still gripping his erstwhile attacker's crotch with his left fist, Gaston proceeded to hammer his face to raspberry jam with the other. The railing gave and as the semiconscious victim fell away Gaston let go with a shrug and turned to see how the others were making out with Captain Gringo.

The one he'd kicked the wind out of was still sitting up, making funny noises as he tried to breathe. So Gaston kicked him in the face and stepped over him as he moved into the main brawl, drawing his revolver.

One of the men piled on Captain Gringo saw him coming and shouted a warning as Gaston swung his pistol barrel down to split his skull. In the meanwhile, Captain Gringo had gotten his hands and knees under his center of gravity and was coming up, whether they wanted him to or not. Somebody yelled, "Hold him!" and another gasped, *"You* hold him! He's too strong to be human!"

Gaston began to sing "Here we go gathering nuts in

May" as he went into a sort of sissy-looking dance, kicking people in the head as chance warranted. Captain Gringo was up now, and while he didn't dance as well, people flew farther when he hit them with his big and thoroughly annoyed fists. By the time they had five men on the deck or over the side the survivors were leaving in all directions. Captain Gringo dragged one of the men Gaston had kicked silly to his feet, slapped him a couple of times, and snapped, "Who sent you, pronto, or you go over the rail!"

The man muttered something dumb about being a robber. So Captain Gringo picked him up by the front of his shirt and the crotch of his pants and threw him over the rail to land in the mud below. He turned to look for someone more sensible, but Gaston said, "Let's get out of here before the police notice how untidy we were, hein?"

Captain Gringo glanced around, saw nobody else was out in the rain near enough to matter, and said, "Right."

He jogged up the walk, over a bridge, and between other buildings until he noticed the catwalk was turning into a brick paved walk between showy flowering bushes of some kind. He stopped on the edge of a wide grassy expanse, turned to look for Gaston and, finding himself alone, walked on. He saw he was on higher ground and that plaza ahead had to be the main part of town. He found a peon selling fruit under an arcade and asked directions. The peon said the U.S. Consulate was the building near the church with the American flag in front of it. That made sense.

As he legged it across the plaza in the rain, Captain Gringo spotted the Stars and Stripes though there were other flags hanging damply over other stucco and tin buildings all around. It was hard to make out the pattern of a sopping wet flag, but he spotted the French and Dutch colors, the white German ensign, and, to his momentary surprise, the British Union Jack flew, or rather, drooped, a few doors down from the U.S. Consulate.

That figured, when you thought about it. Tucupita was a seaport and provincial capital, so naturally most trading nations would have their consulate here. Britian wasn't at war with Venezuela and the U.S., yet. But as an old army man Captain Gringo knew flags only flew in rainy weather during time of war or serious emergency. The various consulates had their flags out not to ruin them but as beacons for their

nationals in case anyone had to run for cover when the shit hit the fan!

Everything was up to date at the U.S. Consulate. The marine guards stood at parade rest with chromed sword bayonets on their bolt action Krag rifles. Since neither of them even looked at him as he entered the doorway between them, he almost wondered what the hell they were doing there. A civilian might have *really* wondered, but, as an old army man, Captain Gringo knew the military mind, or what passed for a military mind in certain circles. Had he been the military attache, here, he'd have had them on the roof behind some sandbags. The marine detachments guarding U.S. installations around the world weren't supposed to be doormen. They were there in case the local unwashed came in a bunch to send the Yanquis up in smoke.

It was lighter inside than out in the overcast. Edison bulbs were set in the hubs of the revolving electric fans overhead. As he felt a chill from the wet air moving over his wet clothes, Captain Gringo wondered if they could switch the lights on without turning on the fans, and decided they probably couldn't. An officious-looking girl with Hispanic features sat at a desk in the center of the foyer. She looked the soggy Captain Gringo over, dubiously, and said in Spanish, "You are tracking water on the floor tiles, Señor."

He replied in English, "There's a lot of that going around, lately. I'm Major Marvin, Sis. So if you don't intend to mop up after me you'd better tell the boss I'm here. He's expecting me."

She literally leaped to her feet as she replied in perfect English, "Forgive me, I took you for a native, Major. Come with me. I have orders regarding you."

He followed the snooty-looking she-male down a corridor, lighting a claro as he admired her rear view. He considered patting her on the bustle as she paused to open a frosted glass door for him. But he decided he'd only carry his arrogant act as high as a major's rank rated. You'd have to be

122

at least a bird colonel to goose girls working for the government these days. She led him into what looked like a draftsman's office, where three men were busy at drawing tables and another was climbing out from behind a desk as the receptionist announced Captain Gringo as Major Marvin.

The department head of whatever department this was held out a hand and said, "You're a little late, Major. But we can fix you up before lunch if I'm correct about your needs. The chief explained your problem."

The head whatever was a few years older than Captain Gringo albeit a bit officious for anyone under sixty. The soldier of fortune looked around and asked, "Right. Just what is it you guys do here?"

The older American said, "Forgery, mostly. This is the documentation section. If anyone asks, we're supposed to be cartographers, mapping the delta for our allies in Caracas. As you can see, our official job calls for all sorts of paper and inks of every color. My name's Smith, if anyone asks. You can call me Smitty, Marv. But I gather you don't want to be Marv anymore, right?"

This was too good to be true. All he needed to hear, now, was that the receptionist put out. But he noticed she'd left. So he nodded and said, "Yeah. I seem to have blown my cover as a retired army major. I take it you guys can fix me up with another American passport?"

"American, British, French, hell, Russian or Turk, if you want it. We have all sorts of blanks and rubber stamps. The idea is to use a lot of rubber stamps and smear a little grease and graphite on the pages, see?"

Captain Gringo saw how an American consulate would have all the blank U.S. papers it might need, but he was curious about the others. So he asked, "Are you sure your fake foreign stuff would stand up to a real going over by a pro?"

Smitty looked hurt and asked, "What do you think we are, amateurs? Of course our workmanship stands up under scientific scrutiny. We're the guys who figure out the tests, so we know how to beat 'em."

He stepped over to his desk and picked up a mock British passport, handing it to Captain Gringo as he explained, "Look at that paper. We're not talking about some back street forgery with a jeweler's glass and a crowquill pen,

123

damn it. We had Whitehall's paper chemically assayed and ran off our own, duplicating the fiber, sizing, and finish. We make our duplicate rubber stamps from photographs taken from real visas. You want us to fill this out for you?"

"Hardly. I'd have a hell of a time passing as a Lime Juicer, even if that passport passed inspection. I just want to be another American travelling under another name. I'd better drop my military cover and say I'm a reporter or something."

Smitty shook his head and said, "Bad move. Journalist is the most common cover for a secret agent, and they know that even in the sticks. Why don't we make you a geologist? Nobody knows how to talk to a geologist, and the job fits a guy wandering around down here. Standard of Ohio's been prospecting for oil in Venezuela, lately. They haven't found any, yet, but the British are drilling for oil in Trinidad, right off the coast, so this delta ought to be a good place to look for it, right?"

"Yeah, it sort of explains Whitehall's sudden interest in this swamp, too. I like it, Smitty. Let's make me a geologist named, oh, Rogers?"

"Richard Rogers? Catchy name. Okay, let's have your old passport and I'll get the boys right on it."

Captain Gringo managed not to show his sudden dismay as he asked in a desperately casual tone, "Oh, do you need my old papers? I left them back at the hotel, but I can get them soon enough."

Smitty glanced out the window and said, "Hell, it's raining fire and salt. Be quicker to play it by ear."

He picked up a blank from his desk and said, "Here, sit at my desk and fill this out. Say anything you want and I'll go over it and edit out any traps you write yourself into. Don't make up a phony oil company you work for, for instance. Use a real street for your home address. You'd be surprised how many guys get nailed by some bush league customs agent with a few city directories and a copy of the Wall Street Journal in his desk."

"I can see that. But isn't it pretty easy to check out real addresses and companies?"

"Sure, if anyone takes the trouble to write a letter and wait for a reply six or eight weeks later. No minor official's about to spring for long distance cable charges unless he's

sure he's on to something. Trust me, Marv. I've been in this game a while."

Captain Gringo sat down and tried not to smile as he started to forge a new identity. He knew Smitty was no fool. Had he really been a Major Marvin on a real mission he'd have never gotten this cooperation just by walking in off the street. But people never suspected anyone they'd been introduced to by someone they already trusted.

Nancy's introducing him to her husband had led the late diplomatic courier, Gordon, to vouch for him at the consulate. The front office accepting him as a neighbor of the Gordons' had led in turn to these government forgers accepting him as one of their own. It was too good to be true, but what the hell, it was about time his luck changed. He'd been getting shot at by total strangers a lot, too.

It only took him a few minutes to fill out the application blank and he knew a man with any sense would quit while he was ahead. But as he handed the blank to Smitty he found himself saying, "I shouldn't press my luck, but while I'm here, do you suppose you could run off a fake French passport for me, too?"

"Sure, *parlez vous?*"

"No. I never was very good at French, but I'm working with a French agent named DuVal. They probably told you about him, right?"

Smitty frowned and said, "Can't say as they have. What's the deal?"

"Well, he might be able to get by with the papers he has, if the Brits don't know he's working with Uncle Sam. I don't know if they spotted him with me or not, but . . ."

"Hell, Marv. No problem. French papers are easy. Any halfway decent printer can make French money!"

Smitty reached past Captain Gringo and pulled another blank from a pigeon hole, saying, "Lessee, yeah, this is the Frog form. You want to fill it out for him or wait 'til he can come in with you? It's in French."

Captain Gringo smiled and said, "He'd probably feel better doing it himself. But how do I smuggle him into a U.S. Consulate without blowing his cover, Smitty?"

"You can't. The fuckin' Limies are just down the street and they have a spyglass trained on our front door. The British agent watching our back door sits in a private house

to the west, the turd. Can't you fake up something for him, Marv? You must know his cover, right?"

Captain Gringo tried not to laugh as he nodded and proceeded to fill out new I.D. for Gaston. Gaston was going to have a piss poor opinion of American Security when he got his new passport, but with fool proof travel documents their troubles were over. They'd sell the arms cheap, board the first tub out, and let everyone down here have their war in private!

He was still working on Gaston's papers when a tall younger man in U.S. Army dress blues came in with some papers. Captain Gringo looked for a hole in the floor to sink into. There didn't seem to be any. Smitty said, "Howdy, Lieutenant Bronson. Do you know Major Marvin, here?"

Bronson turned toward Captain Gringo with a pleasant smile, blinked in surprise, and said, "For God's sake, what are you doing down here, Mister Walker?"

Captain Gringo sighed and said, "Oh, a little of this and a little of that. It's been a long time, Bronson."

Bronson turned to Smitty and explained, "We were at the Point together. He was an upper classman when I was a plebe."

"Gave you a rough time, eh?"

Bronson laughed and said, "As a matter of fact, old Walker, here, was one of the only upper classmen who never reamed my ass." He turned back to Captain Gringo and added, "I've always meant to ask you about that, Old Buddy. Remember the night you saved my hide on interior guard?"

Captain Gringo's lips felt numb as he murmured, "Oh, I never saw much sense in that hazing shit."

Bronson chortled, "That's for damned sure. I thought I'd shit when you were acting O.D. and caught me off my post."

"What the hell, a guy has to take a piss, he has to take a piss. It was no big deal. That brass cannon you were guarding was left over from the Revolutionary War and stuck in cement, anyway. Who the hell was going to steal it?"

Bronson looked sort of dewy eyed as he shook his head and said, "I still owe you, Mister Walker. Or is it really Major, like Smitty says?"

"Right now I'm supposed to be a civilian named Rogers.

I don't have to tell you what they do back in this office. What are you doing here in Venezuela, Bronson?"

"Officially? Military Attache, of course. Off the record, I'm with G2. Jesus, you must be G2, too, right?"

"Uh, close enough. I'm not supposed to tell anybody, Bronson. Officially, I'm still in Washington, see?"

"Oh, right. If the right hand doesn't know what the left hand's up to, nobody can keep track of the little pea under the shells. You'll let me know if there's anything my section can do for yours though, won't you? I told you I owed you from our days at the Point together."

Captain Gringo got up from the desk and handed Gaston's paper to Smitty, who glanced at it and passed it to one of his draftsmen, saying, "Good. Short and simple. Make sure you don't put any back dated stamps connecting this M'sieu Chambrun with French Guiana, though. The lime juicers are keeping an eye on all the colonies down the coast while they expand north."

He turned back to Captain Gringo and Bronson to say, "It'll take us an hour or so. You want to wait or come back for 'em?"

Before Captain Gringo could answer, Lieutenant Bronson said, "You'll have lunch with me, Old Buddy. Come on, I'll show you the way, I understand the provincial governor is coming to lunch, here, today."

Captain Gringo followed him out into the hall, but he must have shown a little green around the gills because Bronson stopped him and asked, "What's wrong? You look like you're fixing to vomit!"

Captain Gringo was. He knew the governor. The governor knew him. They'd parted last on friendly terms, aboard that steamboat he and Gaston had deserted, but the Venezuelan official was going to be very surprised to learn he was a recently arrived U.S. agent. Could he fake it? Did he dare?

He said, "I'm wet as a drowned rat and you may have noticed this isn't my best dinner jacket, Bronson."

"Hell, nobody cares. Who dresses for lunch in this steaming swamp, anyway? Come on, I'll introduce you to the local international set. Some of the ladies aren't bad, and all they do down here is sleep and screw."

Captain Gringo remained rooted and shook his head.

"I'll have to level with you, Bronson. I don't want to meet anybody in high circles right now. I'm supposed to be a guy travelling in low circles, see?"

"Oh, sure, stupid of me. I thought you just needed a shave. I forgot all about that crazy story about you. But it's coming back to me, now. You were supposed to have gotten in some sort of a jam out west a while back, right?"

"Yeah. I take it you read it in the Army Times?"

"Sure. I knew right off it was some sort of plot to remove you from the active list. They wrote you up for a Dishonorable and then they let you officially escape, right?" Bronson laughed, boyishly, and added, "Boy, the bullshit some people will believe. You remember Chandler, in my class at the Point? He was with me on Governor's Island when that story broke, and the asshole said he thought you were *guilty* of those crazy charges!"

Captain Gringo swallowed and said, "Chandler always was sort of slow. You weren't fooled, huh?"

"Hell, no, I served under you at the Point, remember?"

Captain Gringo remembered, and it made him swallow again. Bronson had been one of those lower classmen who just couldn't keep out of the upper classmen's way and he'd felt sorry for the kid. He'd never dreamed, the times he'd covered for the harrassed plebe, that the shoe might be on the other foot. The Golden Rule made a lot of sense, when you gave it time to work.

Bronson said he had to go to lunch, but he led his guest to a small secluded study down the hall and said, "You can wait for your papers in here, Old Buddy. Hardly anybody comes in here, but there's a lock on the door if you really want to be alone. Are you sure you don't need anything? I could bring you a sandwich or some smokes."

Captain Gringo shook his head and said, "I've eaten and I've got some smokes. You run along and show the flag." But then, as Bronson turned to leave, he said, "Hey, Bron?"

"Yeah, Walk?"

"This war shit. Do you think the Brits are really going to invade?"

"Sure looks like it. I can think of a lot of people I'd rather fight."

128

"That makes two of us. I guess, if push comes to shove, you'll be okay here behind your desk, right?"

Bronson shook his head, grimly, and said, "Desk, hell. I've put in for a field command. I hope the Brits are bluffing, but we're not sure, and if the balloon goes up you'll find yours truly on the front line with the rest of our guys!"

Captain Gringo had been afraid he'd say something stupid like that. But he'd been young and eager, once, so he just nodded and said, "Good hunting, if I don't see you again."

Bronson left. Captain Gringo took out a smoke and lit up, pacing the floor in his damp clothes. He knew he wasn't really cold enough to be shivering so. Goddamn Grover Cleveland and goddamn Queen Victoria. Neither of them would have to fight this stupid little war they both seemed hell bent on having. Decent kids like Bronson, on both sides, would get to face each other in this green hell, and as if it wouldn't be rough enough on the professionals, a mess of innocent Venezuelan natives would be in the power play's crossfire they couldn't possibly understand. He wasn't putting them down as stupid peons. *He* didn't understand it, either! They probably didn't understand it in Washington or London. Stubborn old people with stubborn old pride were fighting for inches of paper on a country's map none of them would ever see. He had a mad desire to drag old Grover and Queen Vickie into the swamps of the real delta and put them to work with machete and spade for a few days on the beans and rice of the simple folk who had to live off this brutal land. No politician would ever know the map like a peasant who worked it or a soldier who lost a comrade for every acre taken or lost!

But what the hell, there was nothing he could do about it. The U.S. Army had kicked him out on his lonesome ass and they were welcome to this war on their own. He'd never considered his disgrace and renegade status a lucky break, before, but from what he'd seen of the delta around them he was just as glad he'd never have to lead troops through it!

He blew a thoughtful smoke ring and muttered, "Who are we shitting? This is the big one, Old Buddy. The first war with a major power we've had since 1848 and you can't come to the party!"

The door opened and a feminine voice gleeped, "Oh!"

He turned. It was Bubbles from the steamboat. She'd dyed her hair dark brown, but there was no forgetting a chest like that. She recognized him at the same time and said, "Dick, what on earth are you doing here at the U.S. Consulate? Don't you know there's a big reward out on Captain Gringo?"

He swore softly under his breath and said, "Yeah, and I understand they don't like British spies. But I won't tell if you won't."

Bubbles, Maria, Linda, or whoever the hell she was came in and locked the door behind her, saying, "Silly thing, is that why you ducked out on me up the river a few days ago? Whatever gave you the impression I was a British spy?"

"You did. You said you'd been waiting for me up the river to recruit me for some outfit. You talk in your sleep, too. You even answer questions. When I asked you how long you'd worked for Greystoke you said this was your first hitch. I've worked for Greystoke once or twice. He's not only the big British spy master in these parts, he double crosses people a lot. So the rest is history. What the fuck are you doing? You can't take your clothes off in here, Bubbles!"

"Sure I can," Bubbles said, "and a fuck is what I had in mind, you silly old growly bear. We were just getting down to the good positions on that steamboat when you ditched me in some mad snit and . . ."

"Bubbles, for Christ's sake, we're in the U.S. Consulate, in broad daylight, and this study must belong to someone!"

The heroically proportioned, now brunette dropped her dress in folds around her stocking-clad legs and stepped out of it like Venus rising from the foam, only Venus should have curves like that!

Despite himself Captain Gringo felt his erection growing inside his damp pants as he stared at the pneumatic vision headed his way with a brazen smile on her painted lips. He'd had her before, and in many ways, but she was one of those women who acted on one's appetite like potato chips. No matter how many crunches you had of her, you always seemed to want another.

They called her "Bubbles" partly because she was sort of vague about her real name and mostly because Bubbles fit. She was beautifully put together, but seemed to consist of

perfect spheres. Her high-stepping breasts rose like cante-loupes and her deep navel was set like an invisible jewel in the center of a flatter hemisphere of yummy tummy. She shaved her pubis, making it difficult to tell what color her hair really was, and her mons was a cute little ball of flesh, too, slit like a hot dog bun, and, speaking of hot dogs . . .

He found himself unbuttoning things even as he protested, "For God's sake, Bubbles, what if somebody comes?" and she giggled and said, "I hope we *both* come, a *lot!* Why are you acting so shy, you silly? The door's locked."

"I know, but if someone wants to get in . . ."

"They can't. We'll tell them we're fucking and to go away."

"Are you serious?"

"Of course. Wouldn't *you* go away if you knocked on a door and the people inside told you they were fucking?"

He laughed and said, "I guess I would. But you sure are confident, considering where we are."

She moved closer and started to help him strip as she soothed, "Oh, pooh, I'm here on official business. Or at least I was, until I met you again. Where shall we make love, Darling? That leather couch looks comfy."

He dropped his last stitch on the floor, stepped out of his boots, and picked her up to squish across the room in his wet socks as he carried her to the inviting couch. He lowered her and mounted as she giggled and spread her silk sheathed limbs in welcome. The nice thing about meeting old friends was that he didn't need any help in finding his way home. As he sank into her bubbly body, Bubbles started bouncing to meet his thrusts as she closed her eyes and sighed, "Oh, yes, that's ever so much nicer than the last lover I had."

"Oh, you've had someone else since we were on that riverboat together?"

"Of course. Haven't you?"

He laughed and said, "Bubbles, you are just about the wildest little thing I've run into and I've been running a while. Are you really as dumb as you sound or have you found other men find your uncomplicated approach to sex stimulating?"

She wrapped her silky ankles around his waist and started moving from side to side as she replied, conversationally, "I've never seen why sex has to be complicated, Dear. Heavens, if we spent half as much time getting down to

131

eating as we do to even nicer satisfactions we'd all starve to death. Uh, would you move a little faster, Dick? I think I'm coming."

He did and she was. Bubbles obviously enjoyed her healthy orgasms, or she wouldn't have had so many of them, but unlike most women, Bubbles came with the quiet enjoyment of a child sucking a lollypop. She smiled sweetly as a wave of dusky rose swept over her breasts and throat and her voice stayed simply friendly as she murmured, "Oh, that was lovely. Can you keep going, Dear?"

He grunted, "Jesus, shut up a minute!" as he started pounding to satisfy his own lust. Bubbles giggled and dug her nails into his buttocks as he exploded inside her, went limp a moment, and then started moving again just enough to keep it hard. She said, "That's what I like about you. You're so polite in bed, Dick."

"We're not in bed, we're tearing off a quickie on somebody's couch and we're going to get caught! We'd better compare stories before the U.S. Marines kick that door in. I'm supposed to be here as a U.S. officer on some sort of mission. What the fuck are you supposed to be, this morning?"

"A fuck is all I want to be, and it's almost noon, Dear. But if you must know, I'm here as a field rep for Woodbine Arms. Nobody's going to fuss at me. It's all legal and aboveboard. The Americans are backing the Venezuelan government, but they seem to be having a little trouble getting here with the goods. The people I work for, the people who sent me to recruit you, have arms and munitions of war on hand, so . . ."

He stopped in mid-stroke and gasped, "Jesus H. Christ! Are you working for Sir Basil Hakim, the Merchant of Death or whatever the hell he is?"

"Of course. Move it a little faster, will you? Sir Basil heard you were over in the Amazon, raising some sort of hell, so, when he heard you were headed our way he sent me to head you off before any of the other factions could hire you. He said you'd worked for him before and he liked your style. Officially, of course, he'd never admit you were in the game."

The big American managed to crunch his little partner

132

more to her liking as he muttered, "Oboy, I might have known! I'd give you a message for Sir Basil, but there are ladies present. How come you knew Greystoke of British Intelligence so well if you work for Woodbine Arms?"

"I used to work for British Intelligence, but Woodbine pays better."

"So I hear, but I've had a little trouble getting my money out of Sir Basil in the past. Woodbine Arms is a British firm, isn't it?"

"Of course. Why do you ask?"

"Skip it. A dope who thought the world was run on the level might just wonder why a British arms firm was arming people against a British invasion, but knowing Sir Basil, it's a dumb question. Do you suppose the American government knows Basil Hakim double crosses people a lot?"

"I imagine so. It's been in all the papers. If you're getting tired let me get on top."

He shook his head and said, "Haven't time. Aside from not wanting to have to explain this ridiculous position, I have to go see about some papers."

"Oh, Pooh, I wanted to come again. Where are you staying in town, Dick? Maybe we can get together after midnight. I'm having dinner with some Venezuelan big shot, but we could meet later and do this right, huh?"

He started to lie his way out of it. Then, as he felt her contracting teasingly on his shaft he wondered what he was trying to prove. He didn't know any other girls in town and she was fantastic, even on the fly like this. He said, "I'm at the Flamingo. But don't count on me being there."

She didn't answer and he could see why by the flush of her swollen nipples so he pounded her harder, she gasped, "Ohhh, nice!" and he kept going 'til he'd joined her in a happy surprise orgasm.

They lay in each others arms for a few dreamy moments. Then he said, "Gotta go. Who's this clown you're seducing for Sir Basil tonight?"

Her voice stayed innocent as she replied, "A Colonel Porfirio something. He works for some rebel faction, according to Sir Basil, and I don't have to screw him unless he's pretty. They want guns so bad they'll pay double."

Captain Gringo dismounted with a frown, got their

133

clothes, and tossed her dress to her as he sat down to haul his wet pants on, saying, "Let me get this straight—Woodbine Arms is selling guns to the regular Venezuelan army and navy to fight the British Empire, who licenses Woodbine Arms, and then, at the same time, Woodbine Arms is selling arms to the rebels who plan to overthrow the legitimate government and . . . never mind, I never understood all the logic in *Alice in Wonderland,* either."

"Sir Basil says business is business," said Bubbles, demurely, as she began to button her bodice with practiced fingers. He'd never met a gal who could get in and out of her clothes so fast and neat. He nodded and slid into his own clammy shirt as he said, "I told you I've met Sir Basil. By the way, does he really have nine inches?"

"Don't be nasty, Dear. I still wish you'd come to work for us."

"Doing what? As I understand it, Sir Basil has his money on every horse in the race!"

"Of course, that's why he can afford to pay so well. When I tell him we met again I'll say you're thinking about it. He's liable to have you killed if you upset him."

"I told you I knew the little bastard," Captain Gringo said, as he got to his feet. "Let's get out of here. We'll talk about it later, if that Venezuelan you're having dinner with isn't up to your usual standards."

He opened the door and blinked as an upraised fist almost knocked on his forehead. The young marine officer who'd been about to knock on the door looked as startled and said, "Oh, are you folks using the study?"

Captain Gringo saw he was with the snooty receptionist, who seemed to be blushing for some reason. He smiled and said, "We were just leaving. It's all yours, Leatherneck."

Bubbles smiled sweetly and said, "The couch is very comfy. But then, I suppose you two already know that, eh?"

Captain Gringo waited until they were out of earshot down the hall before he exploded in mirth and said, "You've got a nasty sense of humor, but that snooty little gal had it coming. You'd be fun to be around if you didn't run with such a vicious pack."

"Oh, Dear, does that mean you don't want me to join you later, Dick?"

134

"I never said that. I run with a vicious pack, too. I don't see any way you can make a plugged nickel out of murdering me, so what the hell, let's screw some more tonight."

Pneumonia kills as many people in the tropics as the various fevers, so after leaving the consulate with his new I.D.s, Captain Gringo stopped to pick up some dry clothes. The stuff he had on had seen some rough times even before he'd gotten soaked, so he meant to throw it away and start fresh with a new outfit cut more in the local style. He bought a few changes of shirts and underwear while he was at it, packing them in a straw suitcase to carry back to the hotel.

He found his bed still unmade when he arrived. Apparently the little chambermaid was taking her siesta, but who cared? He took his new outfit down to the bathroom, enjoyed a long hot soak, and returned to his room feeling downright civilized.

Gaston was there and, like Captain Gringo, had thought to change into new dry clothes, with or without a bath. Gaston said, "I was wondering where you were, my jolly alley fighter."

Captain Gringo took out Gaston's new I.D., tossed it on the bed beside him, and said, "Here, M'sieu Chambrun. Welcome to the club."

Gaston picked up the passport, examined it, and marveled aloud, "*Sacre*, this is *good*, Dick! Where did you find such an artist in such a little out of the way place?"

"U.S. Consulate. I could have made you a Russian nobleman but I didn't want to turn your head."

He brought Gaston up to date, mentioning that he'd met Bubbles and what she was up to, without mentioning any carnal matters. But Gaston put a finger against the side of his nose and said, "*Ooh la la!* I thought you looked more weary than a fight with mere men should have left you."

"So I'm a friendly guy," Captain Gringo growled, adding, "Speaking of friendly guys, what's the story on our boat load of goodies?"

Frowning, Gaston said, "A curious one. We have a buyer. The Dutchman says something big is about to happen in French Guiana while everyone is watching this part of the coast, so . . ."

"Wait a minute," Captain Gringo cut in, "you say *French* Guiana, Devil's Island and all that shit?"

"*Mais oui.* As you may know, the French government has a *très* droll policy regarding the penal colony down that way. After a man has served part of his sentence on Devil's Island they send him ashore to the main colony under parole, to work out the remainder of his sentence as rather dramatically underpaid labor. For some reason France has had little luck in persuading *free* Frenchmen to go anywhere near French Guiana!"

"Yeah, I heard it was a hellhole. But who needs the guns, the guards?"

"*Mais non,* the guards and colonial police have their guns. The largely convict population plans to declare independence from France. One gathers they are not satisfied with the local pay scale and so forth."

Captain Gringo nodded and said, "Gotcha. But if these guys in the market for a mess of 30-30 haven't been getting paid enough to matter, how can they afford to pay the going rates?"

"Ah, that is the curious part, *non?*" Gaston said. "The Dutchman says some of the planters down that way are also annoyed with Paris for some reason. Perhaps the French government monopolies on trade. At any rate, the ex-convicts shall supply the muscle and the planters shall supply such leadership and financing as a rather mundane revolution might require."

Captain Gringo took out a smoke, lit up, and said, "Well, like Bubbles says, everybody needs guns. France does have a legion detachment sitting on the lid down there, right?"

"Of course. I told the Dutchman they would be butchered like babes, but he was adamant and what do we care, as long as we are not asked to fire any of the weapons we sell them, hein?"

"Okay, when do we deliver and where?"

"We don't have to do a thing, my worried brow. I simply told the Dutchman where the guns and launch are hidden.

136

Tonight, after midnight, he shall have some of his associates pick up and deliver for us."

"Jesus H. Christ! You told them where we hid that launch? Okay, how much front money did the Dutchman give you, Gaston?"

Gaston looked uncomfortable and said, "Uh, Dick, they are on a *très* limited budget. The Dutchman says he will pay us in full upon delivery. After the guns arrive in French Guiana."

Captain Gringo took the cigar from his mouth, stared morosely down at his smaller friend, and said flatly, "You asshole! Assuming they don't double-cross us, which would be a hell of a switch, it's going to take them at least a couple of weeks to run down there and back. The fucking British Navy is blockading the south-east corner of the delta."

"*Merde,* only offshore, Dick. The coast is a maze of lagoons and shallow channels, all the way to the Guianas. I admit there are certain dangers, but look at it this way: better them than us, hein?"

"Yeah, yeah, sure, and they're about to have an all out war down here any minute! I took one hell of a chance getting us those papers, Gaston. We could leave with the next tide if we had our money. But now look what you've done, you chump!"

Gaston sighed and said, "*Eh bien,* I confess I might have been rash. But, as you say, what the hell, hein? Consider that we paid nothing for the guns and ammo we stole while escaping from those mysterious nuns up the river."

"They're not mysterious anymore. It's starting to fall in place. Old Basil Hakim sent those guns up to that fake mission to arm some back country guerrillas working for Cipriano Castro's faction. The little Turk's a two-faced lying bastard, but he sells top merchandise. It's good business to deliver the stuff the customer orders."

"You confuse me, my old and rare. What do we care about Sir Basil and his hardware business? We are not gunrunners, as a rule."

"Maybe not, but we have our own reps to think of. Don't you see what the wise money boys will say if we let ourselves get diddled like greenhorns by a backwoods thug like the Dutchman?"

"It would be *très* embarrassing. But I see no way to get our money, now, unless we stay until he returns."

"Neither do I, you silly son-of-a-bitch! If we leave without demanding our money word will get around that it's not really all that important to pay us, and God knows we've had enough trouble getting paid as it is. If we stay, we'll be sitting right on the front fucking line when the Brits make their power play."

"Merde alors, Dick, we are well inland. The Royal Marines will have to march through many a swamp before they reach the capital, here, *non?"*

"Bullshit. Haven't you been paying any attention to the way Queen Victoria deals in real estate, Gaston? They didn't take India by marching into a mangrove swamp. They moved in to grab Madras, Bombay, and Calcutta right off. Look at the damned map! There are only half a dozen towns in the whole delta and most of them are just villages. This is a deep water port, inland or not. They'll steam up here with the band playing "God Save the Queen" and make this their base of operations."

"And the Americans?"

"What Americans? I just heard the U.S. forces are bogged down between here and Key West. For a guy who talks so big, old Grover Cleveland vetoes military appropriations a lot. So far they've sent a lousy Civil War monitor that figures to turn turtle if they ever fire its guns. If the gunners of the Royal Navy can keep from laughing too hard, they have her on the bottom before she can even fire her guns. We have a marine detachment here in Tucupita. The Venezuelan forces loyal to Caracas probably number a few more. One Battalion of Royal Marines could have them for breakfast, even before the home grown rebel guerrillas start shooting them in the back."

Gaston grimaced and said, "You make the position sound *très* hopeless, Dick."

"It is hopeless. Cleveland's been beating his chest and sounding off about the Monroe Doctrine and now the Brits are going to call his bluff and, damn, those marines and a few army and navy kids I met today are going to get the shit kicked out of them!"

"Perhaps they will have sense enough to run away?" soothed Gaston.

Captain Gringo shook his head grimly, and said, "They won't run. The poor assholes think the world's run on the

138

level. They're expecting help, real help, from the States. The guys at the Alamo were expecting help, too, and you know how that turned out!"

Gaston took out his revolver and began to check the cylinder as he sighed and said, "I keep forgetting your idealistic streak, Dick. But, *eh bien,* if we must fight beside your countrymen, we must fight beside your countrymen. You know, of course, that you are an idiot?"

Captain Gringo started to protest they were only hanging around until the Dutchman got back with their money, but then he laughed, ruefully, and said, "Yeah, I spent four years at the Point and they never sent me into a real war."

"One hears war is hell, Dick."

"Yeah, but would you really like to miss this one?"

"*Oui,* very much. But if you stay, I stay. You have often reminded me I am an asshole."

In Caracas, El Sortilego moved the black bishop to menace a white castle before he picked up the ringing, unlisted phone. His voice did not betray his surprise when he found himself talking to a strange voice. The man at the other end said, "I'm Sir Basil Hakim. You've heard of me, perhaps?"

El Sortilego said, "Of course. I am most curious to learn how you might have heard of *me,* Sir Basil."

"Let's just say we both have crystal balls, El Sortilego. I know your clients pay you to make things happen. May I assume you're also paid to prevent things from happening *to* them?"

"Perhaps. What sort of things might be about to happen to anyone I know, Sir Basil?"

"Your client, Cipriano Castro, for one. I've been trying to reach the bloody bastard all day and he keeps ducking me. I seldom show all my cards like this, but it's getting late in the game. I haven't been paid for the arms I delivered to Castro's rebels. It's going to be even harder to collect in a few days, when he plans to make himself El Presidente. So get to the

blighter and tell him he's not going to *live* that long unless I see some money within twenty-four hours!"

El Sortilego took the castle with his bishop as he considered a bluff, then sighed, and said, "I shall take your voice on good faith, since I, too, keep tabs on other players and we have met, although I doubt if you would know me."

"I know you. You were acting as the head waiter at that dinner the other night."

"Touché, Sir Basil, you are as good as they say. Very well, let us put our cards on the table, man to man. I admit my client has been avoiding you—I advised him to. He has a temper and they say you have, too. I did not think the two of you should discuss your business dealings until we sort them out a bit. Somebody would seem to have thrown a wooden shoe into the works. Our guerrillas never got the guns and shells you sent. I am sure your people acted in good faith. Those so-called nuns of yours insisted under torture that they had not double-crossed us, and we tortured them to death."

There was a long pause before Sir Basil said, in a cobra-calm tone, "All right. You doubtless have a good explanation for killing two of my agents and I'd like to hear it."

"Our people arrived as agreed to pick up the so-called medical supplies," El Sortilego said. "The people at the mission told a wild story about two maniacs highjacking the two steam launches. Your launch crews were not there to verify they had ever arrived. Our man in the field found it most difficult to believe that two men could have taken two launches, crew and all, so I fear he applied certain pressures. The peons at the mission told the same tale, no matter how often they were beaten."

"The peons don't matter. What about those girls I had working for me?"

"Alas, as I said, they died under the perhaps unskilled questioning. But we got the names of the culprits and their story makes a certain sense. You have heard, perhaps, of a Captain Gringo and his friend, Gaston?"

"I have. They're in Tucupita at the moment, under observation by *my* agents there. Are you trying to tell me Captain Gringo highjacked my arms out on the llano?"

"That is what the people at the mission told us."

"Well, the people at your mission are full of it. I know

Dick Walker. He's worked for me in the past. He's good. He's not that good, and even if he was, how in the devil could he be highjacking out on the llano if my people have him in the delta?"

El Sortilego moved a pawn, decided he didn't like it there, and said, "Perhaps they took the launches they stole down the river to Tucupita?"

"Ridiculous!" Sir Basil snapped. "I've had them under observation since they arrived, I tell you. They're staying at the Flamingo, and neither has a steamlaunch under his bed. I had the Frenchman followed to some riff-raff friends along the waterfront. They spent some time in a boat house. My people looked in the boathouse. There is no steamlaunch in said boathouse. One of my other agents picked Dick Walker up at the U.S. Consulate this afternoon. He didn't have my stuff with him there, either. He's working with American Military Intelligence. American Military Intelligence does not highjack steamlaunches. On the other hand, your Cipriano Castro has a rather dreadful credit rating. This wouldn't be the first time he tried to get out of paying his just debts with a wild story."

El Sortilego looked pained, moved another pawn, and said, "Let us admit Castro hates to pay for goods not received. The point is that somebody got the stuff you sent before his boys could pick it up. You know what I think? I think perhaps somebody pretending to be this Captain Gringo is trying to drive a wedge between friends."

"We're not friends," Sir Basil snapped. "I'm an honest dealer and your lad is a customer who agreed to pay on delivery. So I'll tell you what I think. I think the son-of-a-bitch is trying to have his revolution on the cheap! You get to him, *muy pronto*, and tell him if I don't get my money he can commend his soul to Jesus, because his ass will belong to me!"

"But Sir Basil, how are we to have our revolution unless we have the arms? It is true we got *some* arms and ammunition, before the central government broke up our last delivery point. But without those shells for the howitzers you sold us, it would be suicide to stage a coup here in Caracas. Most of the loyalist troops are marching to meet the invasion, but they still have enough here in the capital to stand off rebels armed with only rifles."

"That's your problem," Sir Basil said. "I delivered you enough 155s to blow Caracas flat. You pay me back by killing my field agents and stiffing me on the price. I'll show you suicide, if you don't get some money to me, damned soon! I have to leave on my yacht before the Royal Navy steams in. But I'm leaving more than enough of my secret associates behind to make your lot very sorry you annoyed me. I'm leaving some rather dramatic hardware too. You want shells, for free? I'll give you shells for free! I'll lob a 155 through Castro's loo, and if that won't make an honest man of him, I'll fire one up his arse!"

"Calm yourself, Sir Basil. I assure you you'll get your money, in time."

"God strike a bloody light, I don't want my money in *time*. I want it *now*!"

"But Sir, you must understand it is difficult to raise that kind of money before one takes over the government mint, no?"

There was a long ominous silence before the little Turk at the other end of the line hissed, "You ... son ... of ... a ... bitch! So that was the game all the while, was it? You asked me to arm your jolly revolution, cash and carry, and all the while you didn't have the money?"

"Oh, I assure you, we have wealthy backers, Sir Basil."

"You'd better have. I delivered. I want to be paid. By the way, those two women will cost you a hundred thousand a-piece. Good help is hard to find. I expect the money, as I said, within twenty-four hours."

"I don't see how we can raise such an amount on short notice, Sir Basil, but I will advise my client of your demands."

"Don't advise him. Tell him! Payment in full for the arms, plus two-hundred thousand for blood money, or you'll see blood run like water before you die. You think your country is having trouble with the British Empire? Well, the British Empire is afraid of *me!*"

The line went dead. El Sortilego winced and put the receiver back on its cradle. He moved a couple of chessmen to steady his nerves and then he picked up the phone and asked for a certain number. When the man at the other end picked up, El Sortilego repeated the conversation and added, softly, "You'd better pay him, Cipriano, my friend."

"Idiot! How can I?" the rebel leader gasped. "We need money for the revolution. Laying out such a sum would wipe us out!"

"True, but we would still be alive and there is always another day to stage a take-over. The Crespo government is weak, whether they last through this crisis or not. On the other hand, Sir Basil Hakim was not bluffing when he said even the empire was afraid of him."

"That's crazy, El Sortilego! He's only a businessman, and a rather shady one at that!"

"True, and his business partners include the Prince of Wales and the new young Kaiser. He's quite mad, of course. They say he enjoys doing his own dirty work. But in a pinch he can order wars to start or stop and he knows where all our bodies are buried. Leaving aside his dramatic threats, a call from him to certain interested parties could have us in more trouble than one cares to think about. You pay me to make the future come true for you, Cipriano. Very well, pay him, or you won't have any future at all!"

There was a long pouting silence until the would-be dictator sighed and said, "All right, you've never failed to give the best advice, but somebody is going to have to pay in blood for this!"

"They will, Cipriano," El Sortilego smiled and purred. "I know where this Captain Gringo and his French friend are. Sir Basil refuses to believe they were behind our problems on the llano, but I see it all now. The American is not the renegade they say he is. He's been working with American Intelligence to thwart our plans for their friends in the central government. We shall have to sit this crisis out, thanks to that damned Yanqui. But rest assured there will come another time, and rest assured Captain Gringo will not live to see it!"

As the sun was sinking behind a silver-bronze veil of rain in the west, H.M.S. Pandora lay at anchor just outside the three mile limit on the continental shelf of Venezuela. In

the chart room off the bridge, Greystoke of British Intelligence was having his own argument with Sir Reginald Rice-Davis, Admiral of the Fleet. Around the florid-faced old man's chosen flagship, other British warships lay at anchor, brooding on the quiet copper surface.

Admiral Rice-Davis was a Welshman busting a gut trying to be John Bull English, so it was rather hard to talk to him. He kept waddling up and down the deck with his hands behind him, muttering, "What, what, what?" for no particular reason.

Greystoke said, "We strongly advise against going in at this time, Sir Reginald. We've been getting some disturbingly mixed reports on the situation ashore."

"What, what, what? Bloody nonsense!" Rice-Davis said. "Bloody Yanks are bluffing, and my jolly tars are ready to go! Jolly marines are ready, too, what, what what? Two bloody transports filled with R.M. over there abaft Cruiser Nelson. Be like taking candy from a baby, what, what, what?"

Greystoke nodded and remarked, "If it's true the Yanks are bluffing. But you know Britain can't really afford a war with America, and there are some disturbing indications the Yanks are serious."

"Serious, what, what, what? Who cares if the blighters are serious or not. We whipped them in 1812, didn't we?"

"Not exactly, Sir. It was a draw, and it damned nearly cost us the war we were having with Napoleon at the time."

"What, what, what? We're not having a war with Nappie, now, dash it all. Blighter died some time ago, didn't he?"

"Yessir, and now Her Majesty's darling little nephew, Kaiser Bill, is threatening us with a war that will make all others look like child's play. We're going to need the Yanks' good will in times to come, I fear, and for some reason they get dreadfully annoyed when people shoot at them."

"What, what, what? Nobody wants to shoot at Yanks. Came to shoot at bloody Dagoes, I did. Yanks don't want a war, they have no right to stick their noses in Her Majesty's business, down here. Venezuela isn't an American colony, what, what, what? Dash it all, Venezuela's not even a proper *country!* Rum, lot of fandango dancers with no more claim to this part of the coast than we have. Can't understand the

144

bloody Yanks getting into this perishing mess, what, what, what?"

"Whitehall never expected them to when we announced our border adjustment with Venezuela, Sir. But their President Cleveland seems to think the Monroe Doctrine was given to them as Holy Writ on the Mountain."

Admiral Rice-Davis shrugged and said, "Who the blazes was Monroe? Sounds like a bloody Scotsman, what, what, what?"

"He was an earlier American president, Sir. For some reason he took the position that if the Yanks stayed out of European affairs, the European powers should stay out of this hemisphere."

"Piffle and posh. Arrogant, if you ask me. Europe had colonies over here before there was any U.S. of A! I say, the bloody Yanks were British colonies, too, weren't they?"

"Yessir. I agree the American position is rather weird, but they can be weird people. Meanwhile, if we ever need DuPont powder or Morgan bank loans, it might be a good idea to humor them a bit. I just got a cable from Whitehall: His Highness, Prince Edward, has been working sub rosa to clear this matter up peacefully, with honor to both sides. President Cleveland's still considering a motion to put the matter up for arbitration before an international commission. Our man in Washington says he's not too keen on it, but, on the other hand, he knows his country's not prepared for a war with Great Britian."

Admiral Rice-Davis smiled smugly and said, "Oh, rather, what, what, what? Naval Intelligence tells me there's nothing opposing our landing but a perishing old monitor loaned to the Dagoes by the Yanks. Be jolly target practice, what, what, what?"

Rolling his eyes heavenward, Greystoke said patiently, "There's a U.S. military detachment ashore, too. Our agents tell me they have orders to oppose any landing to the death."

"Oh, rot and piffle! Send my shore patrol to arrest them before they can get in trouble, what, what, what?"

"There's more, Sir. I confess it's the worst news I've had to date. A certain so-called soldier of fortune has been seen going in and out of the U.S. Consulate in Tucupita. They call him Captain Gringo. He's supposed to be a renegade Ameri-

can officer, wanted dead or alive by the U.S. Government."

"Eh, what, what, what, dead or alive, you say? What's the perishing blighter doing at the Yankee consulate if they want him dead or alive?"

"That's a good question, Sir. I confess he had me fooled, too. I've even tangled with him a few times and I always assumed he really was a simple soldier of fortune. But, now that I reconsider, there's been an awful lot of noise everywhere Captain Gringo has shown up. He was seen in Colombia, just before the government was overthrown. Said government was anti-American, by the way. A while back he made holy hash out of Panama and it's no secret the Yanks are interested in events up there."

Admiral Rice-Davis shrugged and said, "It seems obvious his tale of being a renegade is a foxy cover, what, what, what? The blighter is an obvious trouble shooter for G2."

Greystoke nodded and said, "It's beginning to look that way, Sir Reginald. But don't you see, that if Captain Gringo is down here the Yanks must have something serious in mind?"

"Egad! You mean they've sent one bloody chap to oppose a whole British task force? Sounds ruddy wonky to me, what, what, what? Can't stand for it. Won't stand for it. Wouldn't be British to be turned back by one bloody whatever!"

"The whatever is the question, Sir Reginald. I'd like you to hold off until we can get a better line on just what Captain Gringo is up to here in Venezuela. He's only a man, after all, but he's dashedly good at organizing guerrilla groups. I know. I hired him to raid a suspected German base one day, as a diversion, I thought. He and a handful of apparent scum went in and wrecked the place. Neither we nor the Germans have ever quite figured out how."

Admiral Rice-Davis looked at his table map and shrugged again as Greystoke gritted his teeth and braced himself for another "what, what, what." But Rice-Davis said, "Only one thing to do, then. You spy chaps will have to assassinate the blighter. Can't have guerrillas getting in the way. Bloody uncivilized way to fight, and, come hell or high water, I intend to occupy the bloody delta on bloody schedule!"

"But Sir Reginald, don't you see that could mean a war

we don't want, and can't afford to have? Just give me time to find out whether Washington is bluffing or not."

"Piffle and pox! Don't care what the Yanks intend, but if it's any comfort, I can assure you, they most certainly are bluffing. We R.N. chaps have *our* agents out, too, what, what, what? Look out that ruddy porthole and tell me how many Yankee cruisers you see on the horizon! We haven't been at all sneaky about this move, you know. Washington's had plenty of time to place her money where her mouth is, if they mean to play at all. But they're all talk and bluster, I tell you."

Greystoke shrugged in resignation and said, "I wish I was as sure. If we move in, and they fire on us, what happens, Sir Reginald?"

"What, what, what? *Fire* on us? Fire on the Royal Navy? Unthinkable! Just isn't done! The Yankee navy has been begging President Cleveland for more ships and guns and he says they can't afford it. Heard it from a rather decent American flag officer, myself, at Malta this spring. They'll never fire on us. They wouldn't dare. Why, dash it all, a thing like that could lead to *war!*"

Greystoke clenched his teeth to keep from screaming in rage as he realized he was talking to a brick wall, and not a very bright one. He had to get back to his phone and cable network on shore, fast. The only good idea the old twit had was the one about shooting Captain Gringo. That might buy some time by throwing the Yanks off stride. But while stopping Captain Gringo seemed simple enough, who was going to stop Admiral Rice-Davis? He excused himself and headed for the ladder, as he ran his options through again. Maybe he wouldn't kill Dick Walker, just yet. He'd made deals with Captain Gringo in the past and at least the Yank had a brain.

He was on his way to shore in his private launch before he snapped his fingers and murmured to himself, "That's it. A true patriot has to learn to submerge below his principles and this is no time to be sticky about rules. Dealing with the enemy is high treason, but what's a spot of high treason between old friends?"

Greystoke laughed, his mind made up. Captain Gringo was an enemy agent and, it would seem, an even more devious one than the world of international skullduggery believed.

But he was a *smart* enemy and a smart enemy was a lot safer to deal with than a stupid friend.

"I do wish I hadn't double-crossed him a few times," Greystoke sighed as he stared wistfully into the sunset. "It's going to be devilishly hard to convince old Dick I want to be his friend after being his enemy so often. But how does one approach a bloody Yank getting set for a British invasion when he knows you run British Intelligence in this theatre? Let's see, maybe we should do something nice for him before we approach him, eh? Might cheer him up if we shot a few of those Woodbine Arms agents keeping him under observation for that perishing little Turk. On the other hand, wouldn't it be grand if we could get Sir Basil on our side, too?"

Greystoke shuddered as he considered several options. All of them were rather awesome. He lit a smoke and marveled, "I say, if the three of us ever worked on the same side, we could take over the perishing world!"

Gaston left just after dark to see if he could renegotiate their dubious deal with the Dutchman. Captain Gringo had dinner alone in the dining room and was about to go back upstairs when he saw the tall shabby Negro who'd taken them to their rooms when they checked in. The man was wearing his own clothes and looked even shabbier. Captain Gringo nodded to him and asked, "Going off duty?"

The tall Negro nodded. Captain Gringo hesitated, then said, "I hope you won't be offended, but I have a linen suit I was going to throw away, upstairs. As a matter of fact, it's in my waste basket. But, no offense, it's in better shape than what you're wearing. It could use a good laundering, but there are no holes in it. Could you use it?"

The bellhop grinned with delight and nodded, so Captain Gringo led him upstairs to his room. The little chamber maid, Camelia, was caught in the act as she was making his bed. She straightened up like he'd goosed her as Captain Gringo smiled and said, "Better late than never, right?"

"Forgive me, Señor, I have so many rooms to tend and . . ."

"Hey, forget it, Camelia. I'm not complaining."

He took the still damp linen suit from the waste basket and handed it to the bellhop, saying, "Matter of fact, if she'd been earlier this wouldn't be here. Sorry it's a little damp, but it needs a soak in some suds anyway."

The black bellhop held the suit out as he let it unfold and gasped, "El Señor is most generous. This suit is almost new, and I have never owned such clothing."

"Let's not blubber up about it. I told you I was going to throw it away. I'm only glad somebody can still get some use out of it."

The bellhop left, still thanking him as Captain Gringo shut the door in his face. He turned and asked Camelia, "Am I bothering you? I could go back down to the lobby until you've finished here."

The pretty mestiza dimpled prettily and said, "Oh, no, El Señor could never bother Camelia. I was so afraid when those policemen spoke so roughly to me last night. I will never be able to thank you enough for standing up for me."

He shrugged, took a seat, and watched her finish as she smoothed the bed. Standing up wasn't what he had in mind, as he admired her rear view, but she seemed like a shy little thing and what the hell, Bubbles might make it, later.

She'd make it, that is, if the Venezuelan big shot she was having dinner with wasn't good looking. But so what? He'd slept alone a couple of times and it hadn't killed him. Like most knockaround guys, Captain Gringo had learned a long time ago that it was usually a waste of time to make a pass at a waitress or a chambermaid. Any reasonably attractive woman who was willing to put out didn't have to work that hard. And little Camelia was working like a fussy beaver. She already had his bed ready for a West Point inspection, but she kept tugging and tightening.

Her thin, black uniform skirt was long enough to suit Queen Victoria, when Camelia was standing up. Bent over like that, the hem was hiked enough to afford examination of her trim little ankles and muscular calves. In spite of the ritzy-shoddy uniform, the peon girl of course wore rope soled sandals and no stockings. Her legs were darker and hairier

149

than those of Bubbles. Of course Bubbles shaved, all over, and ... Knock it off! he warned himself silently. He knew the trouble his curious dong could get him in if he started comparing possible partners. But Camelia was taking forever to finish and the contrasts between her and his recent sex partner were obvious and intriguing.

Camelia and Bubbles were about as far apart as two women could get without one of them being ugly. Bubbles was a bold, brassy bawd who pampered her pink flesh with expensive perfumed soap and scented talcum. Camelia seemed reasonably clean, but he knew she didn't shave under her arms or anywhere else and her only perfume would be honest female sweat. Bawdy Bubbles took her healthy orgasms like a man. Camelia was a sobber and a moaner if he'd ever spotted one. The little dark mestiza was firm where Bubbles was full-fleshed. The only thing they had in common was that they both looked like great lays. But Camelia had finished and turned around, eyes downcast, so he got to his feet and reached in his pocket to tip her. She seemed to be crying, for some dumb reason, so he left the coins in his pocket and stepped over to her, asking, "What's the matter, Camelia?"

She leaned into him, sobbing, "Oh Señor, I am so frightened. I am finished for the day. Your room was the last I had to do and I confess I took my time doing all of them. Now, alas, they will expect me to go home."

"That sounds reasonable. Where do you live, Camelia?"

"On the east end of town, Señor, by the waterfront. Since my mother died, I have dwelt there alone. Is it true the English are going to bombard us with their big boom booms?"

He grimaced in sudden understanding and said, "They may only be bluffing, Camelia. El Presidente Cleveland and your own Joaquin Crespo have warned them not to. There are American marines as well as Venezuelan troops here to protect you."

She leaned even closer and it seemed only natural to take her in his arms to comfort her as she sobbed, "Oh, I am afraid of the soldados, too, Señor! I hear terrible talk in the barrio. My people are not as united as you Americanos may think! Some of my people think things would be better under

150

the Castro faction. There are others who think we would be more better as a British colony and they wish for the English to win."

"Yeah, but most of your people are loyal to the government they elected, aren't they?"

"Sí, but in times like these nobody knows for sure who one's friends are. I am afraid to be alone when the trouble starts. It is only with you I do not feel fear!" She leaned closer, which was close indeed, as she added, "I think I fell in love with you a little when you stood up for me before those rude police. That is why I lied for you. But I am being silly. You must know why I lied for you, no?"

Captain Gringo felt a sudden chill despite the warm little bundle of fluff in his arms. He patted her back soothingly and said, "I only did what I thought right, Camelia. But what do you mean, you lied for me?"

She snuggled her face against his chest and murmured, "Oh, you know you were here in this room last night while those Americanos were being robbed and murdered. I passed your door in the hall, twice, and heard you moving on the bed." She giggled and added, "I thought for a moment, from the sounds, that you were being wicked. But then I saw the light under your door and knew you had to be alone. Perhaps you were tossing and turning because it was so hot, no?"

"Yeah, it was pretty hot, now that I think of it. But why did you tell the police you saw me downstairs if you knew better, Querida?"

"I did not wish them to be rude to you, too. I knew that, like me, you were the innocent bystander, but you know how the police are. When you made them leave me alone, I thought it was only just that I return the favor. After all, neither of us killed those people, did they?"

He ran that through again for hidden meaning and his lips were a little numb as he laughed, light heartedly, and said, "Well, I can give you my word I didn't stab that poor dame, and her husband was a guy I drank with."

Camelia said, "I know. The busboy said you knew them well. That is why I did not wish the police to question you closely, eh?"

He took her by the shoulder and moved her back to meet her eyes. She looked innocent enough, but he said,

"Let's not pussy-foot about what happened last night, Camelia. Are you suggesting I owe you more than the tip I was about to give you?"

She looked blank and said, "Oh, Señor, I am paid to do the rooms. You do not have to give me anything for my services."

"That's unusual. What do you want, then, Camelia?"

She lowered her lashes, and her dusky face flushed becomingly as she licked her lips and said, "I do not know. I am just afraid to go out into the darkness with all sorts of things about to happen."

"I could run you home. It's early."

"Sì, but then I would still face the night alone. My cabana is so little and the English guns are so big."

"That's true. A sixteen-inch shell would make kindling out of this hotel, too. You're as safe in one part of a small town as another when people start lobbing shells into it. I don't think there's a low spot in town that isn't filled with water. We're closer to the main drag, here, too. If they mean to bombard us at all, El Flamingo's a likely target."

She shuddered in his arms and sighed, "Oh, Dear, I was just about to ask you if I could spend the night with you, but it does sound most dangerous, here!"

He raised an eyebrow as her words sank in. Then he grinned and said, "Dangerous in more ways than one. You'd get fired and I might get powder puffed to death if we spent the night here. Are you serious about wanting to spend the night with me, or are you one of those crazy platonic types?"

She snuggled closer, rubbing her turgid nipples against him as she said, "I am not sure what you mean. But if you take me home, you must promise not to leave me alone in the dark."

The tall Negro Captain Gringo had given his old suit to was unaware of the men following him as he approached a bridge over a side canal of the watery native quarter. There

152

were few street lamps, even in the better part of town, so the tall man in the linen suit was only a paler blur in the darkness as he stopped on the bridge to light a cigarette. One of the men following him murmured, "He's stopped to pull the old chestnut with the casual smoke while he looks back the way he just came. I told you it was Captain Gringo."

His companion said, "I'm still not sure. The light was behind him when he ducked out the side entrance of the hotel, and if we're wasting time tailing the wrong man . . ."

"Oh, shit," his companion cut in, "how many guys that tall wander around a South American town in a European-cut Panama suit? There's nobody else staying at the hotel who comes anywhere near matching his description. Besides, look how he's headed into the slums at this hour. What tourist would be in this part of town, damn it?"

On the bridge, the bellhop scratched his match again and again; it refused to light. His matches were damp, like everything else in Tucupita tonight. The tall Negro shrugged and put his cigarette away to smoke it later. He took a step toward the far side and then a volley of gunshots across the canal flashed orange like a string of Christmas tree lights as the night air, and the man on the bridge, was ripped apart by roaring rifle rounds!

The ambushed bellhop in Captain Gringo's old suit staggered back, hit the flimsy rail, and crashed through it to fall in the canal with a mighty splash as the two surprised British agents hunkered down and listened to the sounds of fading footsteps on wet planking. One of them said, "Jesus!"

The other sighed and said, "Jesus had nothing to do with it. They've run off, whoever they were. Let's see if there's a chance he's alive."

The two men moved forward, cautiously. Nobody else seemed at all interested in the short savage fusilade. People in that part of town tended not to get involved. The agents moved out on the bridge and looked through the gap in the rail down at the ink black water of the canal. The waves of the splash were already settling. One of them said, "He's on the bottom. They got him good."

"Oh, hell, what will we tell Greystoke now?"

"The truth, of course. It's not as if we killed Captain Gringo! Our job was simply to keep an eye on him, and I'd say we did, for as long as he was around. Let's get out of here

153

and find a telephone. His nibs is going to want to know that one player was just dealt out of the Great Game."

Back at the hotel, Camelia was clinging hysterically to Captain Gringo as she sobbed, "Oh, it has started! They are shooting guns outside and now we shall be killed, no?"

"No," he said. "I heard the shots just now. Sounded like a volley of rifle fire. Couple of blocks away to the north-east. They're obviously not shooting at us, so what the hell."

"But, Señor, my poor little cabana is over that way! I can never go home, now. Not until the war is over!"

He nodded and said, "I doubt if they're having a war just yet; but it doesn't make much sense to walk into a gang fight or whatever. Let's just sit tight and see if there's any more noise, eh?"

"Sí," Camelia said. "I think that is a good idea." Then she stepped away from him, flicked off the light, and started to take her clothes off.

He considered saying something dumb about waiting until they got to her place. Then his breath caught as he got a better look at what was going on right here and now. There was just enough light coming over the transome for him to see the petite mestiza, stark naked by the foot of the bed, neatly folding her uniform. As she draped it over the brass bed rail and moved around to draw the covers down, she was bent over again, and nobody could be built that nicely out of flesh and blood. Camelia was a tawny bronze statue, sculptued by an inspired Greek with a hard-on. She climbed demurely into bed and pulled the covers up as high as her perky little breasts, smiling shyly at him in the semi-darkness as she asked, "Don't you want me?"

He realized nobody but an asshole would be standing there fully dressed at a time like this. So he corrected the mistake by shucking his duds and letting them fall wherever they wanted, hanging on to the gun when he dropped the gun rig on his rumpled jacket. Camelia's eyes widened as he climbed in bed, gun in hand. She said, "Why are you

154

going to shoot me? I told you I was most willing, Señor!"

He laughed, tucked the gun between the mattress and the headboard and took her in his arms, saying, "Relax. The last thing I want to put in you is a bullet."

She returned his embrace and matched his foreplay by reaching for his groin as he cupped her heavily thatched lovebox in an eager palm. He felt an odd thrill at the contrast between her and the way Bubbles had felt down there that afternoon. She was even hairier than he'd expected and it would have been repellent had she not been so feminine in every other way. A dark line of fuzz ran up to her navel and the aroused nipples of her firm little breasts were surrounded by whorls of dark down. She grasped his shaft and gasped, "Oh, I don't know, Señor! I did not expect there to be so much of you!"

He said, "I think, under the circumstances, Señor seems a little formal. I am called Dick." Then he parted the matted thatch with his fingers to fondle her engorged wet clit as she relaxed and sighed, "Oh, I don't think I am afraid, after all, Deek!" as she began to stroke him, eagerly.

He rolled to mount her as she spread her slim tawny thighs to welcome him. But as he entered her she bit her lip and pleaded, "Please, be careful with that most dangerous weapon, no?"

He slowly settled into her, wondering if he was going to have his intelligence insulted by the old virgin bullshit. He was polite enough not to remind her this had been her idea, and, after it had been in her all the way, not moving, for a time, Camelia wrapped her arms and legs around him and said, "Oh, you are making me so happy." So he kissed her and began to move as she returned his kiss in an oddly sweet way. It stayed sweet even when Camelia began to move her little derriere in full acceptance of his thrusts. He told himself it was probably just the contrast between a normal peasant girl and the rather raunchy way Bubbles had torn off a quickie with him, earlier. But she was making him happy, too. And he let himself fall a little in love with the first girl he'd met in this crazy country that acted human. Camelia was simple, not too bright, and hardly the sort of girl one took home to mother, but, damn it, he *liked* her, and if the fucking Brits invaded her country, he'd have to do something about making sure she was safe.

155

Sir Basil Hakim was enjoying an opium pipe as a rosy-cheeked boy puffed on his other pipe, when the phone rang by the bed. Hakim put the pipe aside and dreamily picked up the receiver as his love slave went on sucking.

Greystoke of British Intelligence snapped, "All right, you Turkish cocksucker What have you to say for yourself?"

Hakim frowned and said, "I haven't sucked cock since I was a lad in Istanbul. What's made you so surly this evening, Old Bean?"

"You, you son-of-a-bitch! I suppose you're going to tell me those weren't your thugs who just killed Captain Gringo?"

Hakim's eyes widened and he pushed his love slave away as he sat up and replied, "Dick Walker's dead? That's impossible! He's supposed to be spending the night with one of my girls!"

"You have girls, too? Don't play innocent with me, Hakim! Two of my agents just saw Walker killed in Tucupita, and I'm going to have your arse this time! Your chum, the Prince of Wales, won't help you out of *this* one! I happen to know Prince Edward has been trying to patch things up with friends in Washington. You've dangerously misjudged His Highness, Hakim. I know he's a playboy and a rake, but he's a rather decent bloke under all that lard, and you've just messed up a very good idea I had by killing Captain Gringo."

Hakim shook his head to clear it as he said, "As Allah is my witness, I had nothing to do with his assassination. I, too, had plans for Walker. He's done a few odd jobs for me in the past and I've been trying to hire him again. For some reason, he doesn't seem to like me. Damned if I can see why."

"I can. I suppose you didn't know he was a double agent, either, eh?"

"Double what? Dash it all, Greystoke, I told you I've

worked with poor Dick a few times. I know his whole story. He was a U.S. Cavalry officer gone wrong and . . ."

"Bullshit," Greystoke cut in. "He was working for the States all the time. That renegade story was his cover—but that's neither here nor there. The point is that now I can't make my deal with him, and when I get His Highness on the line you're going to pay for it!"

Hakim stood up and stamped his feet, blissfully unaware of the grotesque figure he was cutting for the giggling young fag on the foot of the bed. Sir Basil was a short pudgy man with a white spade beard and an obscenely large penis, limp as a rag at the moment. He blinked away the last opium fumes and said, "Let's stop calling one another names, Greystoke. We're not the only players in this game. I'll admit some of my boys tried to kidnap Captain Gringo and Gaston Verrier earlier today. He unfortunately kicked the daylights out of them before they could persuade him to come see me. I was fortunate enough to have some other bait, female, and I'll find out in a minute why she's not in bed with him at this moment. I give you my word as a peer of the realm that nobody working for me had anything to do with his death. So simmer down and tell me about it."

Greystoke filled the tiny Turk in and Hakim said, "I've an idea who did it, now. A, ah, client I was having trouble with tried earlier to tell me that Captain Gringo intercepted some, uh, merchandise I still haven't been paid for. I know Walker was nowhere near when whatever took place took place, if it ever did. They knew I was trying to recruit him. They must have killed him to shut him up before we could compare notes. But the fools have wasted a good man for nothing. I'm on to the bleeding sods!"

"Tell me who they are, then," Greystoke demanded. "I have a score to settle with them, too!"

Hakim shook his head and answered, "No. You know I hardly discuss my personal dealings with British Intelligence, Greystoke. But not to worry. I'll see they're paid back."

Greystoke's tone sounded more mollified as he answered, "Oh? Your people will take care of the leader of the gang who killed Captain Gringo?"

"Well, hardly the leader. He owes me money and I expect him to be the president of Venezuela in a few years,

no matter how our current crisis is resolved. But I mean to draw his fangs and teach him a jolly good lesson. Tell me about this scheme you had involving Captain Gringo."

Greystoke snorted and said, "Surely you jest. Please don't bother to deny you've been trying to take advantage of this unfortunate business between us and Yanks by dropping your own hook in troubled waters!"

"That's true," Hakim said. "Business is business. But I am having second thoughts about the situation down here. All in all, Washington may have had a good idea when it backed the legitimate government. None of the *other* factions seem to pay their flaming *bills!* Surely, if you thought you could trust Dick Walker, an enemy agent of some sort, you can trust me, a British subject?"

Greystoke said, "I'd trust the Kaiser, first. But dash it all, I can't seem to convince an asshole admiral that the Yanks aren't bluffing!"

The little arms merchant shrugged and said, "They are and they aren't. You know, of course, I have Washington and Wall Street contacts?"

"Get to the flaming point, Hakim!"

"Very well, Grover Cleveland's not bluffing. He's a rather old-fashioned Presbyterian chap with a fatiguing devotion to Old Testament Justice and all that rot. He's given to rather quixotic bursts and he can be most stubborn when he thinks he's in the right. He ordered captured Confederate flags returned to the Southern States a few years ago despite the howls of outrage from the G.A.R. and other professional northerners. He's killed more pork barrel bills than any president since Jackson. He doesn't seem to care a fig for political considerations. He decides what's right, from a rather smug and loftly plane, and then he just goes and does it."

"Sounds like a decent chap, what?"

"It gets more fatiguing. The first time he ran for president his enemies uncovered a scandal in Cleveland's past. Seems he once fathered a child out of wedlock. Only to be expected from a vigorous young lawyer, one imagines. At any rate, his friends advised him to issue a simple denial."

"Naturally, a thing like that could cost a man the election."

"It didn't. Cleveland issued a public statement admitting

his youthful folly. He added that he'd provided for the upbringing and education of his illegitimate child, who was now grown and married and not to be bothered."

"My God, and he *won*?"

"Yes, a lot of Yanks seem to admire his simple views of right and wrong. The smear campaign backfired and he won by a perishing landslide. He's been elected twice and the American people will back him."

Greystoke thought and said, "Hmm, if what you say be true, the Yanks are not bluffing about their Monroe Doctrine after all, even though we can't seem to locate any real forces down here."

Hakim said, "I'm not finished. There *are* no important American forces near enough to Venezuela to matter. Cleveland is standing by his guns, but Congress won't send any. You don't make friends in Congress by refusing to play the patronage game and stabbing one pork barrel bill after another with a pocket veto. Cleveland's put his honor and reputation on the line by invoking the Monroe Doctrine and issuing an ultimatum to the British Empire. His enemies in Congress want to make an ass of him by refusing to send the troops and ships to back his demands."

"Oh, poor chap's in a sticky wicket, then. He'll simply have to back down when our task force steams up the river, eh?"

Hakim said, flatly, "He won't. The handful of military he's managed to post down here have orders to resist any British invasion to the last man. I imagine they will. Halls Of Montezuma and all that rot."

"That's madness," Greystoke said. "Admiral Rice-Davis sings songs, too. What on earth can Cleveland have in mind by ordering those few men to certain death?"

"War," said Sir Basil, bleakly. "Congress is mucking about with the wrong President. There'll be no way they can avoid voting for a declaration of war, once American blood has been spilled. I imagine Cleveland had this in mind when he ordered his men down here to stand and fight."

"But, damn it, Sir Hakim, Britain doesn't want a war with America. Why does Cleveland want a war with us?"

"I don't think he does, but I told you, he's stubborn. If you chaps can keep Admiral Rice-Davis on a leash, the international tribunal may be able to settle the dispute peace-

fully with honor. Cleveland's ready to negotiate. He won't back down unilaterally. You said you had some sort of plan involving Captain Gringo, but Captain Gringo is dead. So what can I do for you?"

Greystoke hesitated again before he said, "Well, you know Dick Walker used to be jolly good at making a lot of noise and raising more hell than one would expect. I have it on good authority that the task force will start with a probing action. Orders are to back off if it looks like the Yanks are really serious. But how serious can a handful of consulate guards seem, even if they go all out with their little pop guns? One imagines a puffed up soft headed sod-like Rice-Davis would take a bit of convincing, eh what?"

Sir Basil smiled, dangerously, and said, "I'll get back to you. I have to wrap a few things up here in Caracas before I deal with Rice-Davis."

Hakim pressed the cradle down and got another number as he sat again and motioned to the waiting boy. As he leaned back luxuriously and took the youth's head in his lap again he said, dreamily, "I want El Sortilego's head. Better yet, leave it in Cipriano Castro's bathroom for him to find. I don't think they understand, down here, how I do business."

By midnight Captain Gringo had been in Camelia more ways than he'd thought she'd go for and he was getting nervous about Bubbles. He'd casually asked the dusky maid, during a smoking break, if she'd ever played three in a bed. Camelia had said it sounded disgusting and added that she'd scratch the eyes out of any woman who looked at her adorable Deek. He'd been afraid she was sort of old-fashioned.

So when they heard a discreet rap on the door as they were going at it dog-style, Captain Gringo muttered, "Oboy" and withdrew to move over to the door, wondering what the hell he was going to say to Bubbles.

But it wasn't Bubbles. It was Gaston. Camelia gasped

and snatched the covers over herself as Gaston came in. He nodded politely, and said, "Very nice. Exclusive, Dick?"

Captain Gringo said, "Yeah. Let's go in the other room," while Camelia covered herself, head and all, either crying or giggling.

In Gaston's room, Gaston said, "That species of a Dutchman is on his way to French Guiana with our launch and the small arms, Dick. I don't think he is out to cheat us. I told them the machine guns were not part of the deal and he left them behind, along with the 155 shells."

"Left them behind where?"

"At his boathouse, of course. Did you think I would run off into the jungle to find them at that cove? It was all *très* proper. I was just with his woman. Unfortunately loyal to the Dutchman but rather ugly in any case. I just missed them as they set out in our launch on their grand adventure. They even left the cases of shells stacked neatly and it must have been most tempting to take the machine guns. I told you he was an old comrade from La Legion."

"Yeah, yeah, so we know where we can get our hands on a brace of Maxim guns, but you let the silly bastards steam off with all the *ammunition!*"

"*Mais non,* we have a couple of belts of ammo attached to the gun and we still have the shells, *non?*"

"Great. What the fuck am I supposed to do with howitzer shells when we don't have a howitzer?"

"I've no idea. But at least the Dutchman did not steal them. His woman says he shall return in about a month, if he and his friends make it."

"Screw the Dutchman. I heard some shooting before."

"Ah, the usual political adjustments before the real fighting starts?"

"Could be. The Brits could be moving up the river right about now. The tide's due in just before dawn."

"*Eh, bien,* that is when *I* would do it, if today were the day. I noticed the old monitor out on the river had smoke rising from her funnel. The Venezuelans may know something we don't, hein?"

"Not that much to know. Every day they delay means a chance an American fleet will come over the north horizon and I don't think the Brits want that to happen. Coming in

with the rising sun behind them and deeper water under their keels make a lot of scary sense."

"In that case," Gaston said shrugging, "what are we waiting for, Dick? There's a smaller launch down at the Dutchman's. His woman is *très* nervous and has agreed to let us have it if we will take her with us, inland."

"We're not going inland, Gaston. I was just talking to that scared little gal in the next room and . . ."

"You call that talking? I have always called it something else."

"Shut up. She's a good kid and I've a couple of friends over at the consulate, too. We're going to have to stop the British invasion, Gaston."

Gaston raised an eyebrow and said, "Let me feel your brow, my ancient mariner. You are obviously *très* delirious. I am not at all certain the American Navy could stop the Royal Navy. Stopping them with a couple of machine-gun bursts is too droll to consider."

"They'll have more 30-30 rounds at the consulate. Wait here, I'll say *adios* to Camelia and get dressed."

"Dick, it's after midnight. The consulate will be closed."

"So we'll wake 'em up, if they're not on battle stations already."

Gaston yawned and added, *"Merde,* I was just looking forward to some sound sleep, too. Have you considered that since you brass-balled your way in and out of there they may have had time to check with Washington by cable, Dick?"

"I have, now. Jesus, Gaston, what makes you such a cheerful optimist? Look at the bright side. If the Americans shoot us we won't have to fight the British, right?"

The lights were burning at the American consulate. The entrance was sand-bagged and this time the marines on sentry duty there were dressed in battle kit and challenged him. He'd have had some trouble getting by a marine sergeant, but fortunately the O.D. standing close enough to yell at was a second lieutenant and Captain Gringo was good at yelling at

second lieutenants. So he promoted himself to a short colonel and bulled on through, with Gaston in tow.

The snooty receptionist wasn't there. He saw light coming from an open doorway and went into a conference room full of military and civilian Americans and Venezuelans, all talking, or rather, yelling at once.

Captain Gringo shouted for order and when nobody listened to him he drew his .38 and blew a divot out of the ceiling. That did it. Everybody froze but one beefy middle-aged man, who frowned and asked, "What's the meaning of this? Who the devil are you?"

"I'm Lieutenant Colonel Walker, G2. Lieutenant Bronson, over there in the corner, knows me. Who the devil are you?"

"I'm Cranshaw, U.S. Council General. Why wasn't I informed the Army had arrived? How many troops have you brought with you, Colonel?"

Captain Gringo pointed his chin at Gaston as he put his gun away and said, "M'sieu DuVal is it. He's with the French, and they're not coming either. I tried to call you from my hotel and the line was dead. I assume all the cable and telephone lines out of here have been cut?"

"They have, goddamn it," Cranshaw said nodding. "But let's get back to what the blazes you're *doing* here!"

"Later. Have the Brits evacuated their place down the street?"

"How the hell should I know?"

"Simple. You send a patrol to look. Bronson, get some scouts down there on the double. If they've evacuated their people after cutting the communication lines we can assume the balloon's going up. Who's in command of the Venezuelans around here?"

As Bronson left the room, grinning, an older officer wearing a chest full of fruit salad on his tropic uniform, moved over to throw Captain Gringo a snappy salute and announce, "Major Hernan Moreno Valdez y Robles, Colonel Walker. What are your orders for my battalion?"

"Battalion? That's all you've got here?"

"Sí, the main forces are far to the south-east, guarding the border with British Guiana in case they invade us as everyone thinks."

Captain Gringo snorted and snapped, "Great. The Brits

163

have the biggest navy on earth, so naturally they'll foot-slog through a couple of hundred miles of unmapped swamp instead of simply steaming in to occupy the main sea port and provincial capital. Where are your men posted right now, Robles?"

"They have set up command posts around the city to control the populace, of course. We are military police, not infantry. Caracas has been warned that several rebel factions may rise to stab us in the back if the British really attack."

"Oboy. I don't know how many rebel factions we have to worry about, but let's worry about the Brits. Does *anybody* around here have an educated guess about enemy strength?"

A man in U.S. Navy tropic whites raised his hand and said, "We've been patrolling the sea in disguised fishing craft, Colonel. They've had what looks like a small task force anchored on the three mile line for almost twenty-four hours, now. But there was no sign of activity at sundown. Looks like a battle cruiser, flotilla of torpedo rams, and some transports. Figuring the Lime Juicers crowd their transports more than we do, I'd say they have at least a couple of brigades of army or marines out there. You say you're all Washington sent?"

"There may be more on the way. Meanwhile, what we seem to have here is a replay of the Battle of New Orleans. The other side must have figured that out by now, too. The Brits are slow learners, but they seldom repeat a mistake and they've had a long time to brood about how they fucked up at New Orleans in 1814. Any armchair general can tell you they never should have landed miles from New Orleans to march through the mud, while Jackson and his irregulars got set up. They'll probably send the transports right into town, behind a screen of rams with the big guns of the cruiser backing them up. We don't seem to have anything worth torpedoing or ramming except that old monitor. But the rams will have four-inch deckguns to pepper us, so there goes the great idea old Jackson had with the cotton bales, even if we had some cotton bales. We can't dig trenches. They'd turn into canals before we could take cover in them. I guess our first move should be to move the monitor downstream, fill its ballast tanks to put it on the bottom, and hope its plates hold when they fire those six-inchers."

Robles looked uncomfortable and when Captain Gringo paused, he sighed and said, "I regret to say my countrymen

164

aboard the monitor are gone. They did not inform us why they were steaming inland up the Orinoco, but one gathers they do not like noise."

The American naval attache started to say something nasty but Captain Gringo silenced him with a warning look and said, "Well, fair is fair and that old tub wouldn't last long swapping shots with a modern cruiser. But we've still got the Venezuelan *Army* and this figures to be a land against sea fight anyway."

Lieutenant Bronson returned to announce, "The British have pulled out. They even took their light bulbs."

Captain Gringo wondered what else was new. He pointed at Gaston and said, "Get a work detail together and go with M'sieu DuVal, here. He'll show you where we have some machine guns and 155 shells. I want 'em inside our lines before somebody else stumbles over them."

Bronson was used to taking orders from his old upper classman and left with Gaston on the double, sans comment. But another army man protested, "What good are 155 shells, Colonel? We don't have any cannons here!"

"I know that and you know that, but the Brits don't know that. Have any of the guards, here, been qualified on the Maxim heavy machine gun?"

"I don't think so. But a lot of them have marksman and sharpshooter's badges and a machine gun's just a fast shooting rifle when you get right down to it, right?"

"Wrong. Putting an unqualified man behind the breech of a machine gun is asking for wasted ammunition and a blown off face. Aiming is easy enough to learn in a day or so, but if you don't know how to adjust the headspacing as the weapon heats up, they tend to blow up at the breech."

He shrugged and said, "We'll cross that bridge when we talk to some of the enlisted men. Who's got the situation map?"

There was an exchange of blank looks.

Captain Gringo manfully resisted a chance to make a crack about chocolate soldiers and explained, sweetly, "A map is a piece of paper showing the lay of the land. A situation map has one's own positions crayoned on it in blue with the enemy positions in red. Sometimes it helps to know where everybody *is*, see?"

Smitty, the draftsman, who'd earlier forged new papers

for him, said, "I'll get a large-scale map of the province, Colonel," and ducked out.

Captain Gringo nodded at the naval attache and said, "We'll put Smitty's map on this conference table. You stand over there and be the Royal Navy and I'll stand here and see what I can do with my blue crayon."

"You mean you want me to mark the positions of that task force?"

"Why, no, I thought you might like to draw some dirty pictures for us."

"Let's not get snotty, Colonel. I can map where they were at sunset, but that's not saying where they'll be at dawn!"

Captain Gringo nodded, grimly, and said, "I know. We'll mark where they were and then try to figure the best way for them to come in. They can't run ocean-going ships up narrow channels. They can't land troops just any old place. You figure where ships can go and I'll figure where a smart land-fighter would want to put him men ashore. Between us, we ought to be able to set up some sort of half-ass defenses."

As Smitty came back in with the rolled map and a box of crayons, the Venezuelan, Robles, said, "I do not like this talk of half-ass defenses, Colonel Walker."

"I don't like it, either, but that's all Jackson had at New Orleans, so what the hell. We don't have to stop them cold. Jackson couldn't have done that at New Orleans if the British had been going all out and to hell with casualties. Jackson blooded a probing action good, so the red coats decided there had to be a better place to invade the Mississippi Valley. They'd have done it, too, if word hadn't come that the war was over."

Council General Cranshaw nodded in sudden understanding and said, "I see your plan. It almost makes sense. It's no secret that everyone thinks Washington is bluffing. If we can hand the invading task force a good shellacking, Whitehall may decide it's cheaper in the long run to sit down at the bargaining table after all, eh?"

There was a mutter of approval, mostly among the civilians around the table. The naval attache shook his head and said, "I know the jerk-off in command offshore. Admiral Rice-Davis is going to take some convincing before *he* backs

166

off! He thinks he's a British Bulldog and I don't see how you stop any kind of dog with a few flea bites!"

Captain Gringo nodded and turned to Robles to say, "We're going to have to use your men, too."

"But my colonel, if they do not watch the people, the people may turn against us."

"We'll have to risk it. That task force is no *maybe*, it's *big!* The handfull of marines here must have extra uniforms. We'll dress as many of your non-coms as we can like U.S. Marines. That way anybody getting cute with spyglasses should assume they're facing a serious joint command."

Robles frowned and said, "I do not understand. For why would my men look more impressive led by U.S. Marines?"

Captain Gringo tried to come up with a nicer answer, decided there wasn't any, and said, "No offense, but we're up against a pig-headed enemy commander with an Anglo-Saxon superiority complex. I know I can count on you and your men. But let's face it, your gunboat crew did run away, and Latins are supposed to do that a lot. Wait! I *know* you and your men are willing to fight, damn it! I want the *Brits* to know it, too. The U.S. Marines don't retreat and those other guys know it. They won't expect native troops led by U.S. Marines to retreat, either, and they'll assume they've had better training than usual down here."

Robles flushed, started to say something, and then he shrugged, saying, "I understand. But what if my men are forced to retreat, dressed as marines or not?"

"We'll all have to retreat, if they really come at us all out. We've got to convince them in the opening round that they're getting into a more serious fight than they bargained for." He turned away, then added, "Let's get that map spread out and get to work, Gents."

Secret Agent Greystoke was sweating despite the cool dawn breezes, as his launch tied up to the torpedo blister of H.M.S. *Pandora* and he was piped aboard. Trusting Sir Basil

Hakim seemed about as sensible as trusting one's canary to the cat, but The Great Game called for risk and the stakes this morning were awsome. Greystoke didn't think of himself as a particularly brave man. As a pro he avoided taking any chances with his precious ass that duty didn't call for. But he really thought it was a bloody shame he'd never get the V.C. for the gut wrenching ride out to the task force with nothing but Sir Basil Hakim's word between him and a rather messy end.

Since he'd helped in the planning, Greystoke knew Admiral Rice-Davis' orders as well as the admiral did. So he wasn't surprised to find the flagship still at anchor and the puffy old Welshman pacing the bridge, muttering, "What, what, what?" as smaller sleeker rams moved in, steaming dead slow for the pencil line of swampline on the western sky line. The transports trailed, with two rams staying by Flag as escort.

As Greystoke joined the admiral on the bridge the older man smiled grimly and said, "You just missed a fine flap, what, what, what? Saw bloody smoke to the north. Sent a patrol boat. Perishing German freighter. Where's this American fleet everyone's worried about, what, what, what?"

Greystoke consulted his pocket watch and saw he'd timed it closer than he really liked to think about. He said, "Odd you spotted a *German* vessel, Sir Reginald. You know, of course, that the Kaiser has offered to sit with the French and other interested parties at the conference table, if Whitehall decides to settle this peacefully."

"What, what, what? Interested parties? Balderdash, say I! Germans have no interest in this border dispute. Kaiser has no perishing colonies anywhere near here. French may be interested. Dutch may be interested. Bloody Germans have no business in this matter. Never have been able to understand that little Kaiser Willy. Met him at Windsor one time. Ugly, strange lad with a withered arm. One of Her Majesty's grandchildren, and just a boy at the time. Stole toys from the other children and had a temper when he had to give 'em back, what, what, what?"

"We know he's a bit, uh, strange, but Germany's on good terms with the U.S. at the moment. Cleveland says he accepts their good offices in this dispute. By the way, we've evacuated the delta, officially, but of course I still have agents

in the field over there. As I was putting out this morning I picked up some rather alarming reports. I don't think the Yanks are bluffing."

"What, what, what? Of course they're bluffing! I have my own sources, too, you know. Naval Intelligence signals the one gunboat they had has made a run for it inland. Nothing to oppose us but a handfull of those rather overrated marines of theirs."

"With 155 shells, Sir Reginald? One of my agents spotted a detachment of U.S. Marines moving heavy artillery shells through town just now. The marines are not alone. There's a large force of Venezuelan regulars led by marine instructors, too. Couldn't get close enough to map their exact positions, but they seem to be setting up all over the place. Martial Law's been declared and all civilians have been ordered to stay indoors. Rather neat move, since it means any of our spies will risk getting shot if they move about enough to help us."

Admiral Rice-Davis moved out on the bridge wing with Greystoke in tow and raised his spyglass to peer at the dim shoreline. He lowered the old-fashioned Nelsonian glass and said, "Hah, humbug and twaddle! Ram Triumphant is well within range and I see no flashing of bloody Yankee guns. They *have* no big guns! My own chaps told me so, what, what, what?"

Greystoke looked at his watch again, swallowed, and said, "It's not that hard to hide a howitzer. My people were quite sure about those shells they saw moving out of an apparent innocent civilian warehouse. We know the Venezuelans and Yanks are working together. We know there are hundreds of sheds and swampy dells no British agent has ever investigated. Seems rather odd to have men bringing up the ammo when one has no guns, doesn't it?"

"Balderdash! If they have any real defenses set up, why haven't we heard about it yet? Look over there, what, what, what? Ram's entered the estuary. Transport of Royal Marines right behind. They haven't fired. They won't fire. They wouldn't dare."

At that moment the ton of high explosives Hakim's agents had planted in the hold of Greystoke's launch with a time fuse exploded in a deafening roar!

Both men on the bridge wing hit the deck as the air was

filled with smoke and flame and the shattered debris of Greystoke's launch. The whole ship tingled to the shock waves of the tremendous explosion as Greystoke grinned like the Cheshire cat and said, "I say, we seem to have been torpedoed, what, what, what?"

Rice-Davis ignored him as he sprang to his feet with surprising grace for such a fat old fart, and darted into the main bridge, yelling at the officers on the deck in there, "On your feet, God strike a bloody light! Can't you see we're under attack?"

He snatched the intercom speaker from its cradle by the wheel and barked, "Damage Control, Report!"

Some idiot started sounding battle stations, forgetting all the battle stations had been manned since dawn. Admiral Rice-Davis yelled, "Avast that bloody noise, goddamn your mother's eyes. I'm waiting, Damage Control!"

A worry-voiced ensign down below the water line replied over the intercom, "Damage Control to Bridge. We're taking a little water in compartment Six but the pumps can handle it easily, Sir. Our blister absorbed most of the explosion and we only sprang a few rivets inside."

Rice-Davis smiled and said, "I say, good show! Any casualties?"

"Nossir. The torpedo blew that launch alongside to kindling wood but her crew was aboard, thank heavens. I say, the torpedo must have hit the launch and exploded her warhead a few inches out from our blister. Lucky thing, too. It must have been a perishing big charge."

Rice-Davis said, "Carry on" and switched to the lookout high above. He said, "Well, Lookout?"

"Sir?"

"I know I'm a Sir. "I'm waiting for your perishing *report!* Didn't you track that flaming torpedo's wake? Can't sink the perishing submarine if we don't know where it is, what, what, what?"

"Uh, submarine, Sir?"

"Right! Submarine! Boat that runs under the water. Do you see any flaming Yankee craft *above* the water out there? Get the wax out of your ears and the sand out of your eyes, lad! We've just taken a ruddy torp like a ruddy sitting duck!"

The officer in the crow's nest protested, "Sir, I don't think the U.S. Navy *has* any submarines!"

"What, what, what? No submarines? Humbug and twaddle! Search the waters for a perishing periscope, Goddamn it! Somebody just torpedoed us and I mean to *sink* the bugger!"

He switched off and yelled to his signal officer down the bridge, "Have our escort sweep 360 degrees for that flaming Yankee whatever. No submarines my sweet Auny Fanny! God strike a bloody light, doesn't anybody around here but me know we're at war with the bloody United States Navy?"

Greystoke joined him, frowning. This wasn't the way the fake torpedo attack was supposed to be affecting the old sea dog. He caught the admiral's eye and said, "It's true the U.S. Navy doesn't have any commissioned submarines, Sir Reginald. I was just thinking about that German merchant vessel you spotted earlier. The new Holland boats can only travel a few miles on their batteries, that's why hardly anybody but the Germans have been experimenting with them."

Rice-Davis frowned and said, "Germans? What Germans? We're not here to fight any perishing Germans! Have it on good authority we're not to fight the Germans for at least twenty years. Kaiser Willy would never attack us while his grandmother was alive. He's always been afraid of her."

"Yes, and he's fond of his uncle, Prince Edward, but hates his young cousin, George. I don't think any German would admit to that torpedo we just took, Sir Reginald, but Whitehall did snub the Kaiser's offer to help negotiate a settlement with Cleveland and *somebody* obviously just tried to sink you."

Rice-Davis puffed back out on the bridge wing, muttering, "Sneaky little bugger. Withered arm, you know. Can't get along with his cousin, the Czar, either. Wouldn't put anything past a lad who'd steal toys under the Christmas tree at Windsor, what, what, what?"

Rice-Davis picked up his telescope and trained it on the western horizon as Greystoke suggested, "Maybe we'd better pull in our horns a bit until Whitehall's had time to digest this mysterious torpedo attack."

Rice-Davis said, "Balderdash! Our lads are up the flam-

ing estuary now. Look like we were *retreating* if we backed off *now,* what, what, what?"

"Sir Reginald, may I remind you this was to be a probing action only? Damn it, somebody just tried to sink you!"

"Piffle. Only ruptured a few plates. Probably meant to shake us up. Take more than a spot of noise to do that, what, what, what? Here, take this glass and tell me if you see any resistance ashore! Our lads will disembark on the Tucupita docks with the band playing 'Rule Brittania' and not a button missing, mark my words!"

Greystoke knew he was probably right. His own bluff hadn't worked, and there was nobody left in the Great Game with a better one.

A Venezuelan scout ran to join Captain Gringo, Gaston, and the others around them on the pickle-shaped point of land just north-east of the endangered provincial capital. The point was well wooded and guarded the approaches up the deep water channel from the sea; but that was about all one could say for it. The ground between the trees was wet sponge underfoot—to dig in was to drown. So Captain Gringo had his mixed force of Venezuelans and Americans behind a hastily thrown together barricade of tree trunks covered with muck. The logs would stop small arms fire—anything larger than that would blow the barricade and anyone behind it to splinters and hash. The scout saluted and said, "They are just around the bend, Colonel Walker. Moving no faster than a man on foot. There are two torpedo rams, buttoned up. Behind them are the transports. The soldados are on deck, for to take the air, and a band is playing."

Captain Gringo nodded and said, "Bueno. Get back to your outpost. Fire your rifle when they round the bend over that way."

"Won't they hear us, my Colonel?"

"Yes, I want them to. Carry on, Sergeant."

He returned the scout's salute and turned to walk back

from the barricade where Lieutenant Bronson and some other soldiers and marines were working, stripped to the waist and muddy as hell. He nodded approvingly as he saw Bronson hadn't been afraid to get his hands dirty and said, "Well, they're coming. I see you guys are set up pretty fair."

Bronson wiped a hand across his muddy face and scowled down at the line of what looked like stove pipes sticking out of the mud at an angle as he said, "We planted 'em like you told us to, Walker. But this isn't going to work."

Captain Gringo stepped over to peer down one of the stove pipes. It wasn't really a stove pipe but an improvised roll of sheet iron, torn from a rooftop in town. He could just make out the brass-fused nose of the big 155 shell nestled in the bottom. He said, "It has to work. The Seminoles used wooden cannon against us in the Everglades and the solid earth around that tin casing should hold better than any goddamn cypress log. If we have the elevation right, the shells should go almost straight up and come down all over the place out there in mid-channel."

Bronson grimaced and said, "I read about the Seminole wars at the Point, too. But those were black powder and ball improvisations. This stuff is H.E. and those shells are *big!* They're going to tumble, too. There's no rifling in those loose fitting tubes, Walker. They may come out, when we light the dynamite fuses down to the charges under 'em. But they're going to come down ass over tea kettle."

"I know. That's why I set the fuses for air bursts. We don't have to hit anything, as long as they go off somewhere in the vicinity of John Bull. I've got to get back to the machine gun nest I set up. When you hear me fire, light the fuses and run like hell. If our big guns don't work, we're going to have some awfully big holes in the ground around here!"

He started back to the barricade nearer the water. But Bronson tagged along a few paces and when they were out of earshot of his work detail, he stopped Captain Gringo and said, "Walker, I have to have a word in private with you."

"Okay, we're private."

"Dick, I take my job as security man here sort of serious."

"As well you should. What's the problem?"

"Uh, I know you from the Point and I never believed that story about you getting in trouble out west, but, well, I had to check. I sent a cable to War, last night, after you'd left."

Captain Gringo pasted a smile across his face and said, "That's what I'd have done. What did War wire back?"

"They didn't. Our wires were cut before I got an answer to my check on you."

"Gee, that's tough. I guess you'll have to wait until this mess is over and communications are restored, huh?"

"Yeah. Meanwhile, I'm sort of taking you at face value and it's going to mean my ass if I'm wrong. So ... am I right or wrong, Dick?"

Captain Gringo shrugged and said, "Depends on what's right and what's wrong. I guess, sometimes it's hard to tell. You want me to back off, if I'm under suspicion?"

"Hell, no! You're the only guy around who seems to know what to *do!* But, for the record, have I your word as an officer and a gentleman that you haven't lied to me, Dick?"

Captain Gringo thought about that. His friend, Gaston, had taught him to be even more *practique* with his professional honor than that court martial and death sentence had in the beginning. Bronson was a poor dumb kid who thought the world was run on the level. Captain Gringo knew Bronson would take his word. On the other hand, they were both West Pointers and they both knew the Code. He looked Bronson in the eye and said, "You have my word I've never done anything I thought wrong and you have my word I'm standing by you on the line today against a common enemy. I've never done a thing that could endanger the security of your post and I'm trying to help you hold this position. Don't push me any further."

Bronson nodded and said, "I was afraid you'd say that. You've been bullshitting us about that story being a cover up, right?"

"What do you think, Bronson?"

Bronson smiled wearily, and held out his hand. As Captain Gringo took it, Bronson said, "Jackson used some pirates at New Orleans, if I recall my history lessons. I can't pardon you like Jackson could, so this is only until the wires are up again and I can't say I didn't know for sure."

Captain Gringo laughed and added, "You always were a

174

Pollyanna, Kid. What makes you think any of us are going to be *alive* when the wires are up again?"

He left Bronson in command of his "artillery" and went back to rejoin Gaston and the others along the barricade. He'd placed the two machine guns side-by-side with the belts feeding from opposing directions. As he dropped to a log seat behind them Gaston said, "I have heard of a two gunman with pistols, but a two gunman with machine guns is *très* unique. I could man one of them, Dick."

Captain Gringo said, "I've a better job for you. Robles has a thin screen behind us guarding the neck of this point from a surprise attack from the mainland. Why don't you go back and see that he's set up right?"

"*Merde alors*, the fun promises to be out here on the point. Who is going to attack us from the rear? Do you think the Brits will land scouts?"

"No, they're too overconfident to worry about that. But Robles is still more worried about a stab in the back and while this point is a good place to dominate the channel, it's a hell of a place to be trapped. I was talking to him, setting up this barricade. He says that aside from the Castro faction, there's a mess of would-be-British subjects we might have to deal with once the shooting starts. I'll listen for your pistol. Don't yell for help unless it looks really hairy to the rear. What are you waiting for, a kiss goodbye?"

Gaston told him to fuck himself and marched away, muttering. Captain Gringo knew he didn't have to worry about his back, now, so he stared out at the blank expanse of sluggish water. The tide was coming in and it looked as if that was all that was coming in. Then he heard a distant rifle and called out, "Okay, troops, this is it!"

The ugly snout of a torpedo ram poked around the bend and he yelled, "Hold your fire. She's armored in the first place and probably won't spot us in the second."

A Venezuelan near him made the sign of the cross, snicked a round in the chamber of his rifle, and rested it across the log in front of him. Others up and down the ragged barricade were doing the same as the long, low ram slid abreast of them, like a big steel cayman. Downstream he heard the distant tinny sound of a brass band playing like they thought they were holding a concert in Hyde Park. He shook his head wearily and said,

175

"That's the trouble with fighting. Nobody but primitive tribesmen and little people for almost a century. Couple of weeks in Apache country would shape you Brits up better for the big one you keep talking about."

The ram passed on as a second came around the bend with the first transport right behind it. He saw the transport deck was crowded with freshly scrubbed jolly lads in pith helmets and tropic full dress kit. He took a deep breath, got a good grip on both machine guns, and opened up with twin muzzles blazing!

He fired one gun at the ram, knowing the slugs bouncing off her plates wouldn't hurt anybody, as, with the other gun, he cut a line of white froth across the water toward the transport's waterline. The men on either side of him opened up with everything they had, of course, and some of them were aiming to kill, but the Royal Marines on deck had taken the hint and were either down or getting there *poco tiempo* as the first rifle rounds started spanging paint off the superstructure over them. The band played on as if nothing had happened. He'd heard they were like that.

The ram stopped dead in the water and began to swing her gun turrets ominously as Captain Gringo tap danced slugs along the rail of the transport and wondered aloud, "What the hell is Bronson *waiting* for?"

The ram fired a salvo of four-inch shells, fortunately high, and some of his men behind the logs flattened in the mud as the screaming shells exploded somewhere in the trees behind them. But most of the defenders, Venezuelan as well as Yank, returned the ram's fire with enthusiasm, bouncing bullets off her armored superstructure as her bridge light signalled the transport to fall back.

Captain Gringo could see the landing force was more annoyed by the small arms fire than concerned. The ram fired again to teach the perishing natives a lesson. Then, like a string of colossal fire crackers, the improvised cannon Bronson and his crew were manning began to go off and even Captain Gringo was impressed.

The earth quivered like jelly as the 155s tore skyward ass over elbows, screaming like banshees as they arched over the river. It got even noiser as they began to burst in mid-air above, between, and all around the British vessels. A lucky hit knocked the funnel off the ram, obscuring her in thick smoke

at deck level as her guns blazed blind. A four-inch gun sounded like a popping cork next to an exploding 155. Some of his men were standing as they cheered and Captain Gringo yelled, "Take cover, damn it!" Unless he'd counted wrong, he'd shot his wad and they hadn't really stopped the Brits with all their wild fire. The last shell fragments were splashing out there on the water and the sudden silence was eerie as the world stood still, teetering on the balance of war and peace.

Then, before he could see what the task force's next move might be, he heard the rattle of small arms fire behind him and, above it, the three rapid shots of Gaston's pistol, held skyward. Captain Gringo swore, shoved another belt in one gun, and lifted it from its tripod to lug it back toward the sounds of skirmishing to his rear. As he dog trotted past the grinning Bronson, Bronson asked what was up and he snapped, "Guerrillas. To the barricade, and stop the fuckin' landing if they try one!"

He tore through some brush and around a big tree to spot Gaston and Major Robles behind a fallen log, their backs to him as they fired at someone beyond. He saw other Venezuelan regulars to the right and left had formed a skirmish line. A couple were hit; the rest were holding. He lugged the Maxim over to Gaston and Robles, and propped the water jacket over the log, snapping, "Who, where, how many?"

"Ah, I was afraid we'd lost you," Gaston said. "That tree line, a hundred meters out. We turned back their first charge, as you can see if you will observe that species in the white shirt over there on his face in the grass. I think they are reforming for a more determined rush. Some of these green troops fired too soon and only dusted their advance skirmishers, hein?"

"My men are good fighters, damn it," Robles growled.

"Children, children, don't fight," Captain Gringo said. "I see a flag over there, eleven o'clock behind that clump of reeds. Looks like the Venezuelan colors, for Pete's sake!"

Robles spat and said, "They have no right to fight under Venezuela's colors, the traitors!"

Gaston said, "This may be true, but here they come!" as, from the rebel lines, someone yelled, "Viva Victoria!" and the tree line exploded in white clad figures, charging with bayonetted rifles, repeaters, fired from the hip as they came. A

bullet spanged off the log they were behind. Another took Major Robles in the shoulder and he spun away to land, cursing, in the mud. Captain Gringo gritted his teeth and said, "All right. We've had just about enough of this shit."

He rose, bracing the Maxim on his hip as he opened up to cut a swathe of death and destruction at the level of the charging guerrilla's white crotches. The other loyal Venezuelans didn't have to be invited to join in. The man carrying the flag screamed as Captain Gringo's hosing lead shattered his flag staff, his left hip, and tore off his balls. A loyalist sharpshooter blew the side of an enemy bugler's face off just as he left his horn to blow something that might have seemed important to him just before he died. The guerrillas were inspired, or maybe drunk. They charged long past common sense. So, when they faltered and began to move back, they were still in the open and it was just as easy to shoot a man running away from you as it was one coming at you. It was more fun, too. The loyalists leaped to their feet to chase the rebels, peppering them rudely and bayonetting any they caught up with. Captain Gringo ceased fire as he saw men on his side in the way. Major Robles had staggered to his feet, drawn his revolver, and was trying to stagger after them when Gaston grabbed him and asked, "*Merde alors,* where do you think you are going, my friend?"

Robles said, "I must lead my men, damn it!"

But Gaston sat him firmly on the log and insisted, "Your men are doing fine. Is this not so, Dick?"

Captain Gringo put the hot gun down and said, "Yeah, they're kicking the shit out of them. I think I just jammed this gun. I have to get back and see how Bronson's making out."

Bronson and the others back at the barricade were making out just fine. As Captain Gringo got there he saw the empty river. Bronson laughed, slapped him on the back, and said, "They turned tail and ran for it! We *beat* them, Dick!"

Captain Gringo said, "Let's not get sickening about it, Kid. They've gone back to think things over with their flag ship and the rest of the fleet."

Bronson sobered and said, "Jésus, do you think they'll come back for another try?"

"I hope not. Now that they know we're serious they won't come in again with the band playing. The fat's in the fire and they'll figure on a no kidding landing under fire."

"Jesus, Dick. How are we to stop them, if they try again?"

Captain Gringo's voice was bleak as he replied, "We can't. If that salvo of HE didn't impress them, nothing we have left will. I don't even have a full belt of machine-gun ammo left."

"Oboy. Maybe it's time to get out of here, huh?"

"You get out of here if you want to. I never said I didn't have *any* ammunition left!"

Out on H.M.S. *Pandora* the Welsh born Admiral Rice-Davis seemed to be doing a Highland Fling in his private quarters as Greystoke sat and watched, bemused. The rams and transports had returned to resume station outside the three mile limit and, thankfully, nobody had been killed in the surprising ambush by the obviously determined Americans. A few men had been lightly wounded by shell fragments. One of said shell fragments rested on Sir Reginald's desk as he danced about in a rage, trying not to listen as Greystoke said, "It's settled, Sir Reginald. I've explained why we can't afford a war with the United States and it's most obvious the Yanks have called our bluff. We're going to have to negotiate our way out of this one. I'm sure Venezuela will give us a few token acres of jungle and all will be right with the world again. Stupid quarrel in the first place, but somebody at Whitehall will muck about with the maps at night after the brighter lads have gone home."

Rice-Davis sputtered, "What, what, what, negotiate? Never! Won't have it! Looks as if we've backed down from a perishing handful of marines!"

Greystoke pointed his chin at the shell fragment and said, "That is not a shard from any U.S. Naval ordinance. It's a field artillery round. The Yanks have been buying those big

155s from the French and they're very good guns. I'm frankly astounded they didn't sink our shore party if it's true they fire that many. I suppose they have orders to avoid a war, too. But if I were you, I'd take the hint."

"What, what, what? Never, by Saint George and the Dragon! Just let my lads regather their wits and we'll show the perishing Yanks who rules the waves! Moving in after ebb tide. Butt, stock, and bayonet. Only way to do it, what, what, what?"

Greystoke grimaced and asked, "Do you have anything to drink, Sir Reginald? It's getting perishing hot as the sun rises."

The older man blinked, nodded, and said, "Of course I have something to drink. Should have said so, if you were thirsty, what, what, what?"

He moved to a sideboard, took a bottle and glass tumbler from it, and put it on the desk near the shell fragment, saying, "Help yourself. As I was saying, we'll let the tide turn, rearm the turrets, fire a few good ones into that bend from out here, with my serious guns, and . . ."

"Aren't you drinking with me, Sir Reginald?"

"Eh, what, what, what? Sorry. Forget me flaming manners when I'm planning a battle."

The crusty sea dog got his own glass and poured it half full of neat scotch before filling Greystoke's. He noted the dismayed look on the spy master's face and asked, "What, what, what, need a chaser? I'll ring for the steward."

But Greystoke smiled and said he liked his malt liquor like a man. So the older man looked mollified and began to sip his drink. Greystoke asked, "What's that, out the port-hole?" and, as he'd hoped, Admiral Rice-Davis lowered his glass and stared out the open port as Greystoke rose to stand beside him. Rice-Davis blinked and would have said another infuriating what, what, what, had not Greystoke shrugged and said, "Oh, stupid of me, just a gull, of course."

"Gull? Of course you saw a gull. What else would you see out a porthole, perishing flying machine?" He drained his glass, slammed it down, and added, "Ridiculous new inventions. Balderdash. Submarines. Flying machines. Never happen, I tell you. Wouldn't be natural."

Greystoke sat down, crossed his legs, and sadly regarded

the old man as he sipped his own drink. He said, "They do have submarines, and they say a lot of people are working on the flying machine. The coming century should be interesting for you Naval chaps, eh?"

"Balderdash. Battleships will always rule the waves, say I. Never saw the sense of converting to steam. Sail was good enough for Nelson, wasn't it?"

"If you say so, Sir Reginald," said Greystoke, with a yawn. The old man paced back and forth, frowned, and said, "I say, I seem to be coming down with that flaming ague again. Bit wonky in the knees all of a sudden."

"Why don't you sit down, Sir? You do look a bit pale."

Rice-Davis shook his head to clear it, staggered over to his bunk, and sat down heavily, muttering, "Can't be ill *now!* Won't have it. Must go back and finish off those cheeky Yanks."

Greystoke lit a cigarette and took out his watch to consult it. The old man tried to rise, stared at him in wonder, and gasped, "I say, by George, you'd best ring for my orderly. I do believe I'm quite ill!"

Greystoke saw he could not rise to get to the bell button. So he blew a smoke ring and soothed, "Lie down and let it take effect, Sir Reginald. You'll be more comfortable, that way."

"What, what, what? Effect? What effect are you talking about?"

"Oh, I just poisoned you, Sir. It's quite painless, and leaves no trace, either."

The admiral gasped, tried to rise, and sank back, weakly, as he said, "I say, that was rather rude of you, Greystoke."

Greystoke said, "Sorry. Had to be done. Queen and Country and all that rot."

"By God, Sir! I do believe you must be a foreign agent, what, what, what?"

Greystoke shook his head and said, "I assure you I'm a loyal British subject with the good of the Empire at heart, Sir Reginald."

"Eh, loyal, say you? What do you think *I* am, a perishing Wog?"

"Sir, I think you're a true blue worthy British gentleman

who's seen his day. Unfortunately, there are a lot of you left, but most are no longer in a position to start a senseless war with the United States."

"You bastard! You'd betray your Queen to the bloody Yanks?"

"No, Sir Reginald. But I assure you I'd murder Her Majesty for our country, if it meant saving us from a ghastly mistake. Like yourself, the Queen is old and out of date as the dodo bird. His Highness, Edward, will mount the throne as an old man, and hopefully die before he can get us into any more of these 'By Jingo' messes you old fools have mucked this century up with. Her grandson, George, will take over in the coming century as a modern monarch, a trained naval officer who doesn't believe in fighting-sail and pointless expeditions to places like Venezuela."

The old man's eyes were glazed and Graystoke felt sincerely sorry for him as he croaked, "But the Yanks, you can't let the Yanks beat us . . ."

"Nobody's beating anybody, Sir Reginald. That's why I can't let you go back for another go at them. Both the Crown and Cleveland will leave the negotiating table with their honor satisfied. Prince Edward is popular in America. He even manages to get along with the French. Britain will be entering the coming century with both France and the United States on her side. A few square miles of jungle and an obsolete admiral seem a small price to pay, but I am truly sorry, Sir Reginald."

The old man on the bunk didn't answer, although his eyes were still open. Greystoke rose, gently closed the dead man's eyes, and pushed the button near the door.

When the steward appeared, Greystoke said, "Admiral Rice-Davis seems to have had a stroke. You'd best get the ship's surgeon. I'll be on the bridge."

He left the steward with the corpse and walked the short companionway to the bridge, where, of course, the other officers were waiting for new orders.

Greystoke said, "I'm afraid the admiral is indisposed, but just now he turned his command over to me."

A rear admiral, almost as crusty-looking as the man he'd just poisoned, frowned and said, "Command over to you, Sir? Why, dashitall, you're a *civilian!*"

"Let's not talk dirty. When you check with Admiralty

and Whitehall you'll discover I hold flag rank and, if need be, I outrank an army general, too. My old school chum, Prince George, arranged this for me when I went to work for Intelligence. But I didn't come here to talk about myself, gentlemen. I want this fleet out of Venezuelan waters and I want it now. Are there any questions?"

A younger officer of the newer breed nodded, knowingly, and said, "Ay, ay, Sir. Trinidad or Guiana?" and Graystoke said, "Guiana, of course. That's where this task force came from. So why don't we just put it back where we found it?"

Considering how close the two sides had come to a formal declaration of war, once the more sensible civilian faction in London wrested control in the field from the jingoists, the crisis evaporated like spit on a hot stove. As the last smoke plumes of the British task force faded over the horizon the cable and telephone connections winked back on as if by magic. Greystoke's field agents simply respliced them in the same secluded jungle nooks they'd cut them less than twenty-four hours before and, for the record, the breakdown in communications must have been caused by the recent rains and some unusual electrical anomaly of the iron rich soil. The Americans and other legations cut off from the outside world for a time accepted this. They were told to. London had cabled Washington that if the perishing matter was really that important it might be a good idea to have a gentleman's agreement, so President Cleveland eagerly accepted third party arbitration, having saved his honor and political neck and pleasantly surprised his bluff had worked for some reason. The military attaches in Venezuela, of course, cabled Washington about their skirmish with the task force, but were advised to forget it. Nobody important had been hurt and officially it hadn't happened.

Within twenty-four hours the Union Jack once more was flying just down the street from the U.S. Consulate and when asked by anyone rude enough to let his curiosity show, the British legation explained they'd been on a picnic in the

woods. Trouble? What trouble? Whitehall hadn't cabled them about any trouble. But then, of course, the wires had been out for a time, eh what?

In Caracas a relieved President Crespo received a hurried phone call from the Loyal Opposition and listened with a wry and understanding smile as a very rattled Cipriano Castro assured El Presidente of his continued support against imperialist aggression.

Loyalist police officials had informed Crespo of the rather messy murder of the shady El Sortilego. His funeral would have to be closed casket. They'd gathered most of him from the various nooks and crannies of his ransanked "Fortune Telling" establishment. But they had no idea just where his head had vanished. Cipriano Castro was said to be trying to raise a lot of money suddenly. He explained he had to pay off some gambling debts, fast.

In another part of town, Sir Basil Hakim was being very reasonable about extending the defeated rebel faction a bit more time. He was keeping a very low profile indeed, after receiving a very rude coded cable from his old drinking buddy, the Prince of Wales. As he waited for the amiable fat future king to cool off he was holed up with a six-foot Negress who offered a change of pace for the jaded little monster. Sometimes it could be amusing to be dominated and the grim sadistic black girl was an interesting switch after the twisted thrill of child molesting. He'd have her killed before he steamed off in his luxurious yacht, of course. It wouldn't do for word to get around that the *Merchant of Death* enjoyed an occasional good cry in the arms of a brutal lover.

By this time, of course, Captain Gringo and Gaston were long gone from the scene. They'd lit out in the Dutchman's spare power launch well before the cables could be respliced and hadn't seen fit to bid formal farewell to the worried Lieutenant Bronson or anyone else who might be expected to arrest them. The Dutchman's woman had told them they couldn't use her man's launch, of course, so they'd stolen it from the boat house during the siesta and now she was mad at them, too, one could assume. It didn't matter. They hadn't told anyone where they were headed.

Gaston was a bit surprised, when the sun came out late that afternoon as they were crossing yet another unmapped

184

lagoon of the vast poorly mapped delta. Gaston turned from the firebox he'd just cast another stick of wood into and said to Captain Gringo, at the helm, "Forgive me, my old and lost, but unless I am wrong about the time and the natural movements of the sun, we seem to be heading south!"

"I know we're headed south," Captain Gringo said. "Everyone will be expecting us to run north. Back toward our usual haunts in Costa Rica."

"I thought that made sense, too, Dick. We have been, how you say, busting the gut trying to reach the Caribbean since we stumbled into this thrice-accursed country."

Captain Gringo nodded and said, "Yeah, and a lot of people know it. It's true we're not wanted and have lots of buddies in Costa Rice, but Costa Rica is one hell of a ways off. We can't go to sea in this wood burning little tub. Do you really want to hug the coast the whole length of Venezuela, Colombia, and Panama after smoking up the Royal Navy?"

"Mais non, the Colombians are after us, too. But, to the south, lies even more trouble, Dick. The next border we come to, that way, is British Guiana!"

"Yeah, I noticed. Calm down, we're not going to British Guiana. There's another Venezuelan seaport on the delta's south side. Curiapo, on the Boca Grande. The Brits bypassed it to make an end run for the main delta town back there, but they tell me lots of ships put in the Boca Grande. I figure it's a day's run, in a straight line. Take us a little longer, winding through all these bayous and lagoons, but what the hell's your hurry? Give 'em time to calm down, right?"

Gaston thought, nodded, and said, *"Oui.* For a moment you had me worried. I thought we were chasing the Dutchman, to get our money for the arms he's running to French Guiana."

"We are," said Captain Gringo, grimly. "It's bad business to let guys screw you, and even if the Dutchman was on the level we can't hang around back there in Tucupita until he gets back with our dinero."

Gaston sighed and said, "Dick, listen to me. I have often told you I thought you were crazy, but this time I am *très* serious! French Guiana is south of British Guiana. You just assured me we were not steaming into the jaws of the doubtless enraged British lion, hein?"

"Relax, damn it. We'll be lucky if that old boiler holds

185

together as far as the nearest seaport. I *told* you we'll board a *ship*. There must be hundreds of coasting tramps running between this delta and French Guiana. We'll steam right by the British colony, sitting in first class deck chairs as we toast the Queen."

Gaston said, "Well, since you put it that way, I won't have to shoot you and turn this craft around after all. *Eh, bien,* we can use the new papers they forged for us, *non?*"

"Now *you're* talking crazy! If I know Bronson, he'll put out an all points bulletin on us as soon as he gets cabled confirmation of his suspicions. For old time's sake he might give us a few days' lead, but he has to make at least a half-ass stab at capturing me for Uncle Sam and the guy's pretty good. He and the others know the names on those fake papers they gave us. So we'll pull a switch and use our old ones. I never showed them to Smitty's forgery team, so they don't know about 'em."

"Ah, *très* sneaky! *Regardez,* I shall tear up my droll new passport *non?*"

"No. Hang on to it. It's a lovely forgery and guys like us never can have too many fake I.D. papers."

"Eh bien, after the heat dies down, as you say, one never knows what one may feel like showing some annoying public official. I had forgotten we meant to get out of here with our old fake passports in any case. It is a good thing you have me along to do your thinking, Dick. At times you can be *très* forgetful."

And so the two soldiers of fortune spent the next two days winding through the delta channels to the steaming port of Curiapo, where indeed they saw several ocean going ships at anchor in the channel and Gaston looked up another old legion deserter to see that the borrowed launch was returned to the Dutchman's woman.

The hotel was shabbier and the chambermaids were ugly, so they only stayed long enough to board a shelter deck passenger-cargo coaster bound for Rio under the Liberian flag with a mixed Latin American crew. The purser hardly glanced at their papers, once he'd seen the color of their money, and they booked adjoining cabins on the port side to avoid the afternoon sun on the way south. The coaster steamed out of the Boca Grande on the late afternoon ebb

tide so there was little time to meet other passengers before it was too late to do anything about it. But that night at dinner Captain Gringo spotted a very beautiful albiet frosty blond sitting at the captain's table. She looked like one of those snooty dames who wore her white gloves and veil to bed. It was impossible to catch her eye from across the salon. The middle-aged Argentine skipper was drooling as he stared at her from closer range, but Captain Gringo didn't think he was going to make it with the willowy ash blond. She was too poised and well-hatted to be a virgin, but if she was travelling alone, she figured to be sleeping alone, damn it.

Gaston spotted her, too, and nudged his younger comrade to slyly say, *"Regardez,* there is a woman worthy of your talents, my adorable child. She likes you, too. I, Gaston, keep abreast of such details, and, speaking of breasts, oh, to be young again!"

Captain Gringo kicked him under the table and said, "Knock it off, you dirty old man. I'm a judge of various kinds of flesh, too, and that one's out of my league."

"Do you want me to see if I can find out who she is and where she's going, Dick?"

"Don't bother. We'll be getting off too soon. That's a two week campaign if I ever saw one, even if I had the kind of money it would take. Finish your fucking food. You're giving me a hard-on."

Gaston reluctantly dropped his eyes to the much less interesting dessert in front of him as Captain Gringo forced himself to look somewhere less painful, too. Gaston said, "I noticed a couple of others, strolling the deck as we came from our cabin."

"I noticed them, too. They weren't bad, but I picked up some books to read back in port. Behave yourself aboard this tub, Gaston. By now the wires are sizzling and we don't want to attract attention by playing musical beds for the ship's gossips."

"Merde alors, it is all very well for you to stay in your cabin and read. I, Gaston, am a man of action. But you are probably right. I shall content myself with renewing my old love affair with my fist, tonight. I am not ashamed to admit this voyage is making me *très* nervous. Would you have boarded if you'd known they meant to put into that disgusting

British port of call in the morning, my old and reckless?"

Captain Gringo shrugged and said, "They didn't list Georgetown, British Guiana, as a regular stop when I bought our tickets, but there's nothing we can do about it, now. We'll only be there long enough to drop off some cargo and if we stay aboard we don't have to go through British customs, so what the hell."

Captain Gringo was still keyed up by the last few frantic days, so he read until late and ignored the sunlight through the porthole to turn over and sleep some more. When he woke again he sat up, startled, wondering what felt wrong. Then, as he wiped a hand across his sleep-puffed eyes he realized what it was. The ship wasn't moving under him anymore. They were anchored some damn place.

He washed and shaved before getting dressed in the new suit he'd picked up in Curiapo to look less suspicious. When he stepped out on deck he saw the some damn place was a river estuary with a little neat white town along the eastern shore. The Union Jack was flying in the breeze above a small fort guarding the approaches to the town. The British flag on shore didn't bother him nearly as much as the one on the stern of a British battle cruiser anchored amid some rams and transports a few cable lengths away. One of the rams looked familiar. It had machine-gun dents all over its superstructure.

He went back to his cabin and decided to skip breakfast. But as he was lighting a cigar, a steward knocked on the door and announced, "All passengers to the main salon with their papers, Señor. We are to be inspected by the authorities here for some reason."

Captain Gringo considered his options. There was no place aboard to hide that the crew wouldn't know about. Jumping overboard seemed sort of dumb in broad daylight. He hid the forged papers the Americans had just given him under his mattress and decided his old fake I.D., so dirty and worn, would be difficult to read. He was dead if he attracted

any attention at all, so he buttoned his jacket and decided to get there before anyone came looking for him.

He met Gaston on deck. The Frenchman smiled wryly at him and asked, "Know any other short cuts to French Guiana, Dick?" and Captain Gringo said, "Shut up and try to look nonchalant."

"*Merde alors,* I always look nonchalant, even when I am wetting my pants. I don't think we're going to make it, Dick. Perhaps if we shot them and commandeered their launch . . . ?"

"Shut up and let's play it by ear," said Captain Gringo as he entered the salon to discover other passengers and crew members sitting about with their papers handy. He noticed the cool blond, in a different hat, sitting alone in a corner smoking a cigarette from a long ivory holder. She didn't return his gaze and it seemed a dumb time to join her. So he led Gaston to another table and they sat down, wearing puzzled smiles, as a trio of white uniformed men in pith helmets moved from table to table with the skipper. The Brits were polite and fast, so, all too soon, they came to Captain Gringo's table and the one with a moustache that looked like it belonged on a toothbrush said, "Just a formality, Sir. But would you be good enough to identify yourselves?"

Captain Gringo handed his and Gaston's grundgy papers to him and the official glanced over them, handed them back, and said, "My word, you chaps certainly have been moving about. Would you be good enough to come ashore with us, both of you?"

"What for?" protested Captain Gringo. "Aren't our papers in order?"

"Oh, there's nothing wrong with your I.D.'s, if those are your I.D.s, but we'd better have a word with our superiors on shore, anyway. You will come quietly, won't you, Gentlemen?"

Gaston tensed at Captain Gringo's side. But the tall American shot him a warning look and rose, smiling grimly. A lot of things could happen in a harbor launch and how accurate were all those ships guns all around in any case, right?

As Gaston rose, too, the willowy blond left her seat across the salon and joined them, taking a small black folder with a gilt crest from her hand bag. She asked the one with

the moustache, "What seems to be the problem, here?" and he touched the brim of his helmet to her and said, "Official Matters, Miss. None of your concern, I assure you."

The blond flipped open her I.D., held it up to him, and said, coldly, "I'll decide that, my good man. I assume you recognize this. Pamela DeVere-Hunt, here. Brevet Colonel, British Intelligence."

"Oh, I say, Mum, I had no idea."

"Quite. Now suppose you tell me why you're bothering these fellow passengers of mine? Haven't you Colonials stirred up enough of a flap with friendly powers in the past few days?"

Moustache flushed and said, "Just doing one's duty, Mum. Co-operating with the American authorities, as a matter of fact. These gentlemen answer to the descriptions they just cabled us regarding a certain Captain Gringo and a smaller non-descript comrade in arms. Chaps wanted for murder in the States, I believe."

Pamela DeVere-Hunt looked even snootier as she said, coldly, "You really are behind the times. Dick Walker, alias Captain Gringo, is dead."

"The Yanks caught him, Mum? They never told us that!"

"Of course they didn't. They don't know. The notorious soldier of fortune was ambushed the other night in Tucupita with two of our agents watching."

"Oh, I say, then who might *this* gentleman be?"

"I've no idea, but since Captain Gringo is at the moment rotting on the bottom of a drainage canal he must be someone else, don't you imagine?"

Moustache nodded and turned back to tell Captain Gringo, "Sorry to have troubled you, Sir. Just doing my job and all that rot. Must say you certainly resemble that other chap. But all's well that ends well, eh?"

Captain Gringo realized he'd stopped breathing when he tried to answer. He nodded, mutely, and Moustache looked around to add, "Well, that's that. Nobody else on board we want. Sorry, all."

Then he saluted the willowy blond in the veiled hat, turned on his heels, and marched out with the others in tow. Captain Gringo smiled at the blond British agent and said,

"That was decent of you, Miss. The least I could offer you would be a drink, right?"

The blond shrugged and moved back toward her table without saying yes or no. Gaston nudged his taller and younger comrade and murmured, "I told you she liked you. I think I'll take a stroll on deck. The girls I mentioned are just leaving."

Captain Gringo saw the salon was starting to clear, but he caught the eye of a waiter and pointed at the blond's table as he moved over to join her. He sat down and asked, "Gin and tonic?" and she said, "Of course. By the way, *are* you Captain Gringo, by any chance?"

"I thought you said your guys killed him, Ma'am."

"Call me Pam. He wasn't shot by British agents. Castro rebels, we imagine. Pity, I'd heard so much about Captain Gringo and now it seems I'll never get to meet him."

"Yeah, life's like that. My name is Dick, by the way."

"Really? You do seem bent on offering a passable substitute for the late Captain Gringo. Where are you and that funny little friend of yours going, Dick?"

"Oh, here and there. Where are you bound for, Pam?"

"Rio, on another case, now that this silly flap over Venezuela is over. But we seem to be aboard a slow boat that makes every port of call. Are those shoulders real, or is that jacket padded?"

He smiled and said, "Little of both, maybe. I'd let you feel my muscles but it's a little public here."

She met his eyes levelly and replied, "I know. Don't you suppose it would be more comfortable if we had those drinks in my stateroom?"

"I'd like that," he said, "but can we assume you're not on the Queen's business, at the moment?"

She laughed for the first time and said, "I hardly think the Queen would approve of what I have in mind. But not to worry. I'm completely on my own at the moment. My assignment in Rio has nothing to do with anything you or the late Captain Gringo would be interested in. Meanwhile, why don't we go to my place and get out of this ridiculous vertical position, whoever you may be?"

THE BEST OF ADVENTURE
by RAMSAY THORNE

RENEGADE #1	(C90-976, $1.95)
RENEGADE #2: BLOOD RUNNER	(C90-977, $1.95)
RENEGADE #3: FEAR MERCHANT	(C90-761, $1.95)
RENEGADE #4: DEATH HUNTER	(C90-902, $1.95)
RENEGADE #5: MACUMBA KILLER	(C90-234, $1.95)
RENEGADE #6: PANAMA GUNNER	(C90-235, $1.95)
RENEGADE #7: DEATH IN HIGH PLACES	(C90-548, $1.95)
RENEGADE #8: OVER THE ANDES TO HELL	(C90-549, $1.95)
RENEGADE #9: HELL RAIDER	(C90-550, $1.95)
RENEGADE #10: THE GREAT GAME	(C90-737, $1.95)